I0709534

"THE RED PLANET TRUCKERS!"
2nd Edition.

By STEPHEN JOHN WILLIAMS

Based on the original internet adventure series:"THE TITANS OF MARS" by Stephen J. Williams historically writing as 'William Alexander Stephens.' It contains the complete first two Seasons of that adventure series from 2016 to 2018 as published on the World Wide Web at the time.

Copyright © 2011-2024 Stephen Williams. No reproduction of any part without permission.

ISBN-SBN: 9781738487516

NOTES:
[1] The front cover illustration is from 'IStock – Getty' Images under license by the Author.

[2] You can contact the author at:
https://stephenjohnwilliams.blogspot.com

[3] Story written with young adults in mind and a larger Font used to assist those who struggle with reading.

[4] Sometimes, within the narrative, I will place little notes which I hope may help understand certain parts of the stories:

CONTENTS:

EPISODE 1: "WSV THE THOR."
START PAGE: 6

EPISODE 2: "WEATHER STATION No.3 (South)."
START PAGE: 23

EPISODE 3: "DISTRESS CALL."
START PAGE: 41

EPISODE 4: "OPERATION MINCEMEAT."
START PAGE: 59

EPISODE 1: "WSV THE THOR."

1. BACK FROM LIBERTY.

The Thor had been resting at Rossington's No.4 Dock for a couple of days, most of the crew had taken advantage of the liberty granted by Captain Jones and had disappeared into that thriving metropolis to drink, fornicate and/or simply visit any family or friends that resided in the large Southern Mars Capital.

Captain Jones had remained aboard with Chief Marcus Enders, neither man had family in Rossington. The Chief had a couple of old friends living in the Ford District, but on the last liberty some weeks ago, he had played poker with them and lost nearly a Month's salary. So, he decided to save what was left of his depleted finances (and pride) and remain on the Thor, it was free food and accommodation after all!

Captain Jones smiled and nodded as the Chief explained for the 4th time that morning, how his two old Rig mates had taken him to the cleaners. Both officers were on the Bridge, looking out over the docks of south Rossington. There was an aging 'Mammoth' Class cargo in the next dock – she was still being unloaded - Jones could make out a couple of dockhands in gaudy yellow suits astride her second trailer. He had quickly guessed the cargo was grain, as the dockhands were lowering two flexible pipes into tight matching orifices on the trailers top deck. There was a slight haze about the rig, Jones knew it was grain dust, but he smiled to himself; it looked like a very light rain shower.

Not that Captain Jones had ever seen a real rain shower; born in the city of Kiev on Mars some 16 years previously [Martian

Years are equivalent to 1.8 Earth Years, so the Captain would be about 29 on Earth] to a mother who really didn't want to be a mother and a father who moved North some two years after his birth - with a woman who worked in his laboratory – Jones did not have the best of starts.

But with his grandfather's love and help, he had turned that around. Jones had passed out of engineering University with First class honours and joined Mars military for a year. He moved from there to the large Wang Corporation that ran rigs of every description, both North and South Mars, reaching the position of XO [Executive Officer] on the new 'Titan' class rig "The Richard Kellogg", running heavy machine parts around the southern mining cities and towns, that's where he quickly obtained his red slip, or Commercial Rig Master's Certificate. His first Captaincy followed quickly, another 'Titan' class rig; "The New Cydonia", a big cargo rig that carried all types of cargo; from fruit and vegetables to housing modules.

He remembered the rig and her crew with great affection, he would probably still be her Captain, but the Weather Service made him an offer he really couldn't refuse. A brand new - just off the launch slips - 'Titan' class Weather Service Vessel; The Thor. She was a 'Titan' Class Rig, weighing some ninety tones, equipped with two huge Dyson rig engines and with a superb specification that made his mouth water. Standing nearly six meters high with full external armour and a double hull; The Thor was designed to withstand whatever weather Mars threw at her – and that could be a lot!

The Thor could haul two, 150 tone trailers with ease over the harsh and unforgiving Martian surface, but the two trailers she normally hauled were specially built for her and the weather service. One contained a fully operational weather station and workshop, whilst the other contained accommodation and mess facilities for the twelve crew members who serviced the vital Weather Stations that covered Mars. She was basically a first class "Battle Rig" adapted for use as a weather service vehicle.

All the weather service personnel were, in-fact, in military service. Knowing what the Martian Weather was up too, was vital to survival on Mars.

The second trailer contained a full medical suite, high quality living modules, a ship's mess and galley with a small cargo storage area. It also carried a couple of drones for observation and exploration. The Thor boasted two fully equipped survival rafts that could carry 16 persons between them and keep the crew safe and alive for up to 5 days. It also carried a small 'Sand-Cat' – a four-person tractor that could travel very quickly over the Martian dust - she was highly maneuverable and basically, a great deal of fun to drive! Her nickname was 'Little Thor' amongst the crew; there was never a shortage of happy volunteers to take her out for a spin!

So, Captain Jones had returned to military service, he had completed his refresher training at the big military base outside of the Martian capitol at Fort Benjamin. It was some 700k from Taylor, the capitol of Mars. Then he had made the very long journey south to Rossington, some of it by military flight, but most by military rigs. He had arrived in the Southern Mars capitol aboard "The General Patton", that's where he met the Chief and found that this grizzled old warrior was to be Chief on his rig; The Thor.

The Chief was actually only 28 years old, which would make him in his late forties on Earth but looked much older. If you only had two words to describe him to people, they would be: Grizzly Bear. Yes, with his full beard and hairy arms, that would be an apt description and with the same attitude as a bear!

But what he didn't know about the engineering status of these 'Titan's' you could chisel on the sole of your shoe and still have room for the long forgotten Gettysburg Address. The Chief had two great loves in his life; Engines and flowers, followed closely by woman and poker. Then you could add illicit booze and the occasional cigar.

The Chief was a real character; the crew seriously respected him and even admired him; you really didn't want to cross Marcus. The last fool to actually upset the Chief suddenly found he had volunteered for a three-month duty on Weather Station 29(N) which is located in the middle of the Cydonia desert, some hundreds of kilometers from any other human habitation.

The three weeks it took to reach the station wasn't even included in the three-month tour, nor was the return journey. He changed his opinion of the Chief from 'bastard' to 'total bastard' and a few other expletives were thrown in. It had not occurred to the fool that Dr. Alexander Enders, the Weather Service Director of Human Resources could be related and suffers the same bad attitudes as the Chief [his brother]. He found that out the hard way.

Apart from that, the Chief was good man to have on your side when the shit hits the fan! The Chief only really liked just three people on the Thor; the captain, his apprentice; Summer 'Sunny' Yelsin and the ship's cook; Frankie 'Fists' Fingermann, who was rather a good chef. He did have one bad habit which kept getting him in-castrated at the Military Prison at Salt Flats; if he didn't like what you said, he wouldn't just disagree; Frankie would answer with his fists. But so far, since being assigned to the Thor, after completing another couple of months at Salt Flats, his behaviour was good. The crew believed it was because the captain treated this small, feisty man with respect, or it was because the captain enjoyed his curries far too much.

Frankie's favourite saying was 'the only difference between me and Chief is I'. Well, that was his opinion anyway……

The Chief's engineering apprentice was young Summer Yelsin, nick-named 'Sunny' by the crew because of her very happy disposition and ever presents cheerful personality. The crew referred to 'Sunny' as the Chief's pet and he looked after her like a father.

'Sunny' would not be on this mission; her mother was re-marrying at their family home in Norfolk. 'Sunny' had been granted ten days leave- but it would take her six days just to travel there and back, to the small farming township located some 25k North of Rossington. The family were called 'Bunker Farmers' and occupied the bottom rung of the food supply chain. They produced basic vegetables like carrots, potatoes and onions.

The other favourite of the Chief was the rig's cat; "Dallas." This mysterious creature prowled the rig with total confidence and freedom. He would turn up in the strangest places: to the delight of the crew and was also a firm favourite of the Chef who kept "Dallas" fed and watered. Actually, he [Dallas] was probably everyone's favourite!

Cats had been carried on the rigs for years and no-one was quite sure how the tradition started, but few crews would depart for sand duty [surface work] without the rig's mascot [and lucky charm] aboard. The Thor's cat was a black & white, one & half year old [apparently a gift for the crew from Vice Admiral's Di-Luk's wife who bred them] and "Dallas" was quite spoilt by the crew.

The cat had its own 'survival suit' - made by the engineering crew - and he was shown on the official crew roster. Whilst he didn't receive any pay for his 'duties', his vet bills and food came out the rig's budget. The numerous toys' and treats he received came from the crew. Dallas's most loved place was the medical bay; he was often found asleep in the mortuary tray. This baffled the entire crew and was definitely a mystery aboard the Thor; because the tray had to be opened and closed with a lever!

The Captain had the Chief's serious respect, he would say; 'I've been on these bloody rig's for nearly fifteen years and he's [the captain] about the best I've served under; and that says it all.'

"We depart at 18.00 hours CST." The captain said simply and sipped his lukewarm coffee. He leaned back in his chair and peered through the bridge windows at the dockside. The old 'Mammoth' cargo rig was still being unloaded; he smiled at its name emblazoned upon the tractor unit's side: "The Fruit Fairy", with a colourful painting of a fly with a fairy outfit on.

"Something from the bloody history books." He mused. There were no flies [or fairies – apparently – on Mars] except in books and films about 'old mother earth'. But then few people – apart from Historians – bothered to watch anything produced back then; it was all irrelevant and affected no-one these days.

AUTHOR NOTE:
"CST means Central Southern Time."

"Aye, skipper." The Chief lifted his PA and looked at the screen, "Don't forget skipper we have a new MO and a replacement Ensign due today." Jones nodded and tapped the screen of his PA; "Just been reading up on the pair, the MO seems pretty solid, but no sand time. It's the Ensign that bothers me; the Thor will be her third rig in well under a year."

The Chief rolled his eyes and laughed; "Maybe she gets sand-sick!" The captain laughed quietly. 'Sand-sickness' was blamed for everything that crew members suffered, on or off the rigs. It covered bad hangovers, bad food and the need to spend a day in bed. What 'sand-sickness' actually was defied all medical explanations that the captain had heard over the years. Maybe the new MO could cast more light on the subject. But the new Ensign will need a close eye, being in service just under a year and the Thor was number three; the omens were definitely not good. The captain ran his fingers over his cropped dark hair and stared at his reflection in the bridge screen; he was 16 years old [that's about 29 years old on Earth] 1.8 meters tall and weighed in at 88 kilos. He was in very good health because he was regular user of the rig's gym and generally took care of himself. From quite a young age, he found he was attractive to girls and women; probably because they considered him 'exotic'. His beloved late Grandfather had laughed about that; "You'll thank your ancestors for those looks one day!"

Staring back at the captain was a good-looking mixed-race male. Apparently, the Captain's Earth ancestors had originated from the African continent, but now had white American and European blood mixed in. There were very few 'black' faces around Mars; everyone accepted that was due to the racial situation back on 'Old Mother' during the early days of colonization.

AUTHOR NOTE:
"PA is the abbreviation used for 'personal Assistant' which is a small – all in one – communications device that is far superior to any of the 'mobile phones or portable computers of Earth's 20th and 21st centuries. Just for your information, Earth is

often referred to as 'Old Mother'."

Not that any of that mattered now.

That's all he needed, a mixed-up Ensign who clearly wasn't sure if she liked life on the sand. Jones always thought that it was odd, that the expression 'sand' was used to describe the Mars surface, when it was clearly was a mix of dust and dead soil. But apparently, according to legend - that in the early years - when Mars was still a colony of Earth; one of the founding crew members had coined the expression 'doing sand time' and it had stuck.

Now, 323 years [Martian Years] after humanity had arrived on the Red Planet; there were vast cities, mining townships, enclosed farms and even two holiday resorts. Water was the key to the new life here. The three vast underground reservoirs, discovered some years after colonization, allowed life to explode across the planet's surface. It was now estimated that some 1,370,000 souls currently inhabited the once dead planet, and the healthy population was still growing – though a lot slower now the immigration ships from Earth had stopped coming - some 80 years ago. Jones stopped smiling when he thought of Earth; obviously he only knew her from the archives maintained by the Mars Government. But she had been quite beautiful, full of blue seas and vast expansive forests and millions of different life-forms; from the huge whales to little insects. The place was crawling with life. Not like Mars: definitely not like Mars.

The Captain shook thoughts about 'Old Mother' from his mind; there was really no point thinking about 'what if's' – the past was in the past - you couldn't change it or forget it; just accept it. And bloody well learn from it!

2. NEW CREW.

The deck intercom buzzed and the Captain smiled at the two faces upon the small screen; "Welcome aboard Peter and which bar did you drag Troy from?" Jones stabbed the release button which opened the forward external pressure door as the two faces laughed and disappeared from view. He glanced at the ship's clock and saw it was 16.20 Hours CST. That was good; the crew had started to arrive back from liberty on time.

"When's departure set for Captain?" The Cook's voice made him spin in his chair and he replied, "18.00 hours cookie, what are we having?" The cook was of small statue, but quite stocky, with long dark hair tied with what appears to be string. He had extensive tattoo's covering his exposed arms and upon the back of his hands. But his chef's whites were immaculate; wiping his hands with a paper towel, he said simply; "Curry."

The captain gave him the thumbs up and told Frankie to have the main evening meal ready for 19.30 hours, "How's Dallas?" He added, the Cook smiled;"The last I saw of him, he was sleeping on the morgue tray in the medical bay. He scoffed a packet of fish beans and drank some cold coffee; He's happy enough." The captain laughed; "That is one crazy cat!" The Chef nodded in agreement; "I'd swear skipper that Dallas is getting bigger by the day. If he keeps growing, we'll need a bigger rig." Then he disappeared down the ladder behind him.

Lt. Peter Gravestone came bouncing onto the bridge, stopping briefly to salute and dropped onto a pilot's seat in front of the ship's dashboard. He glanced out the windows and pointed out the old 'Mammoth' cargos logo; "Why a fly in a fairy's outfit?" He looked quite bemused by it. "Troy is changing into uniform and will man the deck for crew returns; everyone is expected to be here for 17.00 hours, but no word on the new people, I hope they caught the tram early, they're going to be busy because the Rossington Raiders are playing at home tonight and it's the National Hardball semi-final." He added, checking his PA for the third time.

"Expecting something important?" The captain gestured to the Lieutenants PA. Peter half-smiled, but his dark eyes betrayed his concern. "Waiting a call from Nikki, he's gone on a three-day conference to Middleford, and he normally calls when he arrives at the hotel."

Jones nodded; "How long you two been together now Pete?" Peter smiled broadly and with great affection in his voice said; "Nearly two years and our parents said it wouldn't last six weeks!" The captain nodded again; "Yeah parents can get it wrong sometimes." Jones hadn't thought of his parents for some time now, his father Robert was now Principal Scientist at a Government Laboratory in Taylor; they hadn't spoken in two years.

In a small case, in a drawer by his cabin bed was a small photograph of the mother he really never knew. A very pretty woman with long dark hair and a huge smile; her dark eyes had been inherited by Jones. Maggie Jones had left her small son with his grandparents and had disappeared to Shackleton on the ice shelf, with a man who drove 'Snow-Cats' for a living. Jones was just two years old – he had never even spoken to her - she didn't bother to attend his Grandfathers resurrection service.

AUTHOR NOTE:
"There were no real funerals anymore, all dead bodies were given a 'Resurrection' service which basically means the corpse was liquefied and used to help grow the crops that were vital for life on the planet. There were few religious objectors since nearly all religion had vanished; Mars was almost entirely secular."

Jones understood from his father that Maggie now lived back up North, with a sewage farm engineer called Kelvin and she had two daughters, now in their teens. Jones didn't even know what his half-sisters looked like – and frankly - he no longer cared. But on his cabin's desk was a lovely real wood, framed picture, of his grandfather, Joshua. [Real wood was incredibly expensive on Mars because there were few tree's and only one's that died were used for products!]

Jones now understands the sacrifices that the old fella had made to keep the young Picasso at home. He really did miss him these days – especially the late-night conversations when the pair would discuss anything and everything - over a couple of cold beers and a hot curry. But he had passed over two years ago, and Jones had never felt so alone. He vividly remembered the argument with his father at the resurrection ceremony at Rossington. They hadn't spoken since.

"Well, I think our two new ladies have made it." The Chief – smiling - pointed to the dockside, where two Military officers were struggling with their luggage and short skirts; trying to keep both under control as they approached the deck ramp, where 'Deckie' Troy Humbleson asked for their Identity Cards and Posting orders. He also had fellow Deckie Leon Zamaski to help with the baggage.

The captain watched carefully on the deck monitor as the Chief opened the Bridge Deck door and the two girls climbed in. They both saluted and Jones shook their hands in greeting. The new MO [Medical Officer] was quite tall, with thick blond hair and green eyes. Lt. Eve Votech was considered pretty by most who met her, and both the Captain and the Chief would agree with that.

The 14-year-old [25-year-old if on Earth] had completed two years at Medical School [paid on a scholarship by the Military] and now was obliged to complete one year on active service, before return'ng to medical school for a further year and qualification as a Military Doctor with the rank of Captain. "Beauty and brains in one neat package." The Chief later commented.

The Ensign was quite small, very slim with dark hair and eyes; clearly nervous, though the captain was a little surprised at the firm handshake. She was nearly 10 years old [19 years old if on Earth] and had completed 29 Weeks 'sand-time' already; but on two other Military rigs. Ensign Lilly Blissford had been given a 'plum' posting on the MSV "The Admiral Valisky". A massive flight carrier based at Fort Benjamin up North. This rig carried four 'flyers' and boasted a crew of nearly thirty. But the young Ensign had requested a move in less than nine weeks and found herself aboard MSV "The Louise Stewart", a Military supply rig with nine crew and about a third of the size of "The Admiral Valisky". She had lasted just 20 weeks, and then had been transferred to WSV "The Thor" – again - at her own request.

Not the best record in the Military for one so young.

Watching, as the girls departed the bridge for their assigned cabins, the Chief said simply;"That Ensign looks like a shy little girl who hasn't a clue about anything." He sighed and shook his head, then smiling added; "Well, if she's going to make it in service, then The Thor is her best bet Skipper!"

Jones agreed with that deduction; but would she stay long enough to work that out for herself?

3. DEPARTURE.

Lt. Peter Gravestone thought there was something odd about the Ensign, but he couldn't quite put his finger on it. But his attention was drawn immediately to the communications desk, a call from Rossington Transit Control. He flicked the screen into life and smiling back at him was Sol Goldstein, one of the control officers; "Hi Pete, your slot is 18.00 hours through Gate 2 and try to avoid the dirty great cargo sitting out there, you really can't miss it!"

Sol laughed and pointed to a flickering monitor by his side. It showed a 'Goliath' class cargo rig sitting some 1000 meters from the external pressure doors of Rossington's Southern docks.

"The Summer Harvest" was an enormous cargo rig, capable of hauling three trailers and boasted a crew of seven. 'Goliath' class rigs were also the first choice for the cruise rigs that had appeared during the last fifty years and there was several working both North and South Mars. Such as "The Queen Eleanor" which was one of the 'Super-Goliaths'. She was a massive three hundred tone tractor unit which pulled three trailers of happy passengers: all paying a small fortune for the privilege. Every rig Captains dream to command. The 'Queen' was one of three sister rigs, the other two worked up North, "The Queen Victoria" and "The Queen Noor" plied their trade from Mar's Capitol docks, whilst "The Queen Eleanor" worked from Rossington.

Peter had seen her once; when travelling back to "The Thor" from leave – an incredible sight moving over the dusty surface of Mars - "The Queen Eleanor" had just left the Southern Capitol and was heading out onto the sand for a two month 'cruise'.

That's when Peter remembered the Ensign; he had caught a lift on MSV "The Louise Stewart", and she had been on board. Clearly, she had not remembered him. But he remembered what was said about her. He looked across the bridge at the captain, who was giving departure instructions to the bridge crew and Ensign Blissford caught his eye. She was on the duty communications desk and she glanced at him, and half smiled. Peter nodded in return and one thought dominated his mind; should he tell the captain?

"Prepare for departure please!" The captain announced, easing himself into his seat. He looked at the rig's clock: 17.50 hours. "Run the numbers please people!" He added, checking the Navicom; the journey to Weather Station 3(South) was scheduled to take 127 hours or just over five days.

A couple of dock hands, in bright yellow suits, waved from the dockside. "All external couplings and both umbilical cords are free Captain." Peter looked up from his screen and could now feel the power surging through "The Thor" as both her engines were now running. The Chief called from the engine room to say all was on standby.

The Captain studied the instruments on his desk panel; "XO, what's our hull integrity?" Peter's eyes swept his panel and without lifting his head, said simply; "Captain, we're green across the board."

Captain Jones nodded to himself, then looking around the bridge, he smiled and said; "Well, let's get some sand pay!" Slowly, the 'Titan' began to move forward, turning a little to match up with the two huge Internal pressure doors, above which was three large diameter, coloured lights. Red was showing currently. Creeping forward, Captain Jones waited for the yellow light to start flashing. That's when Ensign Blissford said;" We have clearance from Rossington Transit Control Captain." The Inner doors were now moving, opening slowly. The red light had extinguished and yellow was flashing. "The Thor" continued to creep forward under the captain's steady Hand. "Thank you Lilly." He called out.

Within a couple of minutes, the doors had opened enough for the final light to come on and "The Thor" was bathed in a strange green glow. She passed through the Inner Gates with ease and came to a stop before the External Pressure Doors of the Docks. Everyone watched the great Inner doors closing behind the Thor. A similar arrangement of lights above the outer gates was showing red. There was a huge neon sign above the lights: it declared: "WARNING! MARS OUTSIDE – TAKE CARE!"

Peter watched on his rear monitor as the Inner doors closed behind them and he could see on his instruments that the pressure chamber was being emptied to balance with the harsh outside climate.

The yellow light started to flash, and the Outer doors began to open, almost immediately, dust started to pour through the opening, swirling and kicking, growing as the doors opened further apart. A very typical Mars welcome!

"There's bit of a minor duster kicking about Captain." Jones glanced over his shoulder at Specialist Bella Limbstronn, the Thor's Meteorologist. "Can we expect anything worse Bella?" He asked as the rig continued to move forward. The doors were almost open when the green light came on and the Thor moved out onto the Martian Surface. Visibility was just a few meters, and the temperature was already dropping rapidly as the Martian night began.

"Pay close attention to the 'Fru-vision' please, Leon." Jones instructed Kamiski - this remarkable piece of kit - allowed the bridge crew to 'view through' the storm up to 500 meters. "Aye Captain." Leon peered at his screen; it was like viewing a clear evening. He also noted that the 'Collision System' had picked up the big rig and was flashing a gentle silent yellow warning. He informed the captain who nodded his thanks;

"We'll try not to hit her." A quite chuckle rippled around the bridge at that.

"A few high winds and a really low temperature for the night, nothing to worry the Thor about." Bella smiled at the captain, but recheckec her PA, for any latest updates. She was totally responsible for assessing the weather reports streaming into the Thor and she felt the responsibility she carried. If she missed a growing storm; the rig and its crew could be in serious trouble.

Bella was considered to be quite plain by many, except her hair. It had the consistency of a mop head and was dyed a striking blue and blond. 'The chunky monkey' was her nickname, but only behind her back. Say it to her face and you would need a good dentist!

Her father was a cargo Captain of some years standing and Bella, both as a child and then a girl, had often accompanied him on his rig; CV: "The Happy Swan." Since Gustov [her dad] owned the rig, he could carry whoever he wanted. The Chief referred to Bella as the 'other Cinderella' – a rich girl who preferred to rough it and make her own way in life - and he did admire her guts for that.

Starboard of the Thor, Captain Jones could make out the lights of the big cargo rig, waiting for her entry into Rossington. They flashed in greeting and Peter responded by operating a couple of the Thor's front strobes. In the lights, the big rig looked like a wall of steel. Peter could make out its bridge, showing a soft red glow through its windows as they had already switched to 'night lights' while waiting for entry to the docks.

As the Thor moved out onto surface, the bridge lights switched to night mode and the crew was bathed in a familiar red glow. "Cruising speed please Pete." Jones ordered and everyone could feel the power surging through the Thor as the big engines responded.

"Forty-five knots now Captain." Pete replied, he glanced at his rear monitor and could see the solid walls of Rossington City disappearing behind them; the city lights swallowed up by the dust storm and the gathering night. The Thor was now on the sand proper and heading out into the 'great nothing' [a term used by rig crews to describe the Martian deserts].

Ensign Lilly called out to the bridge crew that CV: 'The Summer Harvest' had wished them well and to keep their heads down, as it was pretty wild out there. "Tell them thanks for their concern, but this is a Weather Service rig and we're on the sand whatever the weather!" The captain laughed and motioned to Lilly to send the reply.

"Alright to come on the bridge Captain?" Lt. Eve Votech appeared at the bridge ladder and Jones nodded his approval. She came up behind the Captain's chair and peered hard through the bridge windows at the gathering gloom. "I can't see bugger all!" She spoke with some surprise in her voice. Everyone laughed and Jones said simply' "Welcome to the real Mars, Doc." Captain Jones glanced at the rig's clock; 18.00 hours CST. The Thor had departed on time and was only missing one crew member: Summer Yelsin. The journey to Weather Station No.3(S) had commenced and curry was on the menu! He rubbed his hands together like a happy child and smiled. The new 'Doc' smiled back and Picasso Jones had a nice feeling about her: a really nice feeling which he shook away – for now – and returned to his instruments.

EPISODE 2: "WEATHER STATION No.3 (South)."

4. ROUTINE SERVICE.

A gentle persistent buzz penetrated his dream and Jones awoke from quite a deep sleep, he had been dreaming, but now couldn't recall it. "Bugger." He muttered to himself and sat up; he could see that the bridge light was illuminated on his intercom.

Captain Jones rubbed his face and eyes; his night lamp clicked on and he pressed the intercom switch by his head and heard Peter's voice. He also noticed that the time was 03.15 hours. Jones had managed to garner five hours sleep in one session, which wasn't bad considering the Thor had been on the sand for over five days. "What is it, Pete?" Jones yawned, running his hands through his hair.

"We've arrived at number three skipper and there's a real blaster of a duster raging out there." Pete Gravestone was peering through the bridge windows; he had guessed that visibility was no more than a couple of meters. He could only make out the triangular shape of Weather Station No.3(S) because it's external lighting had switched on with the approach of the Thor. "We are parked up some 600 meters from her on good ground." He added. "Thanks Pete, call a briefing for seven thirty at sunup." Jones lay back and stared at the dull coloured, padded ceiling and walls of his cabin. He and the Chief had cabins on the tractor unit as did Peter, Ensign Lilly and the rig's apprentice; 'Sunny' – the last three cabins were doubles - allowing up to eight people to live on the Thor; if necessary; operationally. The remainder of the crew had their living accommodation in Trailer 2, but the MO had her own cabin within the Medical Suite.

He sipped some cold water from the bottle he kept by his bunk and the morning schedule passed through his mind. Brief the crew first; the service team would consist of himself, the Chief, Tom and Kazza. They would cross the sand to the station and start the maintenance routines, whilst the support team will consist of the MO, who would monitor the survival suit read outs with Bella and Lilly on communications', leaving Pete to manage the Thor with Leon's assistance.

Troy can stand by with the' sand cat' for a rapid emergency evacuation - if required - and Frankie can knock up a curry for lunch. Jones laid back and drifted off into a dream about trees and puddles of water. It seemed only seconds, but his bedside alarm buzzing told him it was five thirty and he pulled himself from the bunk and headed for the 'Misty'.

AUTHOR NOTE:
"A 'Misty' was a Martian term for a 'shower'. It soaked you in thin streams of water [to conserve water] like having a 'bubble bath' without actually soaking. It was very effective."

The captain was on the bridge just before six, watching the 'duster' blowing outside. No one was going anywhere in that, winds gusting at 50kph and visibility down to a couple of meters. They would have to sit it out for now. Still, that would mean everyone could have a good breakfast and relax a little before hitting the sand.

The storm blew itself out by nine o'clock and the Thor became a hive of activity; survival suits were checked and checked again, and toolboxes were loaded onto the 'Beaver' [a small drone used for light loads]. Eve set up a medical control centre on the bridge whilst Bella frequently checked the communications and Lilly made coffee for everyone. The Chief consulted his PA and was satisfied that all technical specifications and blueprints for Weather Station 3(S)

had been downloaded to his and the captain's PA's. Tom checked the spare parts that the routine service called for, piece by piece through their protective wrap, logging each on his PA. He checked everything twice before he was satisfied that it was all correct.

The service team assembled in the suit room and after a quick reminder about safety and emergency procedures. They stepped into their survival suits [known colloquially as 'sand-suits'] and checked everything a third time. The service team consisted of Captain Jones, the Chief, Tom and Kazza. Who, now all suited up, headed for the external pressure lift and squeezed in. "Troy, are you under way?" Jones called into his microphone as he noticed that one 'sand-suit' was already missing from its locker. "Yes Captain, on way now." Troy replied, adding; "I'll be there waiting for you."

"Check read outs please Doc." Jones called into his helmet microphone. "Will do captain." Was Eve's reply, as she scanned the five screens before her. "All normal, so clear to go Captain." She watched on her side monitor as Jones gave the thumbs up. The service mission was on.

The external pressure lift descended to ground level; it was located to the rear of tyre no. 7 on the starboard side of the Thor. As the coor opened, exposing the crew to Mars hostile atmosphere, a little dust swirled about the crew's feet, but the dust storm had gone – for the moment – and in single file, with Jones leading, the service crew started the 10-minute walk to Weather Station No.3, which loomed above them like some metallic pyramid. Jones often wondered about the architects choosing that shape for most of the stations; it appears that the pyramid shape was best suited for the harsh conditions on the Martian surface. He thought about 'old mother' and remembered reading or watching somewhere that the original 'Great' pyramid still stood in the wastelands that now made up most of Earth's surface. "Been sitting there for thousands of years now; those buggers knew how to build for the future. It probably was man's first super structure, that built in ancient times and it's outlasted nearly everything that followed it." He muttered to himself and checked to see if the service crew behind were alright.

Tom kept one hand on the 'beaver' as the drone rattled across the dusty surface. "Keeping a close eye on my instruments, I don't fancy picking them out of the crap around here." He told the Chief, who nodded in agreement. But Jones had to smile to himself, a few hundred meters away was a swirl of dust moving quickly around the weather station. "Troy, you're bloody supposed to stand by with the 'sand-cat', not take her on holiday." He called through his microphone. The ball of dust came slowly to a halt by the external door of the weather station and Troy waved through her windows to the fast approaching group.

"Just doing checks on her Captain, she's not been out in a while." Troy explained over his helmet mic. He had not pressurized 'little Thor' in case the service crew needed to board quickly. Troy had loaded her with the emergency surface stretcher which was basically a trolley with a bag that could be pressurized.

Each crew member carried a little emergency repair kit, which could be used to fix tears or holes in the survival suit and a very small oxygen capsule which was designed to be broken open and thrown in the suit. It gave an extra 10 minutes of breathable air – and those extra 10 minutes - could mean the difference between life and death on the hostile Mars surface. It should be noted that the vast majority of people living on

Mars currently had never walked on her surface!

That incredible statistic was actually true because few people needed to leave the cities, farms or townships and spend time outside on the surface. Military personnel all did 'sand-time' as part of their training and like the crew of the Thor; it was part of their duties. The construction teams that build all and everything incorporated surface training, as did the many various rigs' that traversed Mars. But for the average citizen of Mars, they could die of old age in their bed, never once having placed a foot on the surface of the planet they called home.

Jones and the service crew had arrived at the external pressure door of the weather station and he punched the entry code into the keypad, after cleaning it with his glove. The door slid quietly back and the team entered. The pressure room was lit by two bright ceiling lamps and Jones went to the small control panel located by the Inner door and waited for everyone to enter, then closed the outer door.

"Chief, your blood pressure is up a little, are you o.k.?" Eve's voice came through the helmet speakers, and everyone turned to the Chief, who shrugged his shoulders and replied; "I'm too bloody old for this shit!" and laughed. Tom slapped the Chief's back; "You can ride back on the 'beaver' if you're feeling your age." Everyone laughed and Eve added; "Well, once inside Chief and the atmosphere has kicked in, rest up for at least 30 minutes please." Jones had to smile; he could imagine the chief's face!

The Chief nodded; "Sure Doc, whatever you say." He looked at Jones and rolled his eyes, mouthing; 'Fucking bound to.'

"The helmet cams are still working Chief." Eve said without censor in her voice. The service crew had a few giggles at that one. It took a couple of minutes for the station's atmosphere to stabilize and they entered its control room. They slipped from their sand-suits and started to unpack the maintenance kits. The Chief did as he was advised and sat on a chair with his feet up on the desk. He wasn't a happy man. "You take it easy grandpa." Kazza patted the Chief's head and tried to wrap him in a thermal blanket, borrowed from the aid kit. "Fuck off you little shit!" The Chief snapped, throwing the blanket at Kazza who laughed loudly. The captain clapped his hands; "Come on boys, let's get started, Tom, can you rig up the communications with the Thor and complete the system handshake with her mainframe? Let's get it done."

Tom nodded and Kazza started to remove service panels from the rear wall whilst Jones scrutinized the station's technical specifications. The Chief sat with arms folded, swearing under his breath, he had another ten minutes of 'rest' to go.

5. CATEGORY 3 STORM.

Lilly's voice came over the intercom; "Captain, Bella has an urgent weather report you should know about."

Tom answered, "Put her on, the skippers listening." He gave Jones a concerned look, had that bloody duster doubled back on itself? This routine service was logged at twelve hours and that was generous, but a storm could add hours to the visit. Bella had the service crew's full and undivided attention. "Captain, we've got a category 3 Low coming up fast. Its blowing down from the Easter's [A large mountain range to the South of the Thor's position] with wind speeds between 50kph and 70kph and there's some electric's mixed in." Bella had real concern in her voice, she continued; "I estimate that it will roll over us in about four hours."

"It's already showing on the station's instruments." The Chief tapped the screen on the desk he was sitting at. "There have been loads of reports about a couple monsters blowing about the ice shelf, this could be part of one and maybe it's breaking up." The Chief was right about the ice shelf, which lay behind the Easter Mountain range; numerous reports had come into the Weather Service describing one of the worse winters there in living memory. A storm had cut off Shackleton [a small city located on the iceshelf] for about 10 days a few weeks ago. Weather Station No.7(S) which is near the South Pole had given good warning on the storms approach and that had saved lives, with surface ice workers evacuated to Shackleton and Augusta in plenty of time. Jones nodded and looked quite grim; "Thanks Bella, keep on top of it, I want to know about any changes." He looked round the Control Room and could see the real concern on their faces. "Let's go boys, Chief and Tom, you'll head back in the sand-cat and get some rods raised. Kazza and I will go back on foot. We'll leave the service kits here."

Troy's voice came over the headset's; "Ready to go Captain, I'm outside the door with 'little Thor' fired up." The decision was made, abandon the service visit and baton down the hatches on the Thor and sit it out. What really concerned everyone was the mention of 'electrics' in the storm, lightning and worse: bloody thunderbolts. They could be deadly.

A decade ago, a bolt had struck a 'Mammoth' cargo rig up in Cydonia; it simply blew the tractor unit into several pieces and killed all seven crew members. It had come on them so quickly that they hadn't raised rods or prepped the Life-rafts. Had they received a warning, the outcome may have been very different, but Weather Station 29(N) was totally out of commission with a serious fault, WSV: "The David Miller" had been on route to the station when the tragedy happened.

The Chief of WSV: "The David Miller" had been Marcus Enders and he was part of the search team that scoured the scattered wreckage of the 'Mammoth' – they found no bodies - everything had been torn apart, like some crazed giant had simply pulled the rig into little pieces. The wreck had been recovered the following year and a simple memorial service held for the lost crew of CV: "The Sun King." It had been a terrible time for the Chief: the "The Sun King's" rig apprentice was a 10-year-old Katherine Enders, the Chief's niece, on her second tour aboard the rig. A small stone had been erected at the site with the names of the crew. On the sad anniversary of the tragic event, the Chief gets drunk. When a crew mate, helping him back to their rig after such a session, told the Chief that he drank too much, Marcus replied simply; "Too much for what?"

Weather Station No. 29(N) was now manned, a direct result of the tragedy and High Military Command insistence that the station was in operation 24/7. The military had good cause to be concerned. At the time MSV: "The Admiral Valisky" [Flag rig of the Northern fleet] and her two escort rigs had been in the area of the disaster and had the storm struck her; it would have been a catastrophe on a national scale.

The Military Commander [at the time] Marshal John Cabot-Wayne, under pressure from the Martian President and Senate, ordered personally that Weather Station 29(N) will in future, be manned.

The Chief sat quietly in the 'sand-cat' and stared through the windows as they approached the Thor. Every time someone mentioned a storm with 'electric's' he thought of his niece and how happy and pleased she was with her posting on the CV: "The Sun King".

"I'll see you when I get back Uncle M." Young Kate hugged her favourite Uncle and blowing a little kiss, left for the rig; never to return.

"What do you think Chief, four or five rods?" Tom asked the Chief. But Marcus was elsewhere, scrambling through smoking wreckage, shouting his young niece's name with the terrible realization that the little girl he had known and loved from birth was gone. He frantically searched the wreck site like a man possessed until two of his colleagues dragged him back to WSV: "The David Miller" – his oxygen had run out - and he only made it back with minutes to spare.

But worse was to come. His distraught brother shouting: "For God sake Marcus, you were there, why didn't you bring my little girl home for a proper Resurrection service?" Then Kate's dad collapsing in his brothers' arms, totally broken with grief and sobbing; "Why didn't you bring my baby home?" Marcus said nothing and returned to his rig; never mentioning the incident again.

Around his neck, in a silver locket, he carried several strands of coloured string; the remainder of a bracelet that young Kate had made for him when she was six. "When I grow up Uncle M, I want to be just like you, a Chief on a big rig!" The little girl had exclaimed to her delighted Uncle. He now carried so much guilt for all his encouragement and assistance that he had shown her. Kate's father wanted her to be a doctor [just like him and her mother] and not work the rigs. So, the pain of that guilt burned deep in the Chief's heart; he blamed himself for her death and no Psychologist had been able to extinguish that dreadful flame.

"What do you think Chief, four or five rods?" Tom repeated his question and touched the Chief's shoulder; Marcus looked directly at him and said, "Five. Let's have five out. Troy, pass the bloody message to Lilly to get Leon and Peter haul them from the cargo bay, so they're ready for us." Tom nodded his agreement; "We'll have them in operation in less than two hours!"

"If that storm has real electrics, then we'll need every rod we can put out." The Chief stated, viewing his PA, assessing the best places to mount the rods around the Thor. Quickly he made his decision and passed the placement plan to the bridge and Captain Jones. "Well done, Marcus, we'll run with that, it looks good to me." Jones called to the Chief and then looking behind him, as he and Kazza approached the Thor on foot, he could see the dark sky above the Easter's. "Bella, that bloody storm looks closer than four hours away, can you re-calculate please." Shit, thought Jones, it would take a couple of hours to get the Chief's rods into position and that bastard looks only a couple of hours away.

That's when the dark horizon was split with several bright white flashes and a couple of intense orange streaks. "Captain, it's speeding up, running at 70kph and there are lots of electrics. It may be a Category 3 High now. We've got under three hours, I think." Bella spoke into the intercom as she studied the new Storm module she had recalculated, and it didn't look good.

"We're starting the rod placement now skipper!" Tom shouted as he and Troy pulled the first rod canister from the cargo hold and dragged it some 200 meters west of the Thor. The Chief and Leon were already making their way north, pulling another rod canister behind them.

"We'll be with you in a minute, Kazza and I will do the East. Let's go boys!" The captain shouted, reaching the cargo hold door, where he was surprised to find Frank, suited up and rolling a rod canister towards them." All hands to the deck hey skipper!" He called; "But the lunch curry may be late."

"Better late than never." Kazza grunted as he and the captain started to haul the canister across the dirt and encountered another surprise.

"Bella can handle the comm.'s Captain, Frank and I can do the southern one." It was Lilly; "If that's O.K. with you." She added, taking hold of the canisters strap as Frank pushed another one towards the cargo doors; "It will cut setting up time greatly."

"Are you sure Lilly, that you can manage, it's quite physical?" Kazza asked, already panting from his exertions. "Yes, I can thank you Deck-hand Kamiski." Lilly replied with some authority in her voice.

"Sorry Ma'am, no disrespect intended." Kazza glanced at the captain, who smiled and nodded his agreement; "Have you set up a rod canister before Lilly?" The Ensign gave the thumbs up and her and Frank set off across the dirt, dragging a canister behind them.

Jones looked up at the mountains and knew they just had a couple of hours before the storm hit; "Come on people, let's get this done before that bastard kicks our arse!" Jones could see Tom and Troy heading back to the cargo bay; the west canister had been placed. "North is ready!" Leon shouted as he and the Chief started to make their way back to the Thor's cargo hold. "We'll place number five about 1000 meters from the rear trailer." The Chief called out but staggered a little and Leon took hold of his arm. "Fuck off; I can make it under my own steam!" Marcus pushed Leon's hand away, but Eve's voice came over the headsets; "Chief, I want you back on the Thor now please." there was some urgency in her voice: "Your readout's are off the wall. Return at once."

"It'll wait Doc; don't get your panties in a twist." The Chief now panting openly, he could feel the sweat running down his face and back, but he wasn't about to abandon his duty just because some slip of a girl told him so. "Return to the Thor and help Peter on the bridge Chief, it's not up not up for discussion." The captain's voice ended any arguments the Chief may have put up and Marcus made his way to external pressure lift.

"Tom, you get on board too and ready to fire the rods, we won't have time to place number five." Jones added as they reached the placement for the eastern canister. He and Kazza set to work, placing the canister in an upright position and pulled each of the red release straps which allowed the rod to operate. Jones punched in the grounding code and the base bolts fired, tethering the canister to the ground.

"Let's go Kazza, everyone back to the rig when you've placed your rods." Jones was now watching Lilly and Frank as they struggled to raise the canister. It appeared that old Frank was finding it hard to manage. "How's it going Lilly?" Jones called with some concern in his voice. "It'll be ready in about five." Lilly said, adding: "Frank and I won't let you down."

6. RESCUE ON THE SAND.

Jones looked about him; everyone was back on the Thor save Lilly, Frank and himself. Troy was securing the 'sand-cat' and would be on board in minutes. "I know you won't Lilly, but that storm will be here soon."

Jones walked back to the external pressure lift and opened it in readiness, that's when he saw the dust swirl rolling in from the south behind Lilly and Frank. The original little storm was back. "Bloody shit!" Jones exclaimed; "Lilly, Frank; behind you – move it now!" The dust swirled about the two figures, and they disappeared from sight.

The captain, cursing under his breath started to head towards the rising dust cloud when Peter's voice came through his headset; "Skipper! What the fuck are you doing? Get inside the lift, that fucking monster is almost upon us!" Jones looked behind and the sky was black; there was nothing, but dust and lightning and it was almost upon them. "Fire the rods!" Jones shouted and looked anxiously at where the southern rod had been placed. "Where's Lilly and Frank?"

He heard a loud bang as the Northern rod opened and several snake-like cables exploded into the air, travelling a couple of hundred meters up, waving about like metallic tentacles. The Eastern rod quickly followed, and then the western rod burst into life. It seemed like minutes, but just a few seconds later, the south rod activated; Lilly and Frank had done it.

"Lilly's fine, but Frank is hurt, something hit his suit and there was a pressure and oxygen drop, then nothing. But he's back online, he's got oxygen." Eve shouted through the headset, that's when Jones saw them; Lilly was dragging the unmoving incumbent figure of Frank through the dust.

Jones ran to help, grabbing one arm and together they dragged the unconscious Chef to the external pressure lift door. "Lilly what happened?" Jones asked as they pulled Frank into the lift and closed the door. "Eve stand by, Frank was hit by a sharp rock in the small of his back, it cut through his suit and he suffered a pressure and oxygen loss, but I quickly managed to seal the breach with tape from my emergency kit and throw in an air capsule, I think he'll make it." Lilly panted as the elevator rose. The captain gripped Lilly's arm and said simply: "Well done Lilly, very well done."

Eve was in the lift as soon as the door opened; "Get him to the medical bay quick." She pulled off his helmet and could see no real damage, his eyes were fine, his ears and nose had no blood showing. Frank shook his head slowly and smiled; "Hi doc, how's business? I don't think 'Dallas' will have to give up his bed just yet."

Everyone laughed with relief; "You'll do fine Frank, a couple of days in the Medical Bay with me and 'Dallas' fussing over you, you'll make it." Eve grinned and smiled at Lilly; "Ensign, I think you just saved this man's life." Jones agreed with that, as did everyone else. "That was bloody quick thinking Lilly, considering the stress of it all." Peter patted Lilly's shoulder; "You did the right thing, giving oxygen and sealing the suit, you must have passed out top of the class in ruddy survival training."

"And weightlifting, dragging that lump for nearly a hundred meters." The Chief was sipping water from a cup and looking quite relaxed; "If the Thor ever needs a tug-of-war team, you are in it girl!" Lilly laughed and gave a girlish grin, she started to remove her 'sand-suit' and the Chief offered her some of his water. "Well done Ensign." He added, and then noticed Jones looking at him; "The Doc's fixed me up with some blood pressure pills, I'll be fine."

"No sand time for five weeks Chief." Eve said, helping Leon raise Frank to his feet and remove his survival suit. A small stone, no bigger than a thumb, fell to the floor. Frank pointed to it; "I'll keep that for a souvenir please." Lilly picked it up; "I'll hold onto it Frank, maybe you could get it mounted in a nice frame or something." They both laughed.

"To medical bay please children." Eve smiled and gestured down the corridor, "I need to check you out too Lilly, so come on." Lilly stopped in her tracks and unsmiling said; "I'm fine Ma'am, not a scratch." Eve shook her head and quietly added; "You've no choice, you've been involved in an incident on the sand, where's there has been injuries, just the regulations Ensign."

Jones noticed the alarmed expression on Lilly's face and her previous Captain's reports started to pass through his mind;

had he missed something important there? Then it came to him and he had to smile. The Chief gripped Franks arm and with Leon on the other, they headed for the Medical Bay; "Come on fellow invalids, it's down the yellow brick road to medical land for us."

Jones slipped from his survival suit as they disappeared down the corridor with Eve and Lilly following, the Ensign still gently protesting about regulations. Troy appeared in the doorway of the suit room;" Lt. Gravestone asks if you're heading for the bridge Captain." Jones nodded; "I'm on my way."

"That was something else, she looks so fragile, yet she hauled Frank's arse over a hundred meters in a fucking storm blowing 50kph plus, I wouldn't like to get a right hook from her!" Troy followed the captain to the bridge. "Best call her Ma'am then." Jones smiled at Troy, then added; "Or Sir. If you want." and chuckled to himself. Troy was an affable idiot sometimes. Troy laughed, then stopped with a complete look of puzzlement on his face; "Captain, you don't mean she's one of those transfer people you hear about?" He looked quite amazed. The captain sighed loudly; "Its bloody transgender you twat and it doesn't matter either way. Just accept Lilly for the person she is."

Troy grinned and nodded his head; "Yeah, I'm great at tolerating all sorts of people who are different." Jones stopped in his tracks and pushed a hand through his short hair and turned back to Troy; "It's not about tolerance of anything Troy, it's about simply accepting a person for who they are. Lilly is a very good person and she's going to be a fine officer. She doesn't expect to be tolerated but accepted for the person she is. That's it pure and simple." Jones started for the bridge ladder and Troy thought about the captain's words for a few seconds and then smiled; "Your right Captain, I can accept that. I'm a pretty tolerant person." Troy then headed for the Galley n search of a snack, nodding to himself.

Jones held up his arms in mock despair and climbed the ladder onto the bridge. "Maybe there are some sane fuckers on the bridge." He muttered to himself. Pete was watching the storm from the pilot's seat, whilst Bella was still manning the communications and Kazza was sipping coffee, watching a monitor – it appeared to be some old TV show; he chuckled to himself several times, before he realized that the captain was back on the bridge. He quickly switched it back to readouts from the rig's mainframe. "I find 'Mr. Parker' quite funny too Kazza, but best watched when off duty and not sitting on the bridge." Jones jerked his thumb towards the bridge ladder. Kazza was clever enough to accept the reprimand without comment and head for the galley; he wondered if any food would be dished up as he hadn't eaten since lunchtime.

Kazza had joined the service after leaving University for three good reasons: 1. He couldn't stand living in the small city of Augusta with his parents and two dumb brothers, 2. He didn't want to spend seven hours a day in a computer room or lab and 3. You get three meals a day in the Military and someone else cooks it!

AUTHOR NOTES:
"Mr. Parker is a classic Martian TV series from about fifty years ago which featured a cat [Mr. Parker] who could actually talk to humans. It's considered one of the best comedy series that Mars TV has ever produced."

Kazza Kimiski was the Thor's Systems Specialist; he looked after the rigs computer systems under the careful eye of the Chief [and the captain]. He also carried out most of the service and repair procedures on the Stations, which made life a little more interesting – he also knew that the skills and experience he was gaining would set him up for life - in some cushy number in one of the Capitol cities of Mars. That's where life is at. Kazza had visited Taylor for a short sweet holiday after graduation and loved the buzz of the place; he felt that he belonged there. But such a lifestyle in the Martian Capitol would be expensive and so he made plans. Military service was known to always open doors with the big Martian Corporations and he believed the Weather Service couldn't be that dangerous, not like being in the real military, he had reasoned. So, a couple years of 'sand-time', lots of experience with systems and bingo! The life he wanted and yearned for.

Jones sat in the captain's chair and re-read the Ensign's reports. He closed the PA and with hand on chin, stared at the storm blowing against the front screen windows. The good news from Bella was that the storm's electrics appear to be high in the atmosphere. He glanced across to the busy communications desk to see Lilly relieving Bella; "Frank had made the curry, so Eve is serving it up. It's really good." Lilly turned to the captain and added; "Eve said she's saving you a big plateful Captain." Jones nodded; "Thanks Lilly, I'll have it later. Bella, I need new models on this storm, can you have them done by the morning please." Bella agreed and left the bridge for the galley; she actually didn't feel hungry despite not eating since breakfast. But she wanted to have a chat with the Doc and they could sit and talk in the quiet galley when everyone has left.

Jones could feel the Ensign looking at him; "What is it Lilly?" He said, staring at the monitor before him. The young Ensign swallowed hard and nervously said; "Could I ask for a confidential interview please Captain?"

Jones looked up and nodded; "Yes you can Lilly, I think it's somewhat overdue, don't you?" Lilly stared at floor and wiping away a tear whispered; "Yes, you're right, sorry Captain."

"The medical bay tomorrow morning; before I leave with the

service crew; Do you want anyone there?" The captain asked, easing back in his chair and smiling at the young Ensign, Lilly nodded; "Eve, if I may." Jones agreed; "See you tomorrow Lilly and please don't lose sleep over it."

Lilly smiled; "I won't Captain, thank you." Ensign Blissford, somewhat relieved, turned back to the communications desk and saw incoming calls, one from Weather Service Control – marked for the 'Captain only' - and a couple of routine service messages including a weather report.

"Captain, a message marked for you only." Lilly called out and punched the message across to the captain's desk. Jones quickly accepted it and wasn't too pleased with the contents. "Lilly, get Peter and the Chief to the bridge please." Placing hands on head, Jones pushed back in his seat and simply said "Shit!"

EPISODE 3: "DISTRESS CALL."

7. NO CHOICES.

"Normally, fo⁻ a distress call we would up anchors and go at once, but Weather Control has instructed us to finish the service on number three, and then embark." Jones rubbed his chin and pointed to the map being projected onto the bridge windscreen; "Make of that what you will, but we don't have a choice in the matter. This strange little signal is coming from around here, about five hundred kilometers from the start of the ice shelf." Jones pointed to a small twisted valley running into the rear of the Easter Mountains. "Valley Le Mort." He said and smiled at the crew, who were sitting and standing about the bridge listening to the captain's briefing, including Frank who said quietly; "Death Valley."

Everyone looked at Frank who shrugged his shoulders; "It's an old Earth language name, translates as Death Valley." The captain nodded; "Franks right about the name, but the valley was named by someone on Earth centuries ago, even before humanity arrived here. So, it could have been called Happy Valley for what significance the name means." The crew laughed and Jones continued; "So we finish up the service and head south, I calculate about four hours to complete, so we should be underway in about six hours and certainly be on route by 22.00 hrs."

Bella raised a hand; "Captain, why is Weather Control treating this with such a lack of urgency, it is a distress call is it not?" Everyone started to agree with Bella, quietly talking amongst themselves. Jones left it for a few seconds, then raised his hands; "Everyone, everyone please, Lilly our new comm.'s expert will give you the answer on that!"

All eyes turned to Lilly, who stepped forward and flicked a switch on the comm.'s desk. A strange low, almost hypnotic, pulsating sound filled the bridge, everyone stood in silence until the Chief said; "That's the weirdest distress call I've ever heard."

Lilly coughed and motioned for silence; "Because that signal hasn't not been heard on Mars for nearly a century." She stated simply and quietly waited for the reaction from the crew. Everyone was looking at each other; "Did I hear right, nearly a century?" Leon looked quite amazed.

"I'll explain." Lilly replayed the signal and stated, "That was the distress signal for a surface suit from about 215 to 255, then it was changed to a far more high pitched one, which itself was changed about 280/290. But the fact is, that odd distress signal had to be activated during those years of 215 to 255, which means whoever was in trouble, called for help nearly a century ago, hence why there is no rush to attend."

Lilly shrugged her shoulders, continuing; "The interesting thing is that type of distress signal was only used by Mars military, no one else used this type of signal. But according to Military Archives, any suit alarm activations were recorded and there's no record of any being missed. O.K. it was a century ago and maybe somehow it got overlooked. But I probably doubt it. Nevertheless, that's a suit alarm from nearly a hundred years ago."

"So, let's get this right Ma'am, it's a suit alarm from nearly a hundred years ago and it's just been picked up now, how could that be?" Frank sounded quite bemused; "That means, if the poor bastard has been dead for nearly a century, why did they activate it now?" A ripple of amusement swept the bridge, but no-one really laughed.

Lilly nodded; "The suits in those days had a small solar panel on the back of the helmet, which was used to recharge the inbuilt batteries, what we think has happened, is that storms in the area have uncovered a body, and sunlight has reached the panel; its recharged the battery and set off the alarm again."

"Do we know who it is?" Eve asked quietly, but Lilly shook her head; "Military intelligence say they have no records of any missing military personnel who were lost on the sand. But they admit the records may not be complete for certain periods or maybe are still classified."

"Well, that's it for now, let's get this service finished and then we'll recover the poor bastard from the sand." Captain Jones closed down the projection and added; "We've been given the honour and privilege of bringing home a colleague who fell doing their duty. It may be a hundred years ago, but he or she is still one of us; and we will bring them home."

Everyone nodded in agreement; "Spot on Captain, well said." Lilly uttered and resumed her duties on communications, whilst Leon and Peter sat discussing the incident. The Captain and the Chief headed for the suit room with Tom and Kazza. "The answer has to be no Chief; the MO has stood you down from sand-time for five weeks and I cannot over-rule her medical advice." The captain gripped Marcus by the arm and added; "Now stop whining and tell Leon to get down here and suit up." Seeing the look on Marcus's face, he smiled at the Chief and slapped him on the back; "You command the Thor, keep Troy on the bridge with you because Peter will be covering us with the sand-cat."

"You mean I have put us with both her and Troy!" The Chief

exclaimed and raised his arms in mock despair and made his way to the bridge where Eve was setting up the medical monitoring station and Lilly was on communications. Bella was next to Eve and rechecking the weather reports. "The storm has passed over Chief, there's still a bit of wind, but nothing to worry about." Bella scrutinized her readouts and was satisfied that the mission could proceed.

"Captain, the weather is good for go." The Chief spoke into the small microphone; "Peter is suited and bringing the sand-cat around to the station." Jones grunted his agreement. They would have to recover the canisters from the surface after the service was completed. He had a feeling that they would be certainly needed again.

Marcus watched on the suit-room cam as the service team squeezed into the External Pressure Lift, and then Captain Jones looked up at the camera and gave the thumbs up, saying "How's the readout's Eve?"

"All suit readouts are green, good to go Captain." Eve spoke over Lilly's shoulder and then sat back; "Let's hope this bloody service call is dull as dishwater." Lilly smiled in agreement; "Thank you Eve for being with me on my interview, I did appreciate that."

"You did the right thing Lilly, The Captain now knows and has said he will support you. He won't allow bloody bullying on his rig! I would have found out with your first medical. Then I would not have been happy with that, but that's behind you now. You've been given another chance. But frankly, you really had no choice but to accept this one – and it's a good one – so don't waste it." Eve gripped Lilly's arm and raised her voice a little from a whisper; "I wonder who it is?"

Bella looked round and agreed; "I too, wonder who the poor

bugger is, he or she has waited nearly a century for a rescue that has come well late." Bella shuffled her papers about and checked her PA again; there were no new weather reports available for the region. "Chief, the team is at the station." Lilly reported; "The Captain thinks a couple of hours and it will be completed."

The Chief nodded but said nothing.

"I think he's still sulking about being stood down." Eve whispered to Bella and they both giggled, drawing a dark disapproving look from the Chief who muttered; "Bloody women." under his breath.

The maintenance of Weather Station number 3(S) concluded after two and a half hours and the service team returned to the Thor without incident. Bella and Troy had prepared an early evening meal - after Bella received a little surprise in the Galley - she was pulling loose potatoes from a crate, when she screamed so loud and suddenly, that Troy dropped the chicken pieces all over the floor. "There's something moving in the crate!" She yelled, hiding behind Troy who armed with a whisk, peered into the box.

Dallas climbed out the box and sauntered down the table, tail in air, with a complete look of indifference. "How the hell did that stupid cat get in there?" Troy asked, because the crate had been taken out of the locked vegetable store just a few moments before by Bella who shook her head; "That damn cat seems to be getting bigger by the hour."

The pair managed to get a fairly good chicken casserole ready and it was appreciated by the crew, even Frank, sitting in the Medical Bay stroking the mischievous cat, thought it was O.K. There was some left over and Dallas showed his appreciation of their efforts by eating it!

Troy, looking at the empty dish, was not happy; he was going to reheat it later and have it for a bedtime snack. "Bloody furry bandit." He muttered to himself and then realized he had put the plate in one of the kitchen fridges and now it was on the floor; empty. "He's a real fucking cat burglar!" He cursed and threw the plate into the dishwasher and went back to the bridge. The Thor was now on route to the strange distress call location.

8. SECRETS IN THE SAND.

The sun had risen some forty minutes before they arrived at the entrance to Valley Le Mort, which was between two towering cliff fronts of ragged rock, jutting from the Easter Mountains, bathed in dark shadows and littered with boulders and rock fall debris.
"Looks inviting as a bloody cyanide sandwich." The Chief said, easing the Thor down and halting several hundred kilometers away. "This is very good ground Skipper, but there's no way she will make the Valley."

"We'll have to keep her [The Thor] on this ground; the Valley is nothing but sand." Jones instructed Peter; "Tell Troy to prep the 'sand-cat' and it will be Lilly and Kazza with us." Peter nodded and passed the command to Lilly who was on the Commutations desk.

"The signal is a little stronger now Captain, you should be able to locate the body." Lilly was also intently listening through her headset with some intensity, and then Jones noticed the expression on her face; "What is it Lilly?" He said with some concern. Ensign Blissforth nodded and held up a hand to silence everyone for a few seconds, then with some real puzzlement on her face announced; "I think there is a second signal now Captain, much weaker than the first and a little different."

"Isolate it and push it through the speakers." Jones ordered and Lilly tapped at her keyboard for a couple of minutes and a strange, eerie sound filled the bridge. "What the fuck is that?" Tom said openly: he had never heard a signal like that and neither had the rest of the crew who now packed the bridge, all standing or sitting in relative silence.

But it was Kazza, ascending the bridge ladder, who exclaimed; "Wait, wait a tick, I think I've heard that pattern of tones before; when I was at University, and it was really specific to something." He placed both hands on his head and paced the bridge for a couple of seconds, then stopped; "Shit Captain, that's a bloocy cyborg motherboard in hibernation!" The look on his face wasn't missed by his crewmates: Fear; real fear. They all knew what military cyborgs were capable of.

"Lilly, pull that specific sound from the archives." Jones slowly sat down in his chair and sipped some warm coffee, only kazza spoke; "Captain, if I'm right, then that body could be an old Military Grade Cyborg, left over from the Invasion attempt and even lyirg in the sand for almost a century, would not have altered its murderous nature; not one jot."

"Is it one of our old Cyborg's or one of theirs?" Jones said quietly and Lilly answered that particular question; "It's a Mars Military Cyborg Captain." From the bridge speaker came the same distinct sound, "That's from the Military Archives." Lilly said simply. "It's one of ours."

"The Military should still hold disarm codes for it." The Chief announced to the shocked crew, then added; "If it's in any state to do anything; that hibernation signal means it's damaged, awaiting repair and rescue, and we're certainly not bringing it back online, even if it's one of ours."

The captain agreed and made his decisions quickly and

quietly; The Thor would remain parked on the good ground under the Chief's command, Eve would monitor the suit readouts and Bella would handle communications. The search team would consist of himself, Peter, Kazza and Lilly. They would take the 'sand-cat' and enter the valley, using the signal to locate the source and recover the body. For the first time in many weeks, Jones opened the rig's armoury and issued pulse tubes to the search team.

Everyone checked that the 'safety' was on before clipping the hand length, metallic tube to their suit belts. "You are all trained in the use of Pulsars, you know how deadly they are, but if you feel you really must use it, and then act without hesitation." Jones explained as the search team headed for the External Pressure Lift where the final checks on the suits and helmets were made by them [they checked each other.] "I've hooked up the flatbed trailer to 'Little Thor' Skipper, we'll never fit the body in the cab with us four in there." Peter spoke to the Captain as they crossed the sand towards the 'sand-cat'; "It will make it easy for us to lift them into the cargo bay, and then we can retrieve it from there to the Medibay." He added, pulling open the cabin door on 'Little Thor' and they climbed in. Peter fired up the engine, but didn't pressurize the 'sand-cat' – they wanted to be able to move quickly in and out the vehicle – should the need arise.

"Captain, I have a secure link with the Military Control Centre at Fort Benjamin and a certain Colonel James La Strade is in command there. He states that only you are to receive the secure transmissions from the Centre. They are quite insistent about that." Bella spoke with a little sarcasm in her voice. "I've been instructed that if you go down, then it passes to Lt. Gravestone, and then onto the Chief." She added.

Jones chuckled; "Thanks Bella, I do know the Colonel and I would expect nothing less. You had better put him through."

Jones tapped Peter's shoulder; "He was my first rig Captain when I joined the service as an Ensign, he knows his stuff. The last I heard; he was a Major in Military Intelligence. Must be going up the ranks which wasn't unexpected; his Great, Grandfather was Marshall Caleb La Strade of the Invasion War."

Peter whistled in mock admiration; "A total Military man to his regulation blue socks." Jones nodded in agreement and said; "But he's a good man and Officer to have around in a tight spot. Let's get the rundown on this job; Bella is the link ready please?"

"Patching the Colonel through now Captain. I've closed all other channels, but you can still communicate with the search team members on the suit lines. They won't be able to pick up the secure channel." Bella punched buttons and turned to Eve; "This is beginning to turn a little sour I think."

Eve breathed deep; "I agree, the captain's readouts are a little high. I think he is really concerned about this mission." The Chief peered over Eve's shoulder and grunted; "That's OK, a little nerves are good, if there's a fight ahead." He smiled at the girls and returned to the bridge control desk. They both looked at each other and sighed deeply.

"Good morning Pic, is your search team prepped and ready?" Colonel La Strade's voice appeared in Jones's helmet and the captain realized that no-one had called him 'Pic' for a very long time. "Affirmative Sir, we're ready to depart as directed." Jones answered, staring ahead, towards the dark forbidding entrance of Valley La Mort. He looked down to find his right hand was gripping his Pulsar; he had never fired one in anger and really hoped that would not change today.

"I have some background information from Mars Military

Archives that you need to know and understand, about what happened in this area during the Invasion War. Some of it is still classified and cannot be repeated; to anyone. You agree and accept that caveat?" The Colonel spoke softly, but with real authority in his voice.

Jones took a deep breath and agreed; "Yes Colonel, I do completely understand and accept that." He leaned back in his seat and checked that the suit communication line was still active; "You won't be able to hear what the Colonel says but we can still talk to each other." He spoke to the search team and gave them the thumbs up; they all responded with the same signal.

"You of course, know what happed in 227, the attempted Invasion of Mars by forces from the North American Caliphate; everyone learns what happened during those terrible nine days in School and from numerous films and stories produced since. But what happened near Valley La Mort has never been revealed and officially, the mission there during those dark days, is still classified. So, what I'm about to tell you, must remain with just you." The Colonel's voice lacked any kind of emotion, like he was giving a talk to some Military students at Fort Benjamin University.

"I understand Sir, please go on." Jones now had quite a dry mouth; he looked around and could see Peter leaned across the steering wheel, staring out of the windscreen. Kazza was sitting upright, arms folded, looking at the floor. Lilly was leaned well back in her seat, legs crossed and looking quite relaxed until she saw the captain gazing at her. She quickly sat upright and gave him a nervous smile. Jones smiled back, but his attention was quickly returned to the secure channel communication.

"Mars Military Command received information from a very

reliable Earth agent that the enemy was planning something special in that area, during the initial invasion which was to take place here in the North. Military Intelligence dispatched a team to Valley La Mort, their mission was to discover the enemy's plan and prevent its success. The home team was commanded by Captain John Stanner, a former Mars Marine, with Lt. Petra Dreyfuss; a Military physicist and Specialist Kobi Samurri who was trained in demolition. They had three military grade Cyborgs as backup. What was discovered there and what transpired, is classified to this day. Needless to say, the enemy's plan was thwarted obviously, or we wouldn't be having this conversation." A little humour had crept into the Colonel's voice.

"After it was all over, there was a search of the area, but nothing was found. No wreckage, no bodies and no signs of the enemy. The team had vanished completely and within a couple of decades the mission was forgotten and being archived as 'classified' there were no further attempts to discover what happened there. The team is still officially classified as 'Missing, believed killed in action'. If this suit alarm belongs to one of the missing team, it could solve the mystery of what happened there." The Colonel lapsed into silence and Jones asked; "Are there any records of radio traffic at the time; from the team?"

A few seconds passed; "No, sorry Pic, there are no records of any communications with the squad, remaining in the Mars Archives. They must have been disposed of at some time. It has been nearly a century, all we have to go on, is what's in the classified file – and that is not much - I'm afraid." The Colonel replied and Jones muttered; "Shit!" He took a deep breath and said, "Right Sir, with your permission we'll head into the Valley La Mort and start the search."

"Affirmative Pic, good luck and take real care in there." Jones noticed that a little concern had crept into the Colonel's voice; was that a good or bad sign? Jones sighed and gestured for Peter to fire up the 'sand-cat' and it quickly moved away, heading for the Valley entrance. He turned to his colleagues: "There's not much to go on and the bloody incident that occurred here back in 227 is still classified – in parts – so there is much more to this than we'll ever be told. What we know is that three military personnel went missing in this area on some kind of top-secret mission and it's suspected that the suit alarm is from one of them. It also means that we may find another two bodies; if we're lucky."

Lilly leaned forward, a little concerned; "What about the military cyborgs? Have they given us the disarm codes?" Jones nodded and tapped his PA. "The safe word that will make them stand down is 'Hawkins'. If that doesn't work run like hell!" He chuckled at the look on her face and turned back to the windscreen; the valley entrance was in front of them.

9. VALLEY LA MORT.

'Little Thor' disappeared into the dark, shadow filled entrance of Valley La Mort, watched by the remaining crew of the Thor, who were all on the bridge, standing and sitting in silence until the Chief said simply; "The Captain knows what he's doing, they will bloody be alright."

"I don't like the single communications channel, I don't like the fact we cannot speak directly to them and I don't like the sound of this Colonel." Bella folded her arms and sat grim faced by the communications desk. The passing minutes seemed like hours to the waiting crew. "I wonder what the fuck is going on out there." Troy asked after a few minutes; "Bella, can't you ask Military Control for an update?" He added. She nodded and called up Control, but all they replied was the search had started with no results yet.

"They're out on the sand, the readouts show that." Eve informed the crew, as she carefully watched the four suits & helmet readout monitors. "They appear to be fine, sweating a little, but drawing good breaths and all are in good condition." She added, giving a big smile to Bella and the Chief.

"They may have closed the audio and head cam's down, but we can still switch on 'Little Thor's' front camera." The Chief announced with a large grin creeping across his face. Leon leapt into the right Pilot seat and tapped on his keyboard. "We can soon remedy that and chief, if you weren't so hairy and ugly, I'd kiss ya!" He shouted and everyone turned to the front monitor as the screen came to life.

Nothing: the disappointed crew could see nothing but dirt, rocks and cliffs. "They must be to the side of the 'sand-cat' and there's no fucking cameras fitted there." The Chief spate the words out in frustration and the sense of disappointment were palpable amongst the crew on the bridge. Everyone sat back and started to talk quietly amongst themselves until Frank quickly appeared on the bridge with a large tray of sandwiches, followed directly by Tom carrying cups of coffee.

"Scoff's up." Frank said and shook his head; "Typical, all this going on and we're looking at bloody sand and rocks........ and what the hell is that?" Everyone turned back to the little monitor as Frank tapped the screen; "Just there, near the bottom of that sheer cliff face, where that really big black shadow is."

Tom looked closely and nodded; "That's a cave entrance, a big one. But that's no surprise, The Easter's are riddled with huge caverns, it's said they run for hundreds of kilometers deep underground with some caves big enough to lose a city in." He stood and stared hard at the dark shadow on the monitor, but his thoughts were interrupted by the chief.

"Good place for an enemy to hide." The Chief growled, then add; "We need to tell the captain about it."

"How can we do that; they have closed all communications off with the search team." Leon stuffed a cheese sandwich into his mouth and looked at the monitor. "What enemy Chief, the war's been over nearly a century and whoever is left on Earth couldn't raise flowers, never mind an army." He muttered.

Tom sipped his coffee and looked hard at the dark shadow and the thoughts of a deranged and damaged Cyborg, hiding out, waiting for a victim, changed his mind. "Your right Chief, we need to get a message to the captain, without Military Control realizing that we can watch through the 'sand-cats' front camera."

"I know how we can." Eve said quietly; Tom, get in your sand-suit, but I won't hook you up to the Medical Monitors – they can read them - but they can't listen in on the suit lines!" The Chief and Tom were already half-way down the bridge ladder before Eve finished speaking. "Fucking genius Doc!" The Chief yelled, heading for the suit room, with Tom following.

Tom found it quite uncomfortable, sitting on the bridge in his sand- suit, worse still; he needed to keep the helmet on for the head microphone to work. "I'm calling the captain now." He spoke, wiping sweat from his brow and said simply; "Skipper, it's me Tom; we need to tell you something, can you hear me?"

"I hear you Tom. A clever, very clever, idea to bypass our eavesdroppers – I'm impressed." The captain certainly sounded surprised to hear from the Thor. "It was Eve's brilliant idea, Skipper, we're watching through 'Little Thor's' front camera's and some thousand meters ahead of you, on the right cliff face is a big cave entrance, big enough to hide an army of deranged Cyborgs." Tom spoke quickly and quietly. "Thank you Tom, Lilly and I will check it out; we won't wave as we pass in front of the 'sand-cat' for obvious bloody reasons." The captain joked and everyone on the bridge turned to the monitor again. The crew was relieved to watch Jones and Lilly pass in front of the camera, heading towards the cave entrance. The fact they were now holding their Pulsars didn't pass unnoticed.

"I told you that the Skipper will be on top form out there." The Chief spoke with real pride and his words were met with universal agreement.

"Listen up everyone, Peter and Kazza have found a body!" Tom was listening intently to his suit communicator; "They're calling the Skipper back." He hesitated for a couple of very long seconds, then added; "It's someone called Stanners, the suit

seconds, then added; "It's someone called Stanners, the suit name tag reads: J E STANNERS. Kazza says the suit distress call is operating. He was face down apparently and so Lilly's theory was right. They are going to place him on the flatbed. But there's no answer from the Skipper or Lilly." Tom could see some anxious faces around him; "The signal may be getting blocked by the caves; those cliffs are almost like granite and the signals won't penetrate it." He added, but couldn't hide the concern in his voice.

"Peter is saying that Stanners looks like he died yesterday, no signs of decomposition; nothing." Tom wiped more sweat from his face and Eve gave him a clean rag and said, "That's not unexpected, there's nothing on the Mars surface to start decomposing, no germs, no air, it's like being kept in a deep freeze – without the ice - of course." Eve returned to the monitor; "What's happening in there?"

There was still no sign of the Captain and Lilly. The Chief didn't answer; he just shook his head and stared at the screen. After a few minutes, there was a huge sigh of relief as two figures emerged from the dark shadowed cave entrance; the Chief noticed that the pulsars were back in their holsters and his sharp eyes also caught the captain pushing something into his small back pouch.

"You can rest easy people, there's a very badly damaged old Cyborg in the cave entrance and looks like it hit the ground at speed. I've disconnected the Motherboard; there are no more signals." Jones spoke with some relief in his voice; "There are a couple of broken open crates in there and footprints all round, whatever was in the cases have gone." He added and stared back at the cave entrance.

"Everyone back on the 'sand-cat' please, we'll take the body back and after a rest, we'll continue the search for the others and we've plenty of daylight left." The captain announced, panting a little, as he and Lilly made their way back to 'Little Thor', where Peter and Kazza had placed the body on the flatbed.

A voice came over the communications systems of both the big and little Thor; it was Colonel La Strade; "Thank you everyone, this is a job well done. Please return to the Thor and standby for any further instructions." The search crew swapped looks and Kazza muttered; "Well that's that then. I don't think." Lilly slowly nodded her agreement and stared at the body laid on the flat bed trailer. Something wasn't quite right about it. She pointed to the body, now face up on the flatbed; "His rank ensign has been pulled off and his holster is empty."

The captain opened the helmet visor and lifted the dead man's head, the hair still felt wet and squeaky clean from shampoo, he eaned close and gently opened the mouth; the teeth were gleaming from being freshly brushed. Jones rubbed the helmet with his fingers and stared hard at his fingertips, then grunted with realization. The others stared at him in disbelief; "What are you doing Captain?" Peter asked incredulously as the captain closed the visor and folded his arms. "Back to the Thor please, I want Eve to have a good look at our friend Captain Stanners." Jones said simply and they climbed aboard the 'sand-cat' in silence.

The 'sand-cat' took twenty minutes to return to the Thor, where the body was loaded into the cargo bay with some reverence and careful handling. Lilly commented on how young and good looking the late J E STANNERS actually was, considering he had been dead for nearly a century. She also noted there was no damage to his suit or helmet.
"He must have run out of air and was asphyxiated." Peter guessed. Jones glanced at him and said quietly through the suit line; "A Mars marine Captain lets himself run out of air on a vital mission, I don't think so." Peter nodded; "So you know who he is Captain?"

Jones said, "Yes and no, but this is not just a corpse collection mission, I think." He pointed to the body and two little red straps hanging loose in the small of the back. "That's where the spare air cylinders would be, but the straps are broken and with some force; the buckles are shattered. They were ripped off, probably just before or just after he was put here." The two climbed out of the cargo bay and dropped onto the surface again, where Jones let Peter into some of the story.
 "He was killed then, or rather left to die without air refills?" Peter looked back at the body as the outer cargo door slid quietly down and sealed itself. "Poor devil, why did they leave him to die, they could have taken him prisoner, question him for information or bloody something; bloody religious nuts." He sounded sad and a little angry.

"I'll brief everyone after some food and water, lots of cold water, but I don't think anyone killed our friend there Peter, so don't get too upset." Jones patted Peter's shoulder and the pair headed for the Thor's external pressure lift, followed by Lilly and Kazza who had closed up the 'sand-cat'.

Bella called the captain to say that Eve had Tom, Troy and Leon move the body to the Medical Bay and Frank was bringing up more sandwiches and drinks to the bridge. "So, whatever happened here back in 227, I think we've only scratched the surface and we haven't learnt all that Valley La Mort has to reveal." Jones said and looked back at the Valley entrance, then closed the lift door; "Let's get some scoff and rest; I think we are going to need it, this mission is far from over." The lift ascended to the suit room where Eve awaited Jones with some expected, but still disturbing news.

EPISODE 4: "OPERATION MINCEMEAT."

10. JOHN DOE.

Eve helped the captain slip from his survival suit and very quietly whispered: "There's a real problem with our friend Stanners; the Mediscan reveals that he died of pneumonia!" Jones eased from the suit and Troy pushed it back into its storage cupboard, hooking it up for replacement of air and to recharge the batteries.

"I'm not surprised Eve." Jones pushed his fingers through his damp hair and saw the look of amazement on her face. "Our friend had been prepared at an undertaker's for his expected Resurrection Ceremony. Hair washed, teeth cleaned, and make-up applied, I bet his body still smells of the antiseptic that hospital's wash the corpse down with after death. What else can you tell me?" Eve shook her head and smiled:" Yes it does, the Chief said you would be on top form out there!"

Jones laughed and took her by the shoulder: "Let's go and take another look at 'John Doe." The pair made their way to the Medical Bay, followed by the Chief and Tom.

Lilly was waiting for them with some printouts clutched in her hands. "The Human Archive Service cannot identify his DNA, which is quite incredible. They have no record of him as an individual, but say he's closely related to a family called 'Dunning' who reside at a farmstead near New London."

"Thanks Lilly, now how long has he been dead?" Jones directed his question to Eve, she looked down at the body, then back at him: "Approximately 96 years."

"Christ, I hope I look that good after being dead for nearly a century!" The Chief muttered and everyone smiled;" He was nearly 15 [27 in Earth years] when he died." Eve added. The captain rubbed his chin and instructed Lilly to get hold of someone in the 'Dunning' family who may have information about an ancestor who died young and of pneumonia around the time of the attempted invasion.

Jones noticed a strange faraway look on Eve's face as she adjusted the sheet around the body. "What is it Eve?" He asked and she sighed; "According to Military Control, because the body has no near relatives to object and it's in such good condition; they want to hand it over to Project Cenotaph."

He folded his arms and said; "I thought that was just bloody rumours. I mean bringing dead people back to life - years after they died - that's just nuts!" The Chief agreed and Tom added; "I heard they have tried about three times and nearly succeeded, except for one small problem."

"What was the bloody small problem?" The Chief asked and Tom laughed; "It was like Frankenstein's monster, they had to bloody resurrect the bodies really quickly!" He looked down at the body and said quietly and sadly; "Sorry John Doe, we can't help you."

"Well, that's High Command's call, hopefully the other two may have descendants who may care, thats if we manage to find them." Jones spoke with a little anger in voice. He had heard lots of gossip and 'skuttlebug' about the so called 'Operation Cenotaph' when he was on an Officer's course at Fort Benjamin, and it was all about the Military's near-mythical research station called – appropriately - 'RS13'. Even its actual location was classified, but the general rumour circulating was that Research Station Thirteen is hidden up on the Ice Shelf: well away from most of Mars population.

"Well, I'm going to grab some scoff and plenty of cold water before I go back out there." The captain said and headed for the galley; "I hope Frank has knocked up something good." Eve covered the body with the clean white sheet and slid the tray back into the refrigeration unit, that's when she noticed Dallas sitting on her chair; "Sorry old friend, your bed is needed by someone else." She said softly as she stroked his neck and Dallas lay down on the chair and cat napped.

Eve joined the Captain in the Galley, where he was enjoying a vegetable casserole with mash and a couple of large cups of cold water.

"Message from Military Control at Fort Benjamin Captain." Bella appeared in the Galley doorway and handed Jones a piece of paper. He read it with growing interest. Everyone in the Galley fell silent and Jones looked up to see everyone looking at him. "It appears Colonel La Strade is going to visit us with a Military search team; weather permitting." Jones placed the paper quietly down on the table and continued eating. "When will he arrive Skipper?" Peter asked, sipping water from his cup. Tom answered that; "It would be a six-hour flight just to get to Rossington and that's with clear weather all the way."

"So don't expect to see him quite yet." Jones spoke to Eve and finished his meal. He turned to Kazza and slid a small black object across the table; "Do you think you could get that back online?"

Kazza picked up the slim plastic rectangle and studied it. He chuckled; "Captain, the last time I saw one of these, it was in the bloody Telecommunications Museum at Taylor." He turned it in his hand and with a soft click the device opened. "The battery is totally dead; I need to find a way to recharge it once I've cleaned the crap out."

"That was in the sand near those two opened crates." The captain quietly informed Kazza and Tom, who was now also studying the old phone. "Yes, I think we can get this museum piece up and running Captain, but you won't be able to call anybody; the satellite that serviced these phones is long gone." Tom chuckled to himself.

"I don't plan to make any calls, but I would love to see the videos on it." Jones smiled at Tom and they both nodded. "Where better to store any last messages." Tom commented and he and Kazza left for the Thor's workshop. Peter sat back in his chair and pushed his plate away; "So, if that's not mister Stanner on the morgue tray, then what the hell happened to him?" The captain held up his hands: "No idea, but someone dumped that body on the sand in Stanner's surface suit, not forgetting to take his weapon and spare oxygen, and if I had to guess, I would say that Stanner did that."

"I think the skippers on the money. It was an 'Operation Mincemeat'." Frankie the Chef sat down and started to eat his casserole with a spoon, taking time out to dip slices of bread in the juice. There was silence for a few seconds until Peter asked: "What the fuck is an 'Operation Mincemeat' when it's at home?" The Chef looked up from his plate and waved his spoon about: "It happened during one of those bloody big wars that the Earth enjoyed so much. One side dumped a dead body on the enemy with false battle plans and the dumb buggers fell for it and got a good kicking." Frankie explained between quick mouthfuls; "That was the code name of the operation: 'Mincemeat'. I remembered it because, being a Chef, I make mince. Simple really." Frankie gave a big grin and started to slurp his coffee.

The Captain and Eve laughed, but Peter just sat looking quite bemused. "So, the body was a decoy, to make the enemy believe they could land here safely and carry out their planned mission?" Peter placed hands upon his head and then smiled; "Stanner; you're a clever fuck!" Jones nodded, sipping his coffee; "What better way to convince the enemy that they're safe in this area, than the battle squad send to stop them, turning up dead in the sand."

Peter took a ceep breath and said:" Yeah, but we still have two Mars Military Cyborg's missing out there and if the old Classified Records are right, two more bodies."

Jones nodded in agreement "Finding the bodies should not be a problem, if the storm has uncovered them too, but I really don't want an encounter with any undamaged Cyborg's; even if they are bloody ours."

"Amen to that." The Chef grunted and started to clear the tables of plates and cups; he placed on the floor Eve's half-finished meal and smiled as Dallas appeared right on cue.

"Are there really a couple of more bodies out there then?" Eve looked quite sad at the prospect of hauling two more long dead corpses onto the Thor. "We don't have room in the Medical Bay for more than one body." She added, rolling her coffee cup about in her hands.

"We'll store them in the cargo hold, keep it unpressurised and no heating. They'll be fine." Jones stood up and nodded towards the door; "Time for another trip to Valley La Mort." Everyone groaned but rose slowly from the table.

11. RETURN TO THE VALLEY.

Leon fastened the captain into his surface suit and carefully examined the seals. "You're checked and ready skipper." Jones nodded and picked up his helmet, he noticed Lilly had appeared in the door of the suit room with a piece of paper. Tom, already suited, was checking Leon's suit with great care and slapped him on the shoulder; "You're ready to go." The search team was to consist of the Captain, Tom, Leon and Bella.

"What is it Lilly?" The captain adjusted the padding in his helmet and was satisfied that all was good. Lilly held up the paper and didn't smile. "Just heard back from New London, the Dunning family can't help. They tell us that there's nothing in the family history that anyone can recall, of a lost ancestor around the time of the invasion." Lilly held up the paper again and added; "But this may be of interest Captain." She handed Jones the paper and he did read it with some real interest.

"It appears that J E Stanners spent some time on Earth just before the invasion and upon his return had suddenly come into a lot of money. He arrived back at Taylor spaceport with a small fortune in gold and rather strangely, the authorities didn't investigate how he got it." Jones spoke quietly and handed the paper to Tom, who half smiled and said simply;"A double agent?"

"Yeah, but which side was he really loyal too?" Jones took a deep breath and pressed the intercom button; "Bridge, is Bella on her way down, we're already suited up here." The Chief answered that Eve was on her way down to speak to the captain. On cue, Eve squeezed into the suit room and taking Jones by the arm, pulled him into the outside corridor and spoke quickly and quietly. "Sorry skipper, I can't allow Bella on the surface." She smiled and leaning forward, whispered in his ear; "Bella is nine weeks pregnant, no way does she do any surface work now, well except in an emergency!" The look of surprise on the captain's face made Eve laugh out loud. "It's quite common with young women you know!"

"Well, you can knock me down with a feather." Jones smiled broadly and then added; "If it's not breaking a confidence, who's the father?" He rubbed his chin, looking quite bemused and Eve whispered in his ear again. "Holy fucking shit!" Jones exclaimed, and then offered apologies for his language. Eve waved his apology away; "I said something similar when she told me."

Jones said nothing for a few seconds, then he chuckled; "I want ring-side seats when she tells him!" Both he and Eve laughed together and shaking his head, he headed back into the suit room to tell Lilly she was going back on the surface. Eve returned to the bridge to oversee the Medical Station, with Bella back on communications.

"Suit up Lilly, Bella will handle communications again." Jones told Lilly and waited while she slipped quickly into her sand-suit and both Tom and he checked her over. When satisfied Jones patted her shoulder and issued the search team with Pulsar's. "Let's go team." Jones said and with an O.K. from Eve on the bridge, the team entered the External Pressure Lift. The captain was still laughing to himself as the lift descended to the surface; the rest of the team looked quite bewildered by the skipper's demeanor and Lilly was wondering why she had replaced Bella at real short notice, but she didn't ask Jones why. She took a couple of little breaths and quickly followed the others out when the lift door opened on the surface. It was still and forbidding with Lilly actually shivering a little, but she stepped out onto the surface. The captain speaking in her helmet snapped her back from her thoughts.

"Leon can drive the 'sand-cat', we'll start the new search from

the cave entrance, and I want to have another look in there."
Jones spoke to Tom and patted his Pulsar; "Keep that handy
Tom, they may be our Cyborg's, but we won't take any damn
chances." Leon pulled himself into the 'sand-cat' and fired up
the engine, again she wasn't pressurized, and the search team
climbed in. Jones looked about him and gave the thumbs up:
the crew responded with the same signal and Leon headed
the 'little Thor' towards the Valley.

Twenty minutes later 'little Thor' arrived back at the dark cave
entrance and the search team decanted onto the surface,
splitting into two groups, The Captain and Lilly made their way
into the cave whilst Leon and Tom started to sweep the Valley
with an Anomaly Rod [an instrument used for finding 'out of
place' objects on the surface].

Jones and Lilly switched on their helmet lights as they slowly
entered the shadowy darkness of the cave, past the now
defunct Cyborg sitting near the entrance and into the inner
recess of the cavern. "Let's have another look at those
crates." Jones indicated towards the rear, where two grey
cases lay open, their lids broken and thrown to one side.

"There's no writing or symbols or anything, they're quite
blank." Lilly leaned into the nearest one and ran her hands
around the inside; "Nothing here Captain." She added with
some clear disappointment in her voice. But the Captain's
attention had been drawn elsewhere; he walked past Lilly and
the abandoned crates to the very rear of the cave. Lilly
watched in amazement as he disappeared into the darkness.
 "Captain! Captain!" She called anxiously and then quickly
followed him.

It was another much smaller cave entrance, slopping gently
downwards, winding away into the darkness. Lilly's and the
Captain's helmet lights simply could not penetrate the real

blackness to any great distance, but Jones pointed to the soft dirt of the small caves floor. "Human footprints." The captain then spotted more sinister marks in the sand. "Cyborgs." He said and kneeling down, closely inspected the clear indications that showed a couple of Cyborg's, accompanied by a single human, had passed through here and into the depths of the cave system.

"There are no return prints." Lilly said, looking about and then yelled; "Captain, the wall over there has a small claw hammer driven into it and looks like a tag attached!" Jones could now see the hammer embedded in the rock face and hanging from it: a yellow tag. "It was probably used to open the crates." Jones muttered, but he gently lifted the tag and read out aloud, the simple sentence written on it; "Suicide is painless for those you love. J.E. Stanner."

Lilly and the Captain exchanged glances and after a few seconds Jones said simply; "Let's go." The pair returned to the cave entrance and emerged back into the sunlight. "Captain, can you read me?" It was Tom's voice; "We've found the woman's body – It's badly shot up - looks like a laser weapon. She's a real mess." Jones acknowledged the call, and they made their way to a small rocky knoll some distance from the cave. Then Leon's voice came online, quite calm and steady; "The other one is here too. But it looks like he was shot in the back."

Jones and Lilly joined up with their companions at the little group of rocks which formed a horse-shoe shape in the dirt and viewed the bodies. The woman was indeed in a bad state, it looked like she had been killed at close range with one of the old-fashioned Laser handguns that were common military issue a Century ago. Tom lifted her right arm, and everyone could see a laser weapon still clutched in her dead fingers. "Died fighting I suppose." He said sadly.

Lilly had turned away from the dreadful sight and Jones gently gripped her arm; "Go fetch the 'sand-cat' - we'll get the bodies onto the flatbed." Lilly managed to smile and said; "Thank you Captain." Then she made her way back to the 'little Thor'.

Jones inspected the young man's body and could see he had been shot through the small of the back and the exit wound was the size of a football; there were bits of bone, cloth and intestines around his hands, which were still clutching his stomach. But it was the look on his face that drew everyone's attention, not the agony of a terrible wound, but something else.

"Surprise?" Tom spoke quietly and he reached down and pulled the dead man's Laser pistol from its holster. "He was killed from behind in total surprise, didn't even have his gun at the ready." All three turned and looked at the woman's body, the arm holding her weapon was pointed directly at where the young man lay. "What the fuck went on here?" Leon sadly asked no-one in particular. He shook his head and added; "This is some fucked up situation, our own military turning on each other in the middle of a fucking war, an unknown corpse dressed up to be someone else and no sign's anywhere of the enemy."

The three stood in silence for about a minute, then Lilly pulled the 'sand-cat' up, just a couple of meters from the knoll, she jumped from the cab with a canvas ground sheet in her arms. "This will help move her body." She said quietly and unfurled the sheet. Jones and Tom wrapped the girl's body in the sheet and Tom noticed something glint in the lip of her helmet. He reached in and pulled the fragile little object out. He held it up and the captain sighed; "A golden Crescent, the sign of the North American Caliphate, she must have kept it hidden around her neck." They finished wrapping her badly damaged body and placed it upon the flat bed.

Leon had also found something on the man's body: a small brown wallet. He held it open for the others to see. A simple picture of a very pretty young woman cradling an infant in her arms, written on the bottom was: 'My Julie and our son Dave.' Each looked at it in turn; Leon muttered something and slowly pushed it back into the dead man's pocket.

They gently lifted his body onto the flatbed and covered it with a ground sheet, fastening the pair down for their journey back to the Thor. Bella then called the captain to say that she had heard from Military Control; they were closed down with bad weather and Colonel La Strade wanted the Captain to make a full report, over the secure channel, when he returned to the Thor.

"Affirmative Bella, tell them I will when I return." Jones climbed into the 'sand-cat' and stared out the windscreen, various thoughts flooded his mind, especially the note Stanner left. Bella called up the captain again to say that Kazza had the relic working and there was a video on it that he should see.

Jones smiled as the crew settled in, Tom turned to him; "I told you that little shit was a wizard with anything electrical." Jones nodded; "Let's get back to the Thor and get Eve to have a look at these two." Leon pulled away from the knoll and Jones looked back at the cave entrance with mixed emotions; he hoped that the old phone could shed some light onto what happened here, all those years ago and was the outcome worth three young lives. He leaned back in his seat and closed his eyes, Stanner's last written words hung heavy on his mind: "Suicide is painless for those you love." Had he disappeared into the deep cave system, knowing he would never return?

12. THE DEAD TELL TALES.

The bodies were examined by Eve where they lay in the cargo hold; there was no more room in the medical bay. The small handheld Mediscan revealed that the woman had died from multiple injuries caused by laser fire; "Someone really wanted her dead, they lasered her about three times. One would have been enough." Eve stated. The girl's surface suit had been removed and everyone could now see the real extent of her injuries. But it was the numerious tattoo's that caught the crew's attention: They were on both arms, her legs and back were covered with Arabic symbols.

"That's verse from the Koran, aint it?" The Chief said as he rummaged through her discarded surface suit and pulled a small plastic card from the outer lining, he held it up and Jones read it carefully: "AB2341JHN7568XX"

"That looks like some kind of launch code." Tom offered his opinion; "Or to arm a weapon." He added.

Eve looked a little puzzled; "if she was a religious fanatic – prepared to die for her cause – then why the tattoo's? I thought their religion forbade tattoos. Bit odd, don't you think?" Jones nodded; what little he knew about the old religions of 'Mother' told him Eve was right. He grunted; "Another bloody mystery."

"Wrap them in sheets and we'll take a look at that old phone." Jones said and he with the Chief and Tom, made their way to the Thor's small workshop, where a very self-satisfied Kazza awaited them. Eve and Frankie set about wrapping up the bodies for their journey to Rossington, whilst Peter and the remaining bridge crew already had the Thor underway.

Kazza handed the captain the old phone and explained how he managed to charge it and break the entry code that protected the contents. "The videos are something else." He said, tapping the screen; "The first one's a bit dark, he must have made it in that cave."

Jones held the phone up for the others to view and a small fuzzy picture appeared upon the small screen: A man in a surface suit, the name tag read M A KHAN; he looked around 16/17 years old with a dark beard and brown eyes. He was speaking into the camera, but of course; there was no sound, as voices cannot penetrate the suit helmet. The crew watched as he pointed to the first open crate, where a Cyborg was pulling the contents out.

It shocked the crew, they couldn't believe it as a naked and obviously dead young male, was laid upon the floor of the cave. "That's our John Doe!" Tom gasped; "No wonder our Human Archives had no record of him, they must have brought it from Earth!" Khan then pointed the phone to the second crate, revealing a strange metallic object that had several small red and green lights illuminated. Khan touched the object and with the same hand made a cutting movement across his neck. He held the phone close to his helmet's face plate and mouthed very slowly: "Everyone." He held the phone to his name tag and shook his head, as if saying "NO."

Khan held up a surface suit with his other hand and showed the name tag to the camera;' J E STANNER', he then tapped his chest and smiled, he placed the phone against the crate. The crew watched as he dressed the corpse, removing the pistol from its holster and then pulling the oxygen cylinders from the rear. The first video then ended. Jones looked at their amazed faces. "Stanner must have filmed that before the body was placed on the sand and before the other team members arrived."

The Chief grunted; "The woman was a physicist; she would know how to arm that bloody thing and she was carrying the firing code." Jones nodded, rubbed his chin and smiled; "I think we could put together a story that fits what we have, but let's get to the Galley, I need coffee." The four made their way to the Mess where Bella was filling cups with coffee and handing out biscuits. They were joined by Frankie and Eve who had secured the bodies in the cargo hold. Troy took a tray to the bridge for Peter and Leon who were driving the rig.

With everyone quietly seated in the Galley, Jones (with Kazza's help and assistance) switched on the next video; "Again, there's very little light, just some coming through a back window." He added, then grinning; "This is really most interesting, they get four out of five for artistic merit!"

The little screen came to life, and everyone chuckled, Lilly looked a little embarrassed and sipped her coffee without comment; that made the Chief and Tom smile; "It's amazing what people film in the privacy of a hotel room." Tom laughed as they watched two people having sex on a large bed.

"That's our dead girl, those tattoos are quite distinctive, and she looks a lot better there than she does now." The Chief quietly commented; "Now who's the lucky fella?" Tom answered that one; "It's Stanner – and this was filmed on Earth - you can see blue sky through the window and a tree." Everyone nodded in agreement and the short film ended abruptly.

"Right, let's put together what we have." Jones leaned back in his seat and sipped his coffee; "A team from Earth slip our radar and deliver two crates to Valley La Mort just before the invasion "Right, let's put together what we have." Jones leaned back in his seat and sipped his coffee; "A team from Earth slip our radar and deliver two crates to Valley La Mort just before the invasion starts: now this is important – they don't activate the weapon because they think the bloody invasion will be successful; it's a back-up plan. They have two agents in the Mars Military or so they think." Jones placed his cup on the table and folded his arms; "In reality, Stanners is a double agent, and his plan is almost copied from an incident that happened centuries ago on Earth, during one of their many bloody wars. He knows that if Petra Dreyfuss gets near the thing, she'll detonate. So, he dumps the body to make her believe he's dead, maybe she'll cancel the mission. But it goes wrong; she thinks her lover and fellow agent has been killed and their plan has been compromised. Petra kills young Kobi Samurri to cover any loose ends and maybe Stanner witness's the killing and knows she will finish the mission; so, he has to make sure she's dead and so kills her."

"He certainly did that." Eve said; "And then some." The crew laughed and the captain continued; "I think Stanners had a last minute change of mind. The enemy had paid him, he would be a hero had the invasion succeeded, living with his lover in a new religious paradise. But it was a total failure, Mars Military lost a lot of good people; but they won." He continued; "Stanner's was now trapped on Mars with a radical girlfriend who wished to be a martyr and take an entire planet with her, including him."

"They [Mars Military] would have charged him with treason and his life would be over. So, the only option open to him is to hide the device where no-one would ever find it; in a cave system that stretches for thousands of Kilometers below the surface." Jones sipped more coffee and added; "He has no he uses the two remaining functioning Cyborgs to carry the very dangerous device underground – they could carry it far into the cave system before their power ran out – and he went with them. The note on the tag points to that. He meant to leave a message."

"He didn't want anyone else to have such a terrible device and he paid with his life." Lilly sounded quite sad and nibbled at a biscuit. "Our John Doe will never be identified now, what DNA records remain on Earth?" She sipped her coffee and replaced the cup upon the table.

"What anything remains on Earth?" Tom replied with some sarcasm in his voice and lots of sadness.. There was a quiet murmur of agreement from the crew and Jones raised an arm to signal the end of discussions; "Right people, let's get to Rossington and La Strade can take care of our cargo. I best call Fort Benjamin and give them some sort of explanation."

Kazza held up a hand with a puzzled look on his face; "Skipper, can I ask something?" Jones nodded and he said simply; "Who the fuck was M A KHAN then?" Everyone then laughed when Jones replied; "I have no bloody idea!"

"Maybe M A KHAN is our 'John Doe', he could have died on the trip to Mars and kept stored by Stanner, who by then swapped surface suits with him and used him as the decoy. That makes sense I think." Tom offered the explanation to the crew who nodded with agreement.

"I like that Tom, I like that a lot." Jones was impressed with that idea, it tied up a very loose end and the 'John Doe' certainly was not Martian in origin; everyone on Mars had their DNA record stored from the very early days of Mars colonization. Maybe the 'Dunnings' of New London were early relatives who had arrived before the Invasion attempt.

Everyone started to leave the table, but Bella asked Kazza to help clear the crockery away as Frankie needed to prep for the evening meal. Eve and the Captain exchanged smiles; "I think someone is about to find out that he's going to be a dad." Eve whispered and Jones agreed; "Have the smelling salts on standby!" He added, shaking his head in disbelieve, but still smiling.

Dallas jumped onto the table and found a shiny new toy to play with; the old phone. Everyone watched as he pushed it about with his paws. "Maybe he's going to call one of his ancestors!" Kazza chuckled, adding; "Is it me or is that cat bigger than yesterday?" and reached to pick the phone up before Dallas dropped it on the floor. That's when it started to ring and vibrate. Someone was calling? There was absolute silence and amazement in the Galley. Then Eve said quietly; "Who's going to answer it?"

ADVERTISEMENT BY THE AUTHOR.

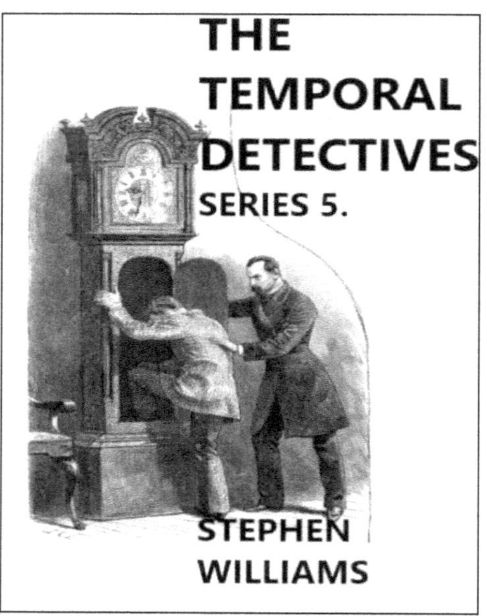

Available on 'AMAZON.COM' and all good bookshops!
Regular and young Adult science-fiction/fantasy, historical
fiction series!

TO VISIT 'THE TEMPORAL DETECTIVES' WEBSITE, SCAN THIS CODE:

Or type: https://temporaldetectives.blogspot.com

PLEASE REMEMBER: ALL STORIES ARE RATED:
AGE 15+ ONLY   or   AGE 12+ ONLY.

13. HOME PORT.

"Here we go Skipper." Frank handed over the small plate and Jones took it with a big smile. "Egg banjo's, just the ticket, thanks Frankie." He happily exclaimed, and sipping his coffee anticipated the delights to come. Lilly took her plate from Frank and lifting the top slice asked: "Why on Mars are they called 'banjo's' Frank?"

"It's a really old military term apparently; anything tasty put between two bits of bread was called a 'banjo'." The Chief answered and eased himself onto the pilot's seat, to check the Navicom. He looked up and sighed: "There they go, talk about being late for your own funeral." Through the large clear windscreen of the bridge, they watched as the steel canisters containing the three bodies recovered from Valley La Mort trundled past, being pulled by a small 'beaver' drone. The MSV: Marshal Alexander awaited them in Dock Bay No.3; then a long journey back to Taylor and some very late funerals with military honours. Everyone watched in silence as they passed.

AUTHOR NOTE:
"I think the Chief is in error here, only a fried egg sandwich was referred to as a 'banjo' - I have this on good authority from a couple of friends in the Army who eat them on a regular basis!"

"I think I will remember the look on Kazza's face, when he answered that phone, for a very long time." Jones laughed; "Though, nowhere near the expression he pulled when Bella told him was going to be a dad." The bridge crew all laughed and Lilly, almost giggling out loud, said: "Fancy getting cold calls for home insurance that's nearly a hundred years old!"

"It was a recorded message, Stanner must have left his answer-phone on and the Acme Home Insurance Company used the opportunity to pitch for a sale." Jones took a bite from his fried egg sandwich and smiled to himself: Miss Carol Dyer of the Acme Home Insurance Company was now dust, even the Company itself folded some forty years ago and I bet Stanner didn't sign up for any policies, considering what he was planning.

"Odd though, that woman sounded quite young, now she's long dead, life can be strange. It's like watching those old films from Earth: everyone in them are now ghosts." Lilly sighed and nibbled at her sandwich.

"When's the wedding Lilly?" The Chief sat back, satisfied that the Navicom was functioning correctly, he also smiled to himself, to say that he was surprised by the events of Bella's pregnancy was an understatement; he was bloody amazed! "They have nothing in common you know, not really, but they have arranged the big day for our next leave; in three weeks time. Her parents are on the way already, they want to meet Kazza." Lilly was grinning, she loved a good wedding and Bella had made it clear that all the crew was invited. Bella and Eve had spent the first day back in the Home Port, looking for a suitable wedding dress.

Captain Jones had managed to persuade Weather Control to stand the Thor down for the day, but Vice Admiral Dr. Chan Di-Luk had insisted that the crew wear Number One dress for the occasion, the only exception being the bride; since the wedding was basically taking place on Military time.

"Kazza had asked the Skipper if he would be best man, but the Captain talked him into picking one of his brothers; keep it in the family and friendly like." Lilly added, dabbing her mouth with a paper handkerchief, she really did like 'egg banjo's' now; "Bella's parents – Grace and Gustov - have booked a flight down here."

Frankie whistled through his teeth; "No expense spared then." Civilian flights were few and far between and really bloody expensive; he cleared the plates and cups from the bridge and pointed to the windscreen: "Skipper, I think you have some visitors."Jones looked to the dock side and saw Colonel Le Strade stepping onto the deck, accompanied by another senior officer; he recognized Vice Admiral Everest Kellamann at once – he had been one of Jones's Military Instructors at Fort Benjamin - when he was a Major in the Engineering department there.

"Shit! Only bridge crew stay here, the rest of you head for cover, that's Vice Admiral Kellamann with Le Strade." Jones stated, and apart from Lilly, Troy and himself, the bridge emptied on his command. Leon opened the external pressure door for the pair and saluted; "Captain Jones is on the bridge Sir."

"Thank you." Kellamann said simply and returned Leon's salute. The two officers made their way to the bridge where Jones greeted them with a salute and handshakes. "Sorry to drop in without notice Pic, but I was here about the three bodies, so I thought I'd deliver the message myself." Admiral Kellamann shook Jones's hand firmly and Jones wondered what message was so important that a Vice-Admiral turned up in person to deliver it.

"This is Ensign Blissford Sir." Jones introduced the nervous looking Lilly to the pair;" She's on Communications presently." Lilly saluted and both men shook her hand. Troy also saluted and stood smiling by the Pilots seat.

"Just the young lady we've come to see." Colonel Le Strade spoke directly to Jones; "Would you call the crew to the bridge please Pic." The captain motioned to Lilly to announce the crew call, which she did with some authority in her voice; that did make Jones smile.

It took a couple a minutes for the crew to assemble with very little chatter and Jones apologized for Peter's absence, since he had been granted a couple of day's liberty to sort out a domestic matter. The Vice-Admiral just nodded; "Your call Pic, you know the man's story and if you think he needs it, then its fine by me." Le Strade clapped his hands and called for total silence, announcing Vice-Admiral Kellamann to the crew. They stood in silence whilst the Vice-Admiral pulled a document from his briefcase and with a smile upon his face read out: "I have the great pleasure and pride in announcing the award of the Silver Star to Ensign Lillian Mary Blissford, Staff 4221 for an act of bravery upon the Martian surface on Week 13, Sol 130 in the Year 323. Ensign Blissford displayed courage and great strength of character in rescuing a fellow crew member during a violent storm, keeping a cool head and acting in the fine traditions of Mars Military Officers. She managed to seal his damaged survival suit and give him oxygen, thereby saving his life; so, it's well done Ensign!"

Vice-Admiral Kellamann started the applause which lasted for nearly a minute, with many shouts of: "Well done Lilly!" from the crew. Lilly went quite red and thanked everyone for their kindness and Eve gave her a big hug and whispered;"Well done Lilly, see our Captain was right about making you stay!" Lilly gave a shy grin and nodded her agreement.

Vice-Admiral Kellamann held up a hand for silence and slowly continued; "Ensign Blissford will be awarded the Silver Star in a ceremony to be held at the Rossington Governor's Palace in three weeks; the medal will be presented by Gaylord Prentiss, the Vice-President of Mars!"

The Chief whispered to Jones and Eve; "The VP is down south to open the new rail terminal and he really does like publicity." Jones nodded, the new rail terminal, build into the North city wall had taken five years to complete and the tracks [when finished] wou d connect Rossington with the two other major cities of Southern Mars: Kiev and Dayburgh. If successful, more tracks and cities would be added in coming years, The North already currently enjoyed a good rail service with five terminals and thousands of kilometers of laid track.

Whilst everyone was congratulating Lilly, Vice-Admiral Kellamann and Le Strade took Jones to one side and spoke quietly. Le Strade made it clear that he was not happy about Jones's failure to inform him about the contents of the phone videos. The Captain could do no more than apologize, but Vice-Admiral Kellamann shrugged his shoulders and sipping coffee that Sunny Yelstin had passed him said; " Don't worry about it Le Strade, I've stopped plans to give that traitorous bitch a military funeral, she'll be resurrected in a quiet little part of Taylor and forgotten. We will leave her name on the War Memorial; removing it would draw attention, as would scratching out Stanners. But the boy has descendants that claimed him; apparently a great, great grandson called Lester Huggins has arranged a private family resurrection in his old hometown of New Paris. The local military will provide an escort for the body; that's the least we can do for him."

"What about the unknown one, what happens to him?" Jones asked accepting a coffee from Leon. "The 'John Doe' has been handed over to a military research station for medical use. Good quality corpses are hard to come by for authorized medical research; He'll be put to good use I'm sure – after all - there is no family to object." Le Strade raised his coffee cup and added; "To our ancestor's and what they all fought for."

Jones, Leon and Kellamann raised their cups and said loudly together; "Salute!"

Jones noticed the sad look on Eve's face, she had clearly overheard the conversation, he raised his cup to her and shrugged his shoulders; the matter was out of their hands and they both knew that.

"You're well prepared for a trip onto the ice-shelf Pic?" Le Strade changed the subject with little subtlety; "Most of your crew have done ice time?" Jones pointed out, that only four members of the crew had 'ice-time' under their belts: himself, the Chief, Kazza and Troy, but he also pointed out that his crew were well trained and would cope professionally with the conditions.

"In my opinion, Weather Station Seven should be manned the whole time, it's far too vital for the Deep South to drop offline for any reason." The Vice-Admiral placed his cup upon the tray that Frankie was holding and touched Jones on the shoulder; "Now the second reason for our visit." Le Strade called the crew to order and the Vice-Admiral addressed all hands and what he stated amazed everyone. "Oh bugger!" muttered the Chief dourly and Jones couldn't agree more with that statement.

14. AN EXPEDITION TO THE EASTERS.

Peter handed his bag to Leon to store in his cabin whilst he headed for the bridge; he was running late because the Rossington Tram Service was being upgraded to ensure that trams were available for the opening of the new rail station.

"Morning Skipper." He called, stepping through the bridge door from the upper deck. He noticed that Jones and the Chief were huddled in front of the large bridge monitor with

Colonel Le Strade. He knew at once they were looking at the Easter's Mountain Range.

"Nice of you to join us Lieutenant." The Colonel gestured for Peter to join the group; "We'll bring you up to speed with this little adventure." Le Strade outlined Vice-Admiral Kellamann's proposal to recover the weapon lost in the cave system under the Easter Mountains. The plan was quite simple; a three-rig convoy would depart Rossington and make directly for the cave entrance that Jones and his crew had found in Valley La Mort. It would consist of the Thor, the MSV: The General Westmoreland under his command [Le Strade's] and MSV: The John Garfield – a Military supply rig - with some scientists aboard borrowed from Fort Benjamin Weapons Directorate. The convoy would camp out in the valley and conduct a search of the cave system, hopefully finding and recovering the lost weapon. The Thor would leave the other rigs in Valley La Mort and continue onto the Ice Shelf to complete the service detail on Weather Station 7(S), they would then re-join the convoy when it departed for home. The military expedition would be commanded by Vice-Admiral Kellamann with Colonel Le Strade as Second-In-Command.

Since it would take about ten days and nights to reach the Iceshelf and the same for the return journey, Bella was advised to remain in Rossington so that her wedding could go ahead; obviously Kazza was advised to do the same! But Bella wanted the crew at her wedding and so the date was pushed back some four weeks and with Vice-Admiral Kellamann's support, Weather Control (South) agreed to the re-arranged date.

Jones was quite happy with Bella and Kazza's decision, he really didn't want a new Meteorologist and Systems Specialist on board with a trip to the Ice Shelf around the corner and with that settled, he and crew could concentrate on getting the Thor ready. The other problem now on the horizon was Peter's personal life; his long-term boyfriend had walked out on him for another man and Peter was clearly devastated by this turn of events. Jones knew that Peter was trying to hide his distress and not very, so he resolved to have a little, quiet personal chat with him as soon as possible. Peter for his part, threw himself into the preparations underway for the trip down to the Polar Cap.

"I have to admire his character, not letting that obvious terrible heartbreak to interfere with his duties. I see young Peter in a different light now." The Chief confided to Eve who agreed with Marcus. They didn't agree on many things, but they did on this subject. "I'm beginning to see why they made him [Peter] a Lt. Commander at such a young age; he's starting to look like a future Rig Captain." Eve commented. Jones would have agreed with the pair, but his attention was now with another couple of visitors to the Thor; the two weapons experts had arrived by military flight and would stay onboard until their ride; MSV: The John Garfield docked in two days' time. Leon was assigned by Peter to bring their luggage aboard and show them to the bridge; they would have cabins to themselves befitting their rank and status. So Lilly moved from her cabin to share with Eve in the medical suite, whilst Kazza and Bella were given permission to cohabit; leaving Tom, who normally bunked with Kazza, ending up sharing with Frankie. Jones knew that would be fine; Tom could share with the devil if he had to!

Peter expressed his surprise, as did the Chief, that the two scientists were not placed in a local hotel. "Maybe the Military High Command doesn't want the pair having contact with other civilians." Mussed Troy, as he helped Leon bring their baggage to the allotted cabins, but Jones knew that was exactly the reason they were here, and he studied the pair as they came on the bridge.

Professor Solomon Jacobson looked like an undertaker! He wore a neat black suit and white shirt with rather strangely, bright red athletic shoes. He was tall and thin, possessing a very pale complexion with big hands and a head of white hair. But had a firm handshake and clear green eyes, the Professor was probably about 27 years old [almost 50 in Earth years]. But it was the voice that everyone noticed, it didn't belong to that body – it was deep and firm - he could have made a fortune doing talk over's for advertisements and movie trailers.

The Professor noted the muted surprise at his vocals by the crew; "When I was attending Kennedy University as a student many years ago, I was a happy amateur Tenor with the 'Presidential Foot lighters', a little group of artists and singers that performed plays and music. We once performed for the then President Sylvester Pullman. I sang 'Amazing Grace'. He's dead now, but I'm sure it was nothing to do with our show." He smiled broadly and everyone laughed.

"Well, next time we're closed down by a storm you can entertain us with a few songs." Peter commented and the Professor agreed with some real enthusiasm. "I already like him." The Chief said quietly, and Eve had to agree with him again – twice in one day would have to be noted in the Rig's log - Jones thought and smiled to himself, then the Professors assistant squeezed through the deck pressure door and announced herself to the assembled crew.

"I'm Doctor Hillary Margot-Jones, I'm far too fat and very loud and I must have a cabin to myself because no-one else would fit in. If I bent down to tie my shoes, the poor soul would fly out the door!" She laughed out loud, like a Hyena with the giggles; she had a bright red and green scarf about her hair and was covered with a shawl that was so colorful, that it could have illuminated a coal mine. Everyone noticed that she was African in descent and her name was 'Jones', everyone also turned to the captain with the same question in mind.

But it was the Chief who had the balls to ask it.

"This is Captain Jones; he commands the Thor and are you two related?" The Chief was desperately trying not to laugh, as he introduced the big cheerful lady to Jones, who stood with a strange grin upon his face and mouth open. Hillary clearly liked the look of Captain Jones and didn't shake his hand but grabbed him by both shoulders and planted a kiss upon each of his cheeks.

"You darling boy!" She exclaimed; "You're a Jones too, how wonderful!" The Doctor clapped her hands together and with some unbridled joy in her voice declared; "And you're black too!" There was embarrassed silence for a few seconds, then Captain Jones smiled and nodded; "Yes, I only noticed it this morning when I was shaving, the shock almost turned me white and I'm still not over it!" Pointing to his face, Jones laughed and shook her hand with some affection.

The bridge exploded into laughter and Lilly whispered to Eve – between giggles – "Can we now call him Captain Darling?" She asked, grinning broadly. Eve said no quietly and had herself a little fit of giggles.

The Thor's guests were shown to their cabins, after Hillary was prized from the Captain's arm by Eve and Lilly, who quickly escorted the wonderful Doctor to her birth, but not before she had kissed Jones again and promised they would have a real chat about possible relatives. "Oh; such a darling boy!" She informed the girls as they left the bridge; much to the captain's relief.

"Coffee please Frankie." He whispered and slumped down

upon the captain's chair and ran both hands through his hair; "I must keep telling myself it's only for two days!"

The crew's evening meal was punctuated with raucous laughter, and everyone agreed that Peter had summed up the visiting pair perfectly; "They are Mar's answer to Laurel and Hardy!" He said, clearly in a better mood than of late. "They must be related in some way; otherwise, it's a bloody hell of a coincidence." Tom offered his opinion to Kazza and Bella, who held hands under the dining table and smiled a great deal at each other. "Frankie took the captain dinner in his cabin, and I think Eve may have to prescribe tranquilizers!" He added, starting the laughter up again.

"The Captain will be fine, he'll cope, he always does." Lilly said, feeding Dallas ice-cream with a spoon while he sprawled across her lap; "I really have to admit she's a real character, especially for a scientist that's a weapons expert." She rubbed his neck and wondered how much bigger this cat could get; he seemed to have doubled in size over the last few weeks.

Eve sipped her coffee and couldn't argue with that deduction, two quite colourful characters that made their living creating death, they certainly didn't fit anyone's idea of Military Scientist's, no matter how hard you tried. Eve noticed that Troy was reading his PA for the third time with a quizzical look upon his face; "What's so interesting Troy?" She asked.

Troy looked up and smiled; "Just reading about Professor Jacobson, he is one intelligent bloke, he has two degrees from Kennedy University; one in weapon systems and the other in a subject I've never heard of and will struggle to pronounce."

Eve smiled and gestured Troy to hand her his PA; "Let me have a look." She read the page and handed back the device with a strange expression on her face. "What else is he qualified in, apart from blowing up people." Leon pushed his empty plate away and gulped down some cold fruit juice; "I bet it has nothing to do with fashion." He laughed to himself.

"Archaeology, he's an Archaeologist." Eve spoke quietly and placed her cup upon the table. Only Troy didn't know the meaning and Lilly had to explain it to him. "But there's sod all to dig up on Mar's, except some of the early settlements that failed or some of the abandoned farms or mines, so there's nothing really ancient on Mars." Troy reasoned and wandered off with Leon to relieve the bridge.

Eve quietly checked the 'other Jones' for qualifications and sat back a little surprised and stunned. Peter saw the look on her face and asked what she had discovered. Eve spoke quietly; "She's also an amateur archeologist."

Peter and Eve exchanged glances; they both had the same thought; was the fact that both were amateur Archaeologist's of any significance to the mission?

AUTHOR NOTE:
"Archaeology was a 'new' science to Mars! Officially, it limited itself to the excavation of early failed mines and townships but the New Archaeologists obviously had access to the Earth's archives – available on Mars – on Ancient civilizations."

15. CONVOY.

"No wonder they came as a matching pair, the good Doctor Margot-Jones is not only a Weapon's design expert; Hillary is a highly regarded amateur Archaeologist in her own right." Peter pushed the paper across the captain's desk and Jones read that Hillary had carried out several excavations around the site of Mar's sixth city to be built; it had been constructed way back in the early part of the first century, but had been abandoned for almost two centuries.

The small city of Little Moscow had been left to the elements after the people had gone. History informed Jones that the water supply had dried up and that the great storm of 62 had caused serious damage to its infrastructure. The government decided to evacuate the residents to the new city of Kiev, which was then under construction. He also noted that the old city was an ideal training ground for the new discipline called 'Archaeology'. The Chief picked up the paper and nodded; "Now that must be another big coincidence; I don't think." The first coincidence that the Chief referred to was finding out that the Doctor Margot-Jones was not related to the captain.

A check with Mar's Human Archives Service had confirmed that the two Jones's were not descendants of the same family. But the finding did not deter Hillary from referring to Captain Jones as 'her darling boy!' during her two day stay aboard the Thor. Jones for his part, simply seemed to disappear into thin air whenever she appeared, the rumour was that Dallas had shown him several hiding places around the rig.

A new saying amongst the crew was "where's the Captain?" to be answered by; "Ask Dallas!" Jones didn't mind; it made the crew laugh and lifted moral. But one occasion had the crew somewhat mystified; the good Doctor was on the prowl again and Lilly, with Bella and Kazza, was seeking the Captain for the Rig's Chandlers, to approve the new engineering stores delivery.

They came upon Dallas sitting in the lower cargo corridor and for a further laugh, Kazza bent down and asked the cat;" Where's the captain?" They all laughed until Dallas wandered up the corridor and sat by the door to the Engine room office. They followed and with some trepidation Lilly knocked on the door. Captain Jones opened it and asked why they looked so surprised – he also gave Dallas a pat - as the cat disappeared inside.

So the new rumour sweeping the rig was that Dallas the cat understood Martian fully and not just his name and dinner time! Certain members of the crew were now having one-way conversations with the cat. When an amused Jones explained to the Chief, Marcus held up both arms and shook his head. " For Mar's sake! What will happen when old Lionel finds out the crew is talking to a fucking cat! He'll have us all thrown in Lake Placid nut house."

Jones could only smile at that.

AUTHOR NOTE:
"Dr. Lionel's is the Head Psychologist for the Mars Military and known for no sense of humour whatsoever. His famed hospital was located at the small settlement of Lake Placid, on the North -South border, is considered the top clinic for treating mental health issues. A nice place to visit but you wouldn't like to stay there!"

But Captain Jones had other matters on his mind; the Thor was leaving with the convoy at 18.00 hours CST and Peter still had not returned from trying to see his wayward and apparently unfaithful lover. He had called Peter's PA twice without success, finally calling the Dockyard Peace Guard [the equivalent of a Police Service on Mars] who manned the security gates to ask if they would call him as soon as Lt. Gravestone passed through the barriers of the dock complex.

The clock was ticking, and Jones sat on the bridge watching through the windscreen, Leon was at a Pilots seat checking his controls with the Chief. Lilly was on the Communications desk talking to the MSV; The John Garfield about the convoy and Bella had appeared on the bridge with the latest weather reports from Weather Control [South]. She explained that the route had clear weather until it reached the Ice-Shelf proper; then it changed to "AT RISK" with a couple of big storms floating around the place. She and Jones chatted about the baby for a few minutes and Bella returned to the small weather office in trailer No.2; quite happy. When the bridge clock showed 17.10 hours CST Jones was now seriously concerned and told Lilly to get Vice-Admiral Kellamann on the radio, he may be able to find a last-minute replacement for Peter. Maybe one of the Officers, on either of the other two rigs, had their Master's Certificate because going on a twenty day mission with just him and the Chief would be a nightmare and a considerable strain on them both.

Military Regulations demanded that the bridge was always manned by a qualified officer and that would mean doing twelve hour shifts between them. But the thought of exposing Peter's absence weighed heavy on his mind. It would mean the end of Peter's career and possible discipline procedures.

"Are you alright Captain?" Lilly asked with real concern, when Jones asked her to make the call. "I'm afraid that the Vice-Admiral is still in a briefing with the Weapon specialists, but he'll be free in about fifteen minutes. Colonel Le Strade is on the bridge of the General Westmoreland, shall I call him?" Lilly shuffled her papers about nervously and then adjusted her headset as another call came in.

"Oh Captain, there's a call from the Dockyard Peace Guard, Lt. Gravestone has just arrived at the South gate, they are going to have one of their mobile units run him up to the Thor, otherwise he won't make it on time; apparently Peter owes them a bottle." She smiled but didn't notice the look of relief on Jones's face.

"Cancel my call to the Vice-Admiral please Lilly and get Troy to meet Peter on the deck, so they can get his gear aboard quickly, we depart in forty-five minutes." Jones pushed back in his seat and managed to smile.

"Chief, the departure will be as planned. The Westmoreland will lead with the John Garfield taking up the rear; we're the meat in the sandwich." Jones issued instructions to the bridge crew and the Chief made his way to the Engine room with his apprentice Sunny in tow. The bridge was now a hive of frantic activity, with last minutes checks and a flow of messages from the Dock Control room, Le Strade called to say that departure would be on time and wished everyone 'good luck'.

Peter made the deck pressure door with nine minutes to spare and Troy stowed his baggage in his cabin, as the Dock crew sealed hatches and removed power cables, air and water pipes from the Thor; all under the close supervision of the chief: she was now ready to depart.

Through the internal bridge door came Peter, still in civilian dress and he looked quite disheveled and tired. He tried to apologize to Jones, but the captain waved that aside and told him to get to his cabin, clean himself up and get into uniform and get some hot coffee down his neck.

"We'll have a chat about things once we're underway, the Chief can cover." Jones smiled at Peter and gently tapped his shoulder; "You have some very good friends on the Thor, and they will want to help."

Peter nodded and went to answer, but stopped and managed to smile, he had clearly been crying and his distress was obvious. "Come on Pete, Frankie has brewed some great coffee, let's go." Eve took hold of his arm and walked him away to the Galley, she Turned back to Jones and mouthed; 'I'll look after him.'

"The Westmoreland is on the move Captain." Lilly announced and Jones returned to his Captains chair and watched the rig pull from Dock No.3, despite being quite an old rig, the General Westmoreland was still impressive in her Military Colours [various shades of red and grey] she was heavily camouflaged to blend in with the Martian surface and being a battle rig, she boasted some serious and deadly hardware including rockets and pulse cannons with turrets front and rear.

As she passed the Thor, Jones thought how her silhouette resembled those pictures of old battleships that Earth's navies had many centuries ago.

"Steel castles, that's what my old Granddad use to call them." Leon spoke to Tom as they watched the Westmoreland pass; "He served on the old Admiral Kemp for many years, they were based In Cydonia; he met my grandmother there, her parents had a small farm and she came aboard during an open day and that was that."

"Captain, Transit Control has given the green light." Lilly tapped away on her keyboard and Jones ordered the Thor to depart Rossington for the Ice Shelf. He sat and stared at the sun sinking slowly and the night creeping in. he thought about the legends and stories surrounding the 'infamous' Easter Mountains; there had been at least nine or ten rigs simply disappear in the foothills over the years Mars has been inhabited. The authorities had played it down – everyone knew that – it was obvious that the violent and unpredictable storms that plagued Mars had carried the blame. But Jones had a gut feeling that maybe storms were not to blame in every instance. He shook the dark thoughts from his mind and called Frankie to see if there was any coffee on the go.

He remembered some stories about the myths and legends of

'old mother Earth' about a certain stretch of ocean in which numerous ships, aircraft and people simply vanished over many centuries. He couldn't recall the name but thought it strange that Mars could have its own strange little area which appeared to have the same phenomena happening. He now wondered if that was just co-incidence or there was some kind of strange link between the two planets. He dismissed that idea as Sunny appeared with the bridge crew's coffee. He ran his hand over Dallas's head and ears, sipping his coffee. The big cat sat at his feet, as if watching the captain operating the pilot controls of the Thor. Leon grunted, "If he pays much more attention we'll have to watch the bugger closely in case he drives the bloody thing off!" Everyone chuckled at that.

EPISODE 6: "WEATHER STATION No.7 (South)."

16. THE EASTER MOUNTAINS.

"Nothing much going on Skipper, they have closed down for the night." Peter pointed through the windscreen and Jones could see the two rigs parked on good ground, some distance from the entrance to Valley Le Mort. Each was ablaze with lights, but the surface crews had been recalled and there was no obvious human movement about them.

"I understand from the Chief of the 'John Garfield' that come tomorrow, they will drop a couple of drones down that cave you found the footprints in Skipper." Peter sipped his coffee and leaned back in a Pilots seat. Troy was sitting in the other seat, hands on head and feet against the dashboard, he looked up at Jones and nodded; "The mad professor and his assistant are quite excited about it all, they really want to see what the device was, even though it's technology is nearly a hundred years old."

Jones dropped into the captain's chair and peered through the windscreen, the Martian night was already upon them. "External temp please Troy." He said simply, running his hands around the coffee cup in his lap. Troy bent forward and tapped a gauge upon his dashboard; "Minus 35c already Skipper."

Eve and Lilly appeared, laughing together, with Lilly carrying several sheets of paper; she sat down at the Communications desk and smiled at Jones; "Just going to send the routine stuff Captain." Jones nodded and Eve gripped the back of his chair and offered him a couple of sheets of paper; "Do you know anything about this?" She asked; Jones took the papers and cast a quick eye over them and laughed out loud; "That is a cracker! All MO's are to check rig mascots for cat mange?"

"I'm not a bloody Vet you know, how do I know what 'cat mange' is?" Eve folded her arms and ignored the laughter from the captain and the bridge crew. Jones tapped her shoulder and smiled; "Just give Dallas the once over and reply back that he's fine: that'll be good enough for Command."

"He's not mangy, he has a lovely fluffy coat and nice clear eyes; he's fine." Lilly added her opinion to the debate about the rig's cat, Apparently Military High Command had asked all rigs to report any symptoms of 'Cat mange' to Military control and Medical Officers had to carry out the task!

"Notoedric Mange is something we obviously skipped at medical School." Eve shoved the papers back into her blouse pocket and watched the Chief appear on the bridge with Tom. "Found any mange yet?" Marcus chuckled to himself, but Tom looked quite serious and asked if Dallas was alright.

Jones held up his arms; "Come on people, Dallas is fine, he has no mange and he's unlikely to catch it from us, so he is fine and will remain fine. End of discussion."

"Talk of the furry little devil." Muttered Troy, as Frankie appeared with Dallas under his arm. "I've combed and brushed him and checked his eyes and mouth; he's fine." Frankie smiled at everyone and was surprised when the captain threw up his arms and said; "Enough is enough!"

When Lilly explained, Frankie laughed out loud and let Dallas wander off down the Engineering corridor. Frank knew that 'Sunny' always kept cat biscuits near her desk and he guessed that Dallas did too!

Tom handed the captain the service stores listing for approval and peered out at the imposing mountains that rose around them; "They use to be called the Athenian Mountains until about 150 years ago. I saw an old Mars globe in Rossington Museum and that's what they were called."

Lilly looked up from her messages and asked: "Why did they have their name changed Tom?"

"I can answer that one; my great, great grandfather was involved with the expedition that caused the name change." The Chief motioned to Troy to stand and dropped into the seat as Troy stood. "Thanks boy, Tom is almost right, but it was about 120 years ago that a famous Geologist brought an expedition here, to survey and map the mountains and cave systems." The Chief gave his coffee a stir and sucked the spoon. "His name was Professor Bellman Easter and they had three old "Scanna" rigs for the trip. They lived in pressurized containers dumped inside one of the big caves and one of the rigs would run back to Rossington for supplies; a six-week turnabout in them days!" The Chief slowly sipped his coffee and continued; "My bleeding great, great grandfather Lester was a young 'deckhand' aboard one of the rigs called 'The Salamander's Hat' and family legend is that he spent nearly twenty weeks around here and he almost died of boredom!"

"Yeah, that's the expedition everyone really remembers, but there was an earlier one, way back in the first century that came to grief here, they lost five people in the cave system, they simply vanished. No bodies, no distress calls; no bloody wreckage, they just disappeared down there." Everyone turned to Kazza as he spoke, stepping off the bridge ladder with a large cheese sandwich clutched in his hand. He stood by the captain's chair and grinned. ""That's right Kazza, there was an earlier trip and it had to be evacuated because of a really big storm, I think it was 62; the year of the Global storm." The Chief nodded and added; "I vaguely remember it was headed by some scientist with a really funny name, something like Slobboski or similar. Professor Easters was a real success; he mapped nearly a third of it. But never came across the missing bodies."

"I wonder if our friend Stanners bumped into them." Troy grinned and popped a sweet into his mouth; he really did like mints. There was a quiet chuckle from the crew and Lilly said: "So the Mountains should be called the 'Slobbo Range' or similar."

"If there was any justice in this world, but Easter's was the big success and poor Slobboski's was a glorious disaster – you don't get whole mountain ranges named after you - if half your team die." Jones placed his coffee cup on the dash and flicked through his paperwork. "You may as well name a rig after 'Wrecker Rogers'." Everyone laughed; they all knew the legend that was 'Wrecker Rogers'.

Except Lilly, who asked the Chief; "Who was 'Wrecker' Rogers and what did he do?"

The Chief rubbed his hands together and smiled broadly; he loved the chance to retell the tale of 'Wrecker Rogers': "More urban legend than truth, Ronnie 'Wrecker' Rogers was a rig Captain who managed to crash four expensive rigs, way back in the last century, for no apparent reason and was blacklisted by all the big rig companies; he struggled to find work for years. Travelling all over Mars in the hope of getting a rig to command, he was near to despair when finally, a small mining company in Cydonia gave him a 'water bucket' to command [the slang name for the rigs that carried water. They normally were old, decrepit and held together with wire, spit and bad welding] The MV: Mighty Oak was a real joke amongst the truckers, people often claimed to have seen pieces fall from her as she approached the docks. The crew was 'Wrecker', a second officer who had one-eye and was rarely The crew was 'Wrecker', a second officer who had one-eye and was rarely sober, a pilot who had done time at Salt Flats prison for various assaults and never spoke – not a single word in years – and a 'Deck-Hand' who was so old that people claimed he shook Taylor's hand when she landed. The Chief was a quiet man who collected labels from toilet rolls and liked music – for years no one had actually seen him - so the rumour was that his dead body was hidden about the rig and the crew divided his pay amongst themselves; they were almost considered pirates by many. But the little rig was tough, and the crazy crew adored her. The rig mascot was a large chicken called 'Chicken' – they couldn't afford a cat even on their combined wages – and it ran water between a couple of isolated mines for years and it was reliable. No storm stopped the MV: Mighty Oak from delivering the water, whatever the weather, she turned up, gaining a quiet respect from Miner's, townsfolk and truckers alike. Then one fateful day, with a full load of several thousand tons, The MV: Mighty Oak struggled through a bad storm to a small mining town, deep in Cydonia, to discover a major disaster was underway. Fire was raging through the small settlement and had almost reached the school and hospital, despite the brave and valiant efforts of the town people. Nothing stood between the raging inferno and the children sheltering in the school and the sick in the hospital – they appeared doomed - lost to the fire.

But 'Wrecker' knew what had to be done. The story says that people watched wide eyed as the old rig headed for the blaze, bit's falling from her sides and roof. They could see the crew on the bridge: 'Wrecker' in the captain's seat, grim faced and determined, The Second officer sprawled across the deck with a bottle in his hand, the mad pilot apparently singing and the old deck hand having a nap. Some claim to have seen the Chief, standing at the Captain's side, gripping 'Wreckers' shoulder and pointing to the blaze. Others say the figure was almost transparent and ghost like. No-one mentioned the Chicken.

Well, the rig disappeared into the heart of the blaze and within a few seconds, she blew up like a steam kettle and the massive explosion extinguished the fire: the young and sick were saved.

There were no remains found of the brave crew and very little of the tough rig, who in the end, lived up to her name. The only find amongst the burnt debris was a toilet roll and some chicken feathers.

There are stories all round Cydonia about sightings of the ghost rig MV: Mighty Oak and her crew, she is still seen today, racing across the sand at sunset, lights ablaze, 'Wrecker' at the wheel, a 'skull & Cross Bones' flag flying from her top deck and bits falling off as she passes the awe-struck witness who would cross themselves and pray hard for their lost souls. To this day, no rig has ever been named after Ronnie 'Wrecker' Rogers, for fear of invoking his bad luck; but several do have 'chicken' in their names......."

Everyone was laughing when the Chief finished the story, though Lilly was a little upset at the fate of the poor chicken. Eve had to wipe a tear of mirth away and sip some coffee; "If any of that is true, I'm a puddle of custard."

"I'd dip my spoon in that any day." Tom confided to the Chief, who had thoroughly enjoyed retelling the tale of 'Wrecker' Rogers after so long. Tom had quite a hidden passion for the 'Doc' and very few suspected the depth of his feelings for the rig's MO. He wanted to run off with her and together, own a small shoe-shop [shoes had an equal fascination for him]; the only problem Tom could foresee would be telling his wife!

"Does anyone know about the ghosts of the Easters?" Frankie was handing out more coffee and everyone was in the mood for stories. "I do." Captain Jones had everyone's attention when he told the tale of 'Easters Ghosts: "Even before the disastrous failure of the '62 Expedition, the Easter's had a reputation for strange happenings, mysterious lights flashing, unknown stuff moving about on rig 'scopes' that simply disappeared and even seeing figures about the cave mouths. Over the years, the stories have spread from rig to rig, city to city and person to person. But the only ones, that appear to have any evidence about them, are the best: for instance, the tale of the time travelling rig."

"This is a cracker!" The Chief interrupted and settled back in his chair with another cup of coffee. The captain smiled and spoke quietly: "Way back in about 180, a cargo rig took shelter in the Easter's during a Category 2 storm – it was a bad one – with high winds and electrics and the rig just made it to cover; it was carrying machine parts for a big Mining Corporation and a crew of five. At first, they hid in a cave entrance, but the storm grew so violent that the rig's skipper decided to risk the soft cave floor and so they moved deeper into the cave. At first, they thought lightening had struck inside the cave because the dark interior lit up with vivid, bright white light. The rig was still moving, and the crew was almost blinded by the light, but the captain managed to stop the rig before she ran into a wall. When the crew recovered their sight, they thought they were all hallucinating- the cave had gone - the storm had gone, and they were somewhere else! For they were parked on long, lush green grass within a forest of huge trees and sky of dark blue with few clouds. The entire crew stared in utter disbelief as strange birds screeched above them and huge reptiles passed in front of the screen.

But they really freaked out when the 2nd Officer screamed out the time on the rig's chronometer – it was showing Week 23 Sol 237 Year 165,097,672 - Apparently the rig had been thrown back in time some 165 million years! In a panic the skipper ordered the rig to reverse, but as she violently lurched backwards, the collision alarms sounded and they were utterly horrified by what they saw: a gigantic, savage reptile gripping the rear trailer with long dark claws. The captain, recovering his wits, pulled the rig forward and free of those monstrous fingers; everyone heard the scratching and scraping as the rig moved away.

Suddenly they were back in the bright light and then the cave. Everyone stood in silence and disbelief – the storm had passed over and so the rig crept slowly from the darkness - they headed for Shackleton cargo docks and decided that they had suffered some kind of 'group hallucination' and agreed not to speak of the incident. But some days later, they arrived in Shackleton and docked – the cargo was unloaded - but only after several dockhands called the captain's attention to the large scratches' across the top of trailer 2.

Some photographs were taken of the scratches', but the company thought they were minor damage and did not hold a Board of Inquiry. So, the incident was forgotten and now, years later, the rig has long since been scrapped, the crew are all dead and the only 'proof' are those photographs which languish in the Museum at Dayburgh and few even know they exist."

Jones finished speaking and several members of the crew applauded; they were enjoying a night together, drinking coffee and relaxing before venturing onto the Ice-Shelf. Tom was about to partake in the story telling with the grisly tale of 'The Death Rig of old Cydonia' when Lilly held up her hand, as she answered a call on the Communication's desk. "What is it

Lilly?" Jones asked, waving the crew into silence.

"It's the General Westmoreland; apparently Weather Control South has lost contact with Weather Station 7(S). It's gone off line completely!" Lilly looked quite concerned and added; "Vice-Admiral Kellamann wants us to leave at once for the Ice-Shelf and you're to call him when we're underway Captain."

"Oh Shit!" Muttered the Chief; "That's an Emergency Call all right; seven can't be offline at any time really. The shit will hit the fan now." The captain nodded his agreement; they would have to leave at once. He quietly gave orders to up camp and get moving towards the Ice Shelf.

17. EMERGENCY SERVICE CALL.

The Thor had struggled through the ice-storm with little damage and was approaching 'Alexander's valley' where Weather Station 7(S) was located. A weather station had existed in this area since the very early days of the service and the current station had been built some 70 years ago, to replace a much older structure. Originally designed to be manned, the crews had been removed some twenty years ago due to cutbacks and problems with the isolation of the place. High Command made little or no comment on the stories that swirled about the place, especially the terrible gruesome murders some forty years ago.

The official line was that one of the crew had an extreme mental episode or breakdown and took an axe to his weather station colleagues – there was only two survivors from the crew of nine - the station cat called 'Snuggles' and the young Ensign on Communications duty. He managed to barricade himself and the cat in the battery store which had extra strong doors and walls. He had already sent out an S.O.S but knew that help from Shackleton [the nearest city] was six days away. Apparently, he survived his self-Imprisonment on a bag of sweets and two bottles of cold tea. Finally, unable to reach his victim, the crazed killer apparently opened the external pressure door and ran, quite naked, out into the bitter darkness and the body was never found. Number Seven had been automated since the crews were removed and received a visit from Weather Service rigs twice a year for maintenance and servicing. This was only its second or third major failure, but it would leave the Deep South vulnerable to surprise storms and that could mean loss of lives.

"About another thirty Kilometers' and she'll be in view." Peter stared through the darkened windscreen [to prevent 'snow-blindness'] at the bleak white landscape and sighed with relief The Thor and her crew had endured six days and nights of a really bad ice-storm, with very strong winds and drifting ice curtains that plunged temperatures to the very working limits of the rig.

Troy nodded and glanced down at the 'scope' where a little strange bleep caught his eye. He tapped at his keyboard and studied the monitor with real interest; it showed, some sixty or seventy Kilometers to the rear of the station was a tiny flashing light; an unknown contact? The computer showed no identifying signature, and the contact was far too small to be another rig. He shouted over to the captain; "We have an unknown contact at the rear of the station and...." He stopped in mid-sentence: the contact was gone. He tapped the screen and re-ran the scan: nothing. He sat back and rubbed his chin, wondering if he should inform the chief. He decided not to.

Jones was sipping coffee and reading the dispatches from the convoy and messages from Weather Control (South). They were demanding constant updates on the Thor's arrival at the defunct weather station – whilst the convoy had - so far, drawn a blank in its search for the lost weapon. "Must have been a bogeyman Captain, it's gone." He informed Jones and added; "I'll report it to the Chief, he may want to recalibrate and run a test." Jones nodded and adjusted his seat and called to Lilly; "Pass on Peter's assessment to Weather Control; they may not call us for at least another two flipping minutes." Lilly smiled and turned back to her communications screen. She was quite tired and drained, but she was very quick to acknowledge that so was everyone else, the last six days had been a nightmare. But the Thor had got them through it – and the captain of course - she glanced back at him, sitting in the captain's seat, surrounded by papers and coffee cups. To young Lilly he was a hero, holding the crew and rig together in some pretty desperate times. She had also come to realize that the captain was a very charming, strong and handsome man. Suddenly he looked back at her and she went a little red, and then slightly jumped as Eve touched her shoulder.

"Anything new on the chatter box?" Eve asked with a big grin and Lilly shook her head and took a drink from her cup of flavoured water, but Peter called over; "If you hang about Eve, the station will be in view in a few minutes, it's quite an impressive sight."

Eve patted Lilly on the shoulder and spoke softly; "Almost as impressive as the captain, don't you think Lilly?"

Standing out against the snowy skyline, encircled by grey and white hills, Weather Station Number Seven South was a large black box, constructed of real stone and steel plates, the external lights were off, and she stood in mute darkness. "It's massive!" Eve exclaimed with real surprise in her voice.

"The number of women who said that to me." Troy muttered and laughed to himself, popping another mint into his mouth.

They had a strange tang to them; but made him feel great.

"Crew call please Lilly." Jones said simply, staring at the dark, silent monolith. It filled him with a strange disquiet, a feeling he couldn't quite put a name too. He was still staring at the windscreen when the crew assembled in silence. The Chief had to repeat himself twice; "We're all here Skipper." Jones pulled away from the foreboding sight and greeted the crew with a tired smile; "Right chief, what's your thoughts?"

"Something is well amiss; the lights haven't come on at our approach, that's bad." The Chief folded his big arms and shook his head; "The Emergency system appears to have failed. We may have to work in suits until we get the bloody environment back online." He spoke directly to Jones who could only agree with him.

"Two teams I think Chief. You, Tom and Kazza work on the Weather systems whilst I'll handle the Environmental Engineering with Lilly and Leon." Jones was already formulating the service and repair schedule. He told Lilly to pass a situation report back to Weather Control and also inform Vice-Admiral Kellamann. "I know we're all tired, but we need to get a grip on this and quickly."

'Sunny' held up her hand and spoke quietly: "Can I please go with your team Captain?" She smiled at Jones and she reminded him of a schoolgirl asking the coach to join the Hardball team. He glanced at the Chief who smiled and nodded his agreement. "O.K. Sunny, you can assist me. Right, Peter you can handle the rig with Troy. Eve and Bella on Medical and Communications and finally, Frankie can keep the coffee going and knock up a curry and lots of sandwiches." The last part of his statement received unanimous agreement. Frankie produced a big grin and gave the thumbs up; "Nice and bloody hot, just as you like it!"

The thought of a steaming hot curry produced a big smile on Jones's tired face; "O.K. people lets prep, the sooner we're in number seven, the sooner we can get the job done and head for home and the wonderful prospect of a wedding and a great party." All but the bridge crew scattered to collect surface suits, toolboxes and repair kits.

Jones was impressed that the two teams were ready within the hour, Eve and Bella had set up the Medical Monitoring Command desk with great efficiency and Peter had pulled the Thor to within thirty meters of the station. "We on good ground skipper and the E.P.L. is facing the stations external pressure doors, you've a ten- or fifteen-minute walk ahead of you. I'll pass you over to Bella."

Peter handed the microphone to Bella who reported that the ice- storm was almost quiet and that she was asking to launch the small drone, so that the Thor would have some warning about any serious changes to the weather about them.

AUTHOR NOTE:
E.P.L. is short for External Pressure Lift, which is located near Tyre No.7 on the Thor.

The captain listened intently through his helmet speaker and gave Bella permission to launch; Troy would fly the drone from the bridge and that certainly put a smile on his face, piloting the drones or driving the 'Sand- cat' made his life aboard worthwhile; he celebrated with another mint. Jones, with Leon, Lilly and Sunny entered the External Pressure Lift and Eve gave the thumbs up for surface time. Bella informed the captain that there was a small sandstorm blowing about, but it was well within the safety parameters for the suits.

Jones was first onto the surface and whilst visibility was poor, he could easily make out the door of Station Seven some meters away. But he still insisted that everyone cable up, and the team made its way across the dirt towards the station in single file, joined by the safety cables.

Glancing over his shoulder, Jones could see the E.P.L. ascending up to the Suit Room to collect the Chief's team. Leon was behind him with small a 'Beaver' drone that hauled the toolboxes and some spare parts, Lilly and Sunny both carried repair kits and spare oxygen cylinders [to enable a 'hot-swap' of the suit air tanks] if the repairs took longer than anticipated. They arrived at the door in good order, to find the entry panel dark and useless; "We are going have to open it manually!" Jones found the small emergency panel about a meter away and Leon handed him the manual emergency key: a three-pronged disc with a built-in power cell. Jones sighed and cleaned dirt from the emergency panel and pushed the opening device against the panel.

It took five or six minutes before the heavy metal door started to slowly slide back – Leon peered inside with a powerful hand lamp – and what he saw made him shout: "Skipper, the bloody Inner-coor is wide open!" Jones had managed to pull the door back half-way and that was good enough to squeeze through with their equipment.

Lilly shouted that the Chief's team was on their way across the sand and could see their suit lights through the swirling dust.

Jones and Leon were already heading through the Inner door, when the Chief stumbled into the room with Kazza and Tom close behind – their 'Big beaver' drone was too large to fit through the half open door – "It's bloody blowing a fucking gale now Skipper, we need all hands to empty the drone before the storm gets it!"

Jones agreed, but he and Leon continued into Weather

Station 7, they needed to find the Control Room while the others unloaded the big drone of its precious cargo, stacking it against the wall; "Seal up the outer door Chief." Jones ordered, and after a brief struggle the external door slid shut and Jones could now concentrate on opening the control room door. He wasn't too happy when Bella called him with an update on the storm; they were likely to remain in the station for several more hours; "Good job we hauled the extra air-cylinders." He grunted to Leon as they managed to open the door and gain entry to the control suite of the station. The drone had been recalled – after picking up several small and strange - unknown objects at the rear of the station. Troy didn't bother to inform the captain; they didn't appear on the scope; "More bogymen." He told Peter and the bridge Crew though he felt a little strange about them: those several shadowy figures actually appeared sort of familiar to him!

Down the corridor came the team, dragging equipment and having strange shouted conversations with each other, the little 'beaver' drone rattling on the steel floor under Lilly's command. They grouped before Jones, panting and laughing, in good humour despite the tiredness of the last week. Jones shook his head and smiled with some pride; "Let's get it done you bunch of nuts!"

What really concerned Jones was finding the Inner pressure door open. No malfunction should have caused that door to open; especially when they opened the outer door. A dark disturbing though entered his mind; the only possible scenario that could cause such a happening; was the Inner door was opened manually. But there was no-one in the automated station before his crew had arrived on scene.

18. CATEGORY 2 STORM.

"It's been about four hours and according to the Chief, they're

doing well, the major fault was in the battery room control panel. When that died the station went with it. The real odd thing is that the back-up system also failed, and the Technical Directorate boys and girls will want to investigate that one." Peter sipped his coffee and passed the update report to Bella.
 "I'll send it now." She turned to her commutations monitor and started to type.

" What's the estimate now?" Eve nibbled at the slice of toast that Frankie had passed her and checked her monitors again – the Chief was a little in the red - but not a worry. "Yeah Mr. Gravestone; what time should I get scoff ready for?" Frank handed the Lieutenant some toast and topped his coffee up again.

"Make it six Frankie and I need not ask what you've cooked up for the captain!" Pete laughed and quickly returned to the captain's chair, leaving Eve and Bella chatting whilst Frankie made his way back to the galley.

"They've done it!" Exclaimed Troy pointing to the windscreen, the external lights had flickered, then powered on. Bella was really concentrating on a message coming in, but Eve clapped and called out: "Well done!" The station was now illuminated, and Eve could now see the control room lights were activated and figures moving about. "They're doing a cracking job." Pete told Troy who could only agree; the repair and service was likely to last for another couple of hours. The Chief and the Captain wanted a full re-check before leaving the station to itself again.

Bella called the captain with a priority signal from Weather control; "Skipper, Weather Central says well done, Number 7 is back online and has just issued a 'Serious at risk' warning for us; Category 2 High storm, we're strongly advised to seek shelter immediately." She repeated the message and the captain acknowledged.

"Does that mean electrics?" Troy asked. Bella nodded an affirmative. Peter took a deep breath; "Suit up Troy, you and Frankie get to the cargo hold and ready the rod canisters, I think we're going to need them."

Franks face betrayed his feelings about going back on the surface in the middle of a monster storm and Pete gripped his shoulder; "You O.K. with that Frank?" The Chef swallowed hard and nodded; "Don't think there's any choice in it Mr. Gravestone, you can't leave the Bridge, Bella certainly aren't going and the Doc has to stay here and look after the others. That leaves me and Troy. It's not up for argument really, I'll suit up." Peter simply nodded and told Bella to pass the message on that the canisters will be ready when the team returns to the Thor.

The Captain had called the service team together in the quiet control room of the now functioning station; "Right, you know the situation we're in and I'm not about to beat about the bush. With a monster like the one about to roll over us, most of the crew will take cover here; it's far safer in a solid steel building than the Thor. The station is fully online with plenty of air and water. The store has a serious amount of water and emergency rations. Those that stay could last for weeks here."

He looked about their tired faces and continued; "I'll return to the Thor and all the remaining crew on her will transfer here, especially Doc and Bella, we can't separate them. If anything happens with Bella, the Doc is her only chance, and the station has a medical suite." Everyone nodded their complete agreement. The Chief already knew what the captain had in mind and asked; "Who do you want with you?"

"A volunteer, to ride the storm out on the Thor with me, it can be anyone except Sunny, Bella or the Doc." The captain looked straight at the very disappointed girl, who was clearly about to protest her Captain's decision. "It's not up for any discussions Sunny." The Chief gripped her shoulder and smiled; "No-one will think any less of you, I can guarantee that, we all know that you would volunteer, but the captain's right; as usual!" Now everyone voiced their agreement with Jones's decision on Sunny and everyone raised their hand to volunteer. If Jones had felt pride in his crew earlier, it had now doubled. He was a little speechless for a few seconds then he pointed at Leon; "Come on, let's get back to the rig."

Tom spoke up; "Captain, we can get the canisters set up, with the Thor so close to the station; it would only need maybe two, three rod sets." The Chief agreed with that, and the team set off for the Thor, as they passed through the external pressure door they could see the darkness gathering behind them. "It's going to be a fucking monster." Whispered Kazza and hoped Bella and the baby were alright.

Within an hour the crew of the Thor, except the Captain and Deckhand Leon Kamiski, had transferred to the Weather Station. Three rod canisters had been planted around the Rig and despite a search, no-one could find Dallas. But when the last crew member had gone, and the Thor was sealed up for the storm; he appeared on the captain's chair. Jones and Leon smiled at each other; they knew Dallas had volunteered to stay!

The storm hit at 18.20 hrs CST and it was bad.

The Thor was rolling as if she was at sea, the dark sky was violently punctuated with bright flashes and the temperature plummeted, the canisters were fired, and Jones felt the slight rumble as lightening struck the ground around them. All Communications were down; the storm had silenced radio traffic and Leon couldn't even raise the weather station next door to them. The night was a long haul the rig shook, and the bridge received repeated 'collision' alarms. The storm was now over them fully and at 23.10 hrs CST the South canister was hit by a bolt of lightning, which destroyed it totally and even damaged the rear trailer. Jones was relieved to see that Damage Control indicated minor external repairs required.

The double hull of the Thor had held up; so far.

As the night dragged on, so the storm vented its rage with high winds and ice. At one point, the Thor was dragged a couple of meters towards the station despite the brakes being fully applied and was now covered in a shroud of thick ice with the inside temperature so low that Leon and Jones had to wrap themselves up in blankets. Jones tucked Dallas inside his and together they shivered as the storm battered the rig with real ferocity.

The storm was to last three days and two nights; but to Leon and Jones it could have been weeks.

Jones was half asleep on the captain's chair; he could see Leon laid across the pilot chairs, blanket about his legs and Dallas asleep by his head. Jones realised that the crew was right: that cat was getting bigger by the bloody week! He would have to ask the chef what the hell he was feeding him. But Jones was thirsty and sipped slowly from a bottle of water, taken from the emergency ration pack that he and Leon had eaten cold last night. Dallas had enjoyed his most favourite meal: fish beans and cold weak coffee. "He's turned into a coffee head, like the rest of the crew." Leon had happily commented with a weary smile. Jones rose and stared out the bridge windscreen; the sunlight streamed in and the storm had gone. Then the radio burst into life; it was the weather station calling and Jones took the call with great relief.

"Captain, are you O.K.?" It was Lilly, calling from Number Seven's contrcl room, Jones answered affirmative, giving Leon a shake. "Everyone O.K. there Lilly? Leon, Dallas and I are fine, but the Thor has taken a bit of a battering." He replied, glad to hear her voice.

There was silence for a minute and Jones repeated his question and Lilly came back on air; "Captain, there's been some strange happenings here, Bloody Troy disappeared, and we searched and found nothing. Then he was back, and we discovered the closed-up store cupboard and the body. It must have been here for years."

"What the fuck has happened?" Jones was now quite grim, yet another bcdy? He shook Leon and told him that the crew had found yet another dead body from the past. Leon yawned and stroked Dallas; he smiled; "Maybe we should change careers and become bloody undertakers." He grunted and Jones – even tired – had to chuckle at that. "Come on; let's get ready to greet the relief team from the station. I need to look at this blcody body and I hope they have some frigging breakfast on over there." He patted Dallas and with a big sigh; headed for the suit room.

ADVERTISEMENT BY THE AUTHOR.

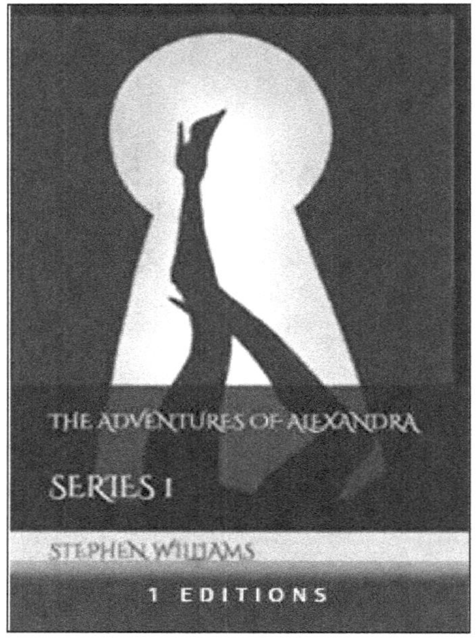

Available on 'AMAZON.COM' and all good bookshops!
An ADULT fantasy fiction series about a character from 'The Temporal Detectives' book series.

Visit the 'Alexandra' website: scan this code

Or type: https://**xxxalexandra.blogspot.com**

EPISODE 7: "MURDER, MADNESS AND OLD GHOSTS."

19. THE CORPSE IN THE CUPBOARD.

Soon after Peter returned to the Thor and relieved Jones of the bridge command, the captain headed for Station Seven, passing Frankie and Sunny in the service corridor - having just removed their surface suits - he nodded to Frankie; "Curry I think." and made his way to the suit room.

On the surface, he approached the dark square block with some real trepidation; not another bloody dead body from the past he thought; the Thor's morgue was getting more use than a local Undertakers, he sighed and jabbed the opening sequence into the external door control. Marcus and Eve helped him out of the surface suit and Marcus muttered; "This way skipper, it's in the old crew quarters which haven't been used for years."

Jones followed Marcus and Eve down the softly lit corridor in silence. He could see Tom and Lilly standing by a half-opened storeroom door, they both smiled and Lilly waved her torch; "In here Captain." She pointed her lamp towards the door. "It's in quite a state; I don't want to see it again."

Jones tapped her on the shoulder and nodded; "Go and get Troy to bring a body bag, we'll transfer the remains to the Thor's morgue." Jones slowly squeezed through the doorway and immediately noticed the plates that had been wielded over the doorway, lying to one side. Then he saw the corpse, face down on the floor; Lilly was right, it appears to have decomposed being sealed in the cupboard, but had a curious appearance, like it had been mummified.

"The storm broke through that vent and almost pulled a plate from the door; that's how we saw the handle and knew there was a door hidden behind it. "The Chief pointed to the rear wall, where Jones could see the repairs carried out by the crew. The wall had been shored up with steel plates and beams.

"That's a good job Chief." Jones nodded his appreciation, turning back to the dead body.

"I think he's been dead about forty years. The Mediscan said a white male aged about seventeen." [That's about 30 in Earth years] Eve gently turned the corpses' shoulder a little, revealing his name tag: "WS Engineering Specialist ROLLO THAMES." She said quietly and noticed a broken red crayon, lying to one side.

"That was some fucking turn up; the infamous Rollo Thames or what's left of him." The Chief grunted and pointed to the dead man's back and shoulders, adding; "Three deep wounds. Eve thinks they were made by an axe." There was silence for a few seconds as Jones considered the Chief's words; if this body was really the supposed mad axe murder of Station seven, then it means the sole survivor fooled everyone back then and played that gross masquerade for almost thirty years. Jones sighed and looked about the grim little room; it contained a weak ceiling lamp which gave very little light and three shelves which were bare of goods. Then, in the far corner, something caught Jones's eye as his torch passed over it.

"What's that?" He motioned to the shiny object and Eve picked it up. Placed in her open palm, she held it out to the others. It was a very old-fashioned Crew Badge; "CAROLINE PALMER." Jones stated and took it from Eve, pushing it into his pocket. "That type of badge hasn't been worn for almost a century." He added softly and then, removing it again, studied it closely.

In the bright light of his torch, everyone could see that the pin had fragments of grey cloth still attached. Eve pushed back her hair and with some emotion in her voice; "It must have been ripped off, who was she and what the hell happened here?"

Tom held up his PA and said; "She's not on the crew list, all the other victims were known and accounted for, she's wasn't one of them." He started to tap at his PA adding; "I'll check the name."

"What's the story Chief?" Jones shone his torch upon the dishevelled remains of Rollo Thames; a man history had confined to the annuals of gruesome murder and depraved insanity; "If it wasn't him, then it could only have been the young Ensign, logic dictates that. Frigging sweet Mars: what a bloody turn up: the young, sweet faced Ensign was a crazed axe waving murdering psychopath!"

"Bugger, hit me with a shit stick!" Tom exclaimed, then looking around added; "Caroline Palmer was the Medical Officer here at Station Seven some ninety years ago. She simply vanished one night, never seen or heard of again and if that's not enough, her Military File is still Classified to this day!"

The little group exchanged glances and Jones held up a hand; "OK, but we'll concern ourselves with this mess for now. "He pushed the name badge back into his pocket; "What's the story about the storm, Troy going missing and this poor sod?" Jones needed answers, so the Chief recounted the crew's time sheltering in Weather Station 7(South): "Lilly was first to mention Troy's strange behaviour, she noticed that he kept laughing to himself and just wandering off, sometimes walking away in the middle of a conversation. She reported it to Eve, and they went to find him. Doc wanted to give him the once over, make sure he was OK."

Eve nodded; "You can imagine I was quite concerned about his behaviour. Lilly said, he had told her that he had seen things around the station. Strange lights and noises that made him afraid, he seemed upset, and so we went to find him."

The Chief continued: "That was the first problem; we simply couldn't locate the daft bugger! We split into three groups of two and searched everywhere and found nothing. The radio was down and the storm was on us. Then problem two appeared; a breach in an old vent, the storm had got it. So, Tom, me and Pete suited up and located the trouble. It took a couple of hours to shore everything up and return pressure to the corridor. No one noticed that a wall plate had come lose or the handle was now revealed. When we returned to the Control room, Troy still hadn't been found so the search continued.

Then we found him, which was not a big surprise, but where we found him was; the very corridor we had worked in! Tom and the Doc found him against the wall we had repaired, sitting with his legs drawn up and whispering about seeing people about the place that weren't any of us. He claimed that a woman had walked through a wall in front of him, pointing to the wall opposite. That's when Tom noticed the loose wall plate and the door handle."

Eve took up the story again:

"I gave him a mild sedative and with Kazza's help took him to the medical bay. Soon as I pulled the sweet bag from his hand and noticed the odd colour the mints had become; I pretty much knew what had happened. The MediScan confirmed my diagnosis; the bloody mints were laced with Lysergic acid diethylamide, better known in days gone by as 'LSD'. The daft twat was high as kite!" Eve managed a small smile and continued; "I gave him something to counter the effects and a couple of hours later he was normal again; well normal as Troy can be."

Tom added, smiling; "Apparently Troy purchased the mints from a street vendor in the wayward Donald Trump district, Rossington's HQ for the recreational drug industry and didn't realise that the nice old man selling sweets was a known drug peddler. Little wonder he was seeing things!" Tom allowed himself a small chuckle; "When Troy asked for his special mints, the old man probably thought he was a new customer and gave him some very special mints."

Even Jones had to smile at that one. But then he looked back at the remains; "Get this cleaned up and I want the station sealed and everyone back on the Thor." That's when Jones noticed Troy in the doorway, clutching a body bag with a very concerned look on his face. "Sorry Captain, I thought they were just mints, I didn't know they were spiked with STD, honestly." He looked quite down trodden and was surprised when everyone started to laugh. Eve sucked breath through her teeth and resisted the fit of giggles that were desperately trying to escape; "It's 'LSD' you twat, 'STD' means sexually transmitted disease!"

Jones shook his head and fought really hard not to laugh out loud; "OK Troy, no real harm done, I'll see you on the rig and we'll put this little incident to bed." The Chief took hold of the body bag and motioned to Tom; "Come on Tom, let's get this poor sod to the morgue."

Jones and Eve watched the removal of the very, very late

Rollo Thames with some sadness; they both knew that the message Jones would send to Military High Command would make one family very happy and relieved, the other: sad and heartbroken.

As the pair walked into the corridor, Eve gripped Jones's arm and spoke barely above a whisper; "Troy said a woman walked through the same wall, where we found that hidden door. Then inside, we find the crew-badge of a woman who disappeared nearly fifty years before the murders even took place; that's some coincidences don't you think?"

Jones nodded; "Let's deal with poor old Rollo first, then we'll have a dig at finding what happened to Caroline Palmer and why her file is still now apparently classified." They reached the corridors internal pressure door and stepped through; Jones operated the closure switch and watched the solid grey slab slide quietly across the opening. Eve stopped in her tracks and breathed quite deep a couple of times; Jones could see a strange expression on her face; "Can you smell that?" She asked a puzzled Jones who took a couple of deep breaths himself. "Only your perfume, smells like flowers, what's it called?"

Eve looked about and whispered closely into the captain's ear; "I'm not wearing any perfume and I would certainly not wear a perfume that smelt as old fashioned as Commander Taylor's socks." They both glanced about and with quite quick steps, made their way to the Station's control room.

AUTHOR NOTE:
"Commander Margret Taylor was the first human to set foot on Mars in the Martian Year 1 or Earth year 2032."

20. PAREIDOLIA.

Tom had been very busy digging into the circumstances of the murders some forty years previously; "You can imagine there's tons of stuff about these killings, books, films and documentary's all over the MSN. The sole survivor Ensign Conway Hallman was just eleven [almost 20 by Earth years] at the time of the murders and this was his first posting. He stuck to his story about Rollo Thames until the day he died – it never altered, he must have been a fantastic liar - because he recounted the details years later and they were identical to the first telling. Quite incredible in itself that. Liars normally always trip themselves up because they can't remember the exact details of the lie. But he obviously did."

AUTHOR NOTE:
"MSN is the abbreviation for 'Mars Social Network' – it's equivalent to the 'WWW' of Earths Internet – when it existed."

Lilly nodded her agreement; "He died about six years ago and he stuck to his story right up to the end, recounting the same details whenever asked."

"Whoever sealed up that small cupboard door did a very professional job: it took a storm to reveal it!" The Chief admired the fine workmanship of the young mass murderer. "But then he had six days to get it right before the rescue forces turned up from Shackleton." He added with a grin. Tom continued; "He was quite a celebrity at the time, the so-called hero of the Ice Shelf. He wrote a bestselling book about it and had a bit part in the first film produced on the story. Young Conway bought his parents and much younger brother a small farm near New Paris out the proceeds. As far as I know, his brother's family still resides there. He never had any children but from social media reports at the time, lots of girlfriends; Quite a playboy by all accounts."

"Some bloody playboy." Grunted the Chief; "He liked to play real hard games." Tom nodded; "Whereas Rollo Thames fitted the bill for a mass murderer, his military records revealed that he had previous convictions for assault as a teenager. His partner had left him, gaining custody of his children, claiming he was violent, and the Chief Medical Officer's file detailed he had received treatment for depression, serious depression. He also had been referred to an 'anger management' specialist. The perfect fall-guy for this crime by any stretch of the imagination, he also wasn't around to argue for himself and for the authorities, it tied the whole terrible episode up in neat ribbons." Tom finished speaking and sat down, sipping coffee and glancing at his PA.

"I still don't understand how Conway never revealed his true self over all those years, he never made one little slip up and was a model citizen until his death. Yet he brutally axed to death eight of his colleagues for no apparent reason and then basically resumed his life. It doesn't make any real sense." Eve folded her arms and nodded at Jones; "It doesn't make any real sense." She repeated.

"I think true psychopaths don't make sense to sane people." Jones spoke quietly and looked at the control room clock; "Let's head back to the Thor." At the captain's command, the little group began to disperse, collecting equipment and the second group back to the Thor was the Chief, Tom, Bella and the Doc. Captain Jones remained in the quiet Control room, now suited up and waiting for Kazza, Troy and Lilly to join him. He looked about the room and checked some of the instruments again; everything was operating to specification. But he felt ill at ease, something about Station Seven made his skin crawl, so many deaths and now the disappearance of the young Medical Officer nearly a century ago. He touched the old crew badge through the skin of his surface suit and sighed; "This place gives me the creeps."

"Me too, I'll be glad to see her on our rear cameras." Kazza laughed, standing in the doorway, suited up and holding his helmet. Jones nodded and smiled; "Let's go Kazza. Frankie is knocking up curry!"

"That'll make the Doc happy; she says we eat far too much curry." Troy peered over Kazza's shoulder and fitted his helmet in place. "Where's Lilly?" He added before sliding the visor down. On cue, Lilly appeared fully suited, and the foursome made their way back to the Thor across the silent ice; the storm had left the ice shelf with an eerie quietness, Mars was rarely peaceful and all four commented on the stillness. Jones glanced back at the dark monolith that was station seven and the control room window caught his eye; the lights were dimming to switch off and just for an instant, he thought he saw a shape, a figure of someone. He stopped in his tracks and called up the Thor; "Peter, are all the crew back except us?" Everyone in the small group was now looking at the station, but the control room was in total darkness. Peter confirmed that the crew was all present – except for the captain's party of course. As Jones turned to continue towards the rig, he caught the look on Lilly's face; she mouthed some words he couldn't make out and her face showed some real bewilderment. He patted her shoulder and pointed to the Thor and the group returned without further comments.

Jones sat on his chair and watched the station disappearing on the rear cameras, he sipped some cold water and read a dispatch from the convoy; they still had nothing to show for all their efforts and his report to Military High Command had caused some uproar. To quote the Chief's well used phrase: 'the shit had hit the fan.'

Leon was in the primary pilot's seat, reading instruments and checking the scope, Peter was refilling his coffee cup, so Lilly dropped into his vacant seat and leaned forward to Jones and spoke quietly; "Captain, just as the lights extinguished, I thought I saw someone in the control room. I know you saw it too because why else would you ask about the crew?" Lilly sipped her coffee and appeared quite nervous. Jones smiled at her and said simply; "Pareidolia Lilly, simple as that I think."

"OK captain, but can two people have it at the same time?" She asked, then seeing Peter return, left the seat and sat back at the communications desk. She glanced towards Jones with some concern still on her face and then her attention was taken by incoming messages. The internal phone by Jones buzzed; it was the Medical Suite; "Hi Doc." He answered and after a few seconds placed the receiver down and sat thoughtfully, hand on chin, then rose telling Peter to take over, he was heading for the medical bay to see Eve and Tom.

In the quiet of the medical bay, they gathered about the remains of Rollo Thames, saying nothing until the Chief joined them. Eve slid the body tray back into its refrigeration unit and asked Tom; "Should I start first?" Tom nodded, and Jones could see he was clutching a small blue notebook that was held together with an elastic band.

"I found a couple of things on the body; we should have searched it at the scene. But never mind, the notebook was in his right thigh pocket, and this was around his neck." Eve held up a small silver chain with a crucifix attached. "According to the reports made at the time, they all failed to mention that Rollo Thames had become a Christian just before he started his final tour of duty at the station. I found that out from a grandson who conducted his own investigation, some years later. Apparently, he had given up alcohol and attended services in his local church; he was even in contact with his estranged wife who admitted that finding Jesus had actually changed him for the better. But none of the media services at the time or the authorities wanted that to go public; it didn't quite fit the image of a crazed axe killer." Eve lowered the crucifix and didn't smile.

Tom then held up the fragile notebook and spoke quietly; "He kept little notes about the station, the people, and the weather and so on. The date Conway says the murders took place is in here. Rollo reports that the crew had reported strange sounds and sights since they came aboard and so they decided to hold a séance in the galley, thinking it was great bloody entertainment and just fun. He wanted no part of that, he states it's against God and left them to their own devices.

But Shrivers – the station Manager - was into the occult and convinced the rest to play the game. Just as important, is that Rollo states he sent young Conway to the battery room, he was supposed to have cleaned it up earlier, but had forgotten, so he wasn't present at the séance and the investigation team reported that all the bodies were found in or near the galley. They didn't, of course, find his body."

"A fucking séance? That's just plain crazy." The Chief folded his arms and shook his head in disbelief. He had heard about some crazy things happening at Weather Stations, but that topped them all!

"Shriver's, the Station Manager, was a real odd character; a self-confessed pagan and he had dabbled in the occult for years. He was nearly 38 and this was his last tour [that's almost 70 by Earth years], he had completed over fifteen tours of station 7 over the years. Here's the cruncher: Conway never mentions the séance, not a word – he always said that the crew was at dinner – nothing about communicating with the bloody dead. Back to this, [the notebook] the last page

is interesting, it's clearly written in a hurry and with a crayon."
Tom held up the open page and read softly; "My God what
have we done?"

Tom glanced about and Jones stared at the frantically written
words and took a deep breath; "What the hell did they do
here that caused a bloody massacre?"

"Evil is evil, on Mars or on Earth." Eve held her hand over her
face and looked back at the morgue door which contained the
remains of Rollo Thames; "How could they have got it so
wrong?" She whispered.

"This is all very interesting, but it doesn't alter the facts that
someone had to kill those eight people. We know it wasn't
Rollo – that's a fact – the only other person there, who
survived the killing, was Conway. Therefore, it had to be him.
Indisputable logic from facts, otherwise we're slipping into the
world of madness." The Chief spoke clearly and firmly and
after a short pause, Jones had to agree with him.

The group broke up and Jones returned to the bridge in deep
thought, one part of him agreed with the Chief, but another
part whispered disturbing thoughts of old ghosts and dark
supernatural happenings. Eve followed, and sat next to Lilly,
who was concentrating on an incoming call. "Vice - Admiral
Kellamann on the secure line for you Captain." Lilly called
across to Jones as he eased himself into his chair and sipped
the coffee Leon had passed him. "This was going to be an
interesting conversation." Jones muttered to himself and lifted
the receiver.

21. GOODBYE TO THE EASTERS.

The dark shapes of the Easter Mountains towered above the
Thor as she rolled back into Valley La Mort; "Nice to be back

in the graveyard." The Chief chuckled, sprawled openly in the captain's chair and sipping coffee. Leon checked the scope and could see the flashing dots indicating the presence of the battle rig, General Westmoreland and the supply rig: the John Garfield.

"About twenty minutes and we re-join the convoy." Leon checked the seismic gauges and confirmed the Thor was on good ground. The Chief nodded; "Buzz the skipper and let him know, he's in the medical room with Tom and Eve."

 "No luck whatsoever, they quoted me the good old hundred-year rule. No disclosure of the files content until then, so we have about a decade to wait, "Tom shuffled the papers about; "The Military File on MO Caroline Palmer remains closed to public scrutiny. I think there's a connection between her disappearance and those murders." The disappointment was clear in his voice. Jones took the papers from him and flicked through them; "I can't see a connection between the two, there's a gap of nearly fifty years. The only real tangible connection is the crew-badge and that could have lain there for years. But you've certainly done some digging on this Tom, but I think it's time to step back and leave it to the past; yes?"

Tom said nothing but nodded his agreement. Eve sipped her flavoured water and placed the glass on the desk, carefully avoiding the sleeping Dallas sprawled across her papers, cat napping. "I have to agree with the skipper; once the body is transferred to the 'John Garfield' I think that should be the end of our involvement in this sad story."

Jones pulled his fingers from his shirt pocket and handed Tom the old crew name badge; "You keep this Tom, I think you deserve something at least, I believe young Caroline would thank you for all you tried to do."

Tom pushed the little shiny object into the small plastic box containing all his research so far; "Thanks skipper, I do appreciate that." He said quietly and wandered from the Medial Suite to the Galley in search of coffee.

The phone buzzed, and Eve lifted the receiver, telling Jones that the Thor would re-join the convoy in twenty minutes. She smiled at Jones and sat running her hand over Dallas, who flicked his tail and gave loud short spluttering purrs. Jones watched her slender fingers caressing the cat's ears and neck; it was the first time in his life that he was envious of a cat! He shook the thoughts away and rose to leave. "That was a weird conversation with the Admiral don't you think?" Eve looked up from stroking Dallas and smiled. Jones sighed and slowly sat back down; "You should not have been eves - dropping Eve that was a confidential call."

Eve grinned; "Then you shouldn't take it on the bridge, I just happened to be there, chatting to Lilly, who by the way, thought the Admiral sounded quite odd."

Jones ran his fingers through his hair and had to smile, very little got past the rigs quick and bright Medical Officer. "I thought you and Lilly would pick up on his voice, especially when he stated that they had not found the weapon, and then hesitated, as if he wanted to say they found something else. I think he remembered who he was talking to." Jones leaned back in the chair and glanced at his PA.

"I best go, we'll be with the convoy in a few minutes, and you had better prepare the body for transfer." He didn't relish attending the officers conference call in the galley of the 'General Westmoreland', scheduled for two hours time and there was the awful prospect of bumping into his mad namesake; Dr. Margot-Jones. "I'd sooner wrestle a bear naked." He muttered to himself, making his way back to the bridge. Then he smiled at the thought of the chief and all his moaning about attending the meeting in place of Peter.

The Thor was parked some meters from the supply rig MSV: John Garfield; Jones watched Troy and Tom accompany the big beaver drone towards that rig's cargo hold. He could see the black bundle laid upon the beaver's flatbed: the late Rollo Thames was heading home finally, his reputation reinstated, and his name cleared; that must give some closure to his remaining family Jones thought.

Then he thought about Ensign Conway Hallman's existing descendants, his brothers' grandchildren now owned and operated the farm Conway had purchased for his parents; what would they make of this change of circumstances? Would they really care? A wise man had once said: 'the past best remains buried.' Jones's thoughts were interrupted by Peter who reminded him of the conference call; "The Chief is already on his way to the suit room skipper." Jones nodded and made his way down the service corridor where Lilly and Leon were helping the Chief into his surface suit.

"Why me? It should be Peter suffering this; he's the bloody XO for shit's sake!" Jones pulled his jacket off and grabbed his suit from its storage locker; "Because I was told to bring you, you moaning old git!"

He grinned at Marcus and the Chief just grunted, "Besides all three of us can't go – someone has to be on the bridge - that's military regulations you know." Jones was laughing as he locked up his helmet; the Chief was in a wonderful mood today, 'Sunny' was the only crew member that managed to gain a half-smile off the grizzled old warrior all day.

"Bastards." The Chief said without any emotion and locked his helmet, following Jones into the external pressure elevator.

The pair descended to the surface and made their way to the Battle rig; MSV: The General Westmoreland. Lilly called the captain, informing him that the transfer of Rollo Thames was complete, and Dallas had his bed back. Jones chuckled at that, glancing at the Chief and almost catching a smile on his face too.

The galley of the General Westmoorland was impressive; covered with wood appearance panels and various pictures hanging on the walls. Jones and the Chief studied the photographs of past battle rigs as the room filled up with more officers. The conference table was laid with water jugs, glasses and coffee cups and the decorated side table spread with all kinds of buffet goodies. Two deckhands, resplendent in white steward jackets, offered everyone coffee in delicate little cups and small, sweet biscuits.

"How the other half fucking rough it." The Chief spoke quietly and sipped his coffee, a far superior blend than the normal military issue. Well, it actually tasted like coffee should and Jones didn't refuse a refill from the smiling Mess-Steward. "Lunch will follow the conference sir, if I may take your meal orders, this is today's menu." He handed Jones and Marcus a printed card; they both glanced at each other and picked the beef curry. They knew it would contain real beef. "How the other half fucking rough it." Jones whispered and the Chief chuckled, then Vice-Admiral Kellamann called the meeting to order.

Vice- Admiral Kellamann completed a resume of events to date; the weapon had not been recovered, neither had the body of Stanners or the two cyborgs. But thanks were given to Captain Jones and his crew for the recovery of Rollo Thames's body and getting Station Seven back online despite category 2 storms. He informed all officers that the convoy would depart for Rossington at 06.00 hrs CST with the same battle order as the outbound journey. The Thor would be middle rig again and Jones was happy with that.

As everyone started to relax and savour the thought of lunch, the Vice-Admiral called the table to order again; "I have one last duty to perform before we return to our rigs, today is quite a special one for a fellow officer and we do need to acknowledge that fact. Ladies and gentlemen, I give you Chief of the Rig Marcus Enders who completes fifteen years service today and can now retire with our due thanks and genuine appreciation."

Everyone started to applaud - except the Chief - who fixed a smile upon his face and looked down at the tablecloth. "Now I know why you were such a miserable bugger today." Jones whispered and asked himself how he missed that in the crew's files.

The Vice-Admiral continued; "Fifteen years ago Marcus joined the Military straight from college and completed his initial Engineering apprenticeship aboard that old battle rig: The Lord Nelson. But from there, he attended Fort Benjamin Engineering University, obtaining a 'with Honours' degree. He was promoted to Executive Officer of the Military supply rig; The Don Johnson, but I'm afraid, the call of the engine room proved too much and he became Chief of the battle rig; The Fort William. Chief he has stayed since then and I will confide to all here, turned down various promotions which would mean leaving those precious engines he loves so much. But now his service is complete, I would ask that you raise your glasses in thanks." The Vice-Admiral stood and raised his glass as did every other officer; "Well done Marcus, the old war horse can now head for pastures new with all our thanks; to Marcus!" Everyone lifted their glass and said, "Marcus!" Jones glanced down at his PA and read the new message that Eve had just sent him and smiled.

The Chief sat quietly; his head bowed a little and mumbled his thanks. Jones gripped his shoulder: "Why didn't you tell me?" Marcus looked up, his eyes betraying his sadness; "I didn't want any fuss."

Vice-Admiral Kellamann, still standing, sipped his drink and smiled broadly; "That's unless the old war horse is not quite ready for the paddock yet and may ask for a year's extension of service – which must be granted by an officer of no less than an Admirals rank - so do you wish to extend Marcus?" He looked directly at the Chief. Marcus gulped and looked at Jones who whispered; "Yes." He coughed a couple of times and spoke directly to the Admiral; "May I apply for an extension of service sir?" He glanced about him, no bloody wonder Jones was told to bring him and not Peter; what a fucking turn-up!

The Vice-Admiral eased back into his chair, clasping his hands upon the table and smiled; "You already did Chief, I signed off on your extension this morning and Fleet Command sent their agreement just before this meeting convened; welcome back aboard."

 Everyone started laughing and clapping, Jones noticed the look of relief upon Marcus's face was palpable and he gripped the Chief's arm; "All you have to do is pass the medical and your back." The Chief nodded, a big smile spreading across his face, and then the smile dropped: "What medical skipper?"

"Your re-engagement medical, it's normally done at the Medical Centre in Rossington, but because we stuck here, they have authorised it to be done locally; Eve has already completed it. You passed you silly old bugger." Jones held up the paper a steward had passed him during the Vice-Admirals speech; "I think you owe Eve some flowers and a thank you – but for Mars sake - don't drop dead or we'll all be in the shit!"

Jones laughed and lifted his glass; "Welcome back Chief."
"I would have given anything to see the old buggers face."
Eve folded her arms and looked out the bridge windscreen
towards the dark caves, she would be quite happy to see
them in the Thor's rear cameras. Jones smiled; "It's been a
good day, but we depart at six in the morning and I'm getting
some sleep. I'll see you both in the morning." He nodded to
Peter who was reading his PA in the primary pilot's seat.

Jones walked with Eve back to the medical bay and picked up
the Chief's file; "I'll tuck this away until next year." They both
laughed and then Jones noticed the morgue tray was open
and Dallas was sprawled over it, happily sleeping. Eve just
shook her head; "I really don't know how he does that; I had
the opening lever locked down and he still manages to open
the damn tray." Jones just smiled and shrugged his shoulders;
"Goodnight Eve."

Jones made his way down the service corridor and passed
Tom's cabin, the door was half open and he could hear voices;
speaking low and quietly. He stopped outside; "Goodnight
Tom, we move off at six in the morning." Tom appeared in
the doorway; his face expressionless; "Yes thank you captain.
We know." Jones noticed he had a strange, unsmiling 'far
away' expression on his face, but said nothing.

Jones couldn't see who was in the cabin, but he assumed it
was Leon who shared with Tom. The cabin door slid shut and
Jones started to walk away, but he stopped and took a couple
of deep breaths: flowers. Jones thought he could smell
flowers; he looked about the corridor and quickly made way to
his cabin. There he flicked open his PA and typed carefully
typed a sole word: 'Poltergeist.' He sat on his bunk and slowly
rubbed his chin as he read the article then slowly smiled as
the author's name appeared: Professor Jack Dawes who lived
and worked from a small shop in Rossington. According to

biographical notes Dawes was an acknowledged expert on the occult and was previously a history professor at Kennedy University. Jones sat back and recalled that the mad Professor Jacobson had also attended Kennedy University. They must surely know each other. Jones also noted that Dawes had written a couple of books about the 'myths & Legends' of old Mars. What did catch Jones eye was the allegation that the Colonial Government had banned the biography's of two members of the Founding flight because of statements they made about a possible ancient Mars civilization and the appearance of 'ghosts' during the early years of settlement. He noted that the subsequent Mars Governments had not lifted the bans!

"This professor Dawes must be worth a visit." Jones mused and could hear voices outside his cabin door; he recognized Lilly and Leon's and so opened the door and bade them goodnight. Lilly shook her head and – apparently – repeated her assertion that she didn't wear perfume with that scent, and she hadn't been in their cabin. Leon just smiled and Jones asked what it was about. A grinning Leon confided to the captain that he had just returned to the cabin he shared with Tom and the place smelt of flowers or perfume. Lilly sighed and denied it was her scent and the pair; still quietly but firmly disagreeing with each other, walked on.

Jones returned to his cabin and wondered who Tom was talking with, if Leon had only just returned to the cabin. But he knew now that two other people – apart from him and Eve – had smelt the strange perfume, so that meant the smell was real. He had a strange – but pleasant - dream that night about rain, grass, blue skies and snow-capped mountains.

Unsurprisingly, Eve appeared in his dream which he didn't mind one bit! Jones didn't know where he was: the rig was not the Thor. It was much older in construction and design and the engines could be heard: loudly. He slowly climbed the bridge ladder and stepped onto the platform and stared wide-eyed through the big windscreen at trees and mountains. The sky was an incredible blue with few clouds. But his attention was soon drawn from the amazing sight and to the figure standing by the pilot's chair. At first he thought it was Eve, and then realized it was another young woman, equally pretty but she didn't smile.

She slowly held up her hand and showed Jones a small glass pyramid with bright colours swirling inside. He now couldn't take his eyes off the damn thing: it seemed to mesmerize him. She waved her other hand over it and the view through the rig's windscreen changed to fire and explosions, like he was staring into an active volcano. Then all that was gone, replaced by a deep black darkness that appeared quite impenetrable. Then slowly a dull yellow sun arose over a broken barren landscape and Jones could see figures walking across the dust and dirt. They vanished into a large cavern and suddenly the sun was gone and it re-appeared at an incredible speed: vanishing and re-appearing. Then it was daylight over the barren land. From the dull reddish sky parachutes appeared and something hit the ground and they fell away. The little machine suddenly jerked, then rolled forward, slowly heading away towards a distant mountain range. In the cavern entrance several strange dark figures watched it depart and then turned and were gone. Jones couldn't make out if they were human or some kind of machines. Watching them, Jones suddenly felt a great wave of sadness sweep over him and a strange feeling of pity filled his heart. "Reluctant ghosts." He muttered and suddenly awoke bathed in sweat and stumbled from his bunk and headed for the bathroom, his thoughts, dark and frightening, swirled in his head. Was it a bizarre dream? Or something else? It had been so vivid, like watching a short film, but what the hell did it mean?

EPISODE 8: "LIBERTY."

22. THE WEDDING.

"Old Gustov has apparently spared no expense on Bella's big day!" The Chief adjusted his tie and sipped his wine with a great deal of happy appreciation; "This wine is fourteen dollars a bottle!" Sitting opposite Marcus, Lilly looked quite amazed; "Chief, you can buy a three-course meal with drinks for that." She turned the glass around in her hand and then swallowed it down in one gulp. "But it does taste nice, and the bubbles go up your nose." She added, with a little fit of giggles.

The entire crew had a table to themselves, but obviously Bella and Kazza was sitting at the top table with the respective parents and close family. Kazza kept glancing enviously across at the crew table each time the room was rocked by the raucous laughter coming from it. "Your friends from the rig certainly know how to enjoy themselves, Kazzamondo." His happy new Mother-in-law quipped – Kazza flinched - he remembered the little ripple of laughter that went round the marriage chamber when the Marriage

Registrar read out his full name: "Kazzamondo Rupert Yassimini." Even Bella chuckled, but gripped his hand tightly, whispering; "Sorry, but no son of ours will ever be called after his father!" He had nodded his agreement without hesitation.

There were lots of children around the rig's table for just one reason: Dallas. They had found, if you held your open palm up to him, he would tap it with his paw and if you threw something, he would fetch it back. They ran about the table giggling and laughing; Dallas had a whole new fan club!

At the bar, Gustov asked Jones about the large cat now playing football with the children (he was in goal) the captain shrugged his shoulders and explained [again] that Bella and Kazzamondo [Jones was still chuckling about that revelation] had insisted the whole crew attend the wedding; so that – of course - included the rig's mascot. Gustov sipped his drink and watched the cat save another potential goal – pushing the ball away with his paws - to the delight of the children and keen watching adults. "Tell me again please Captain, what exactly happened this morning." Gustov grinned as Jones recounted the story: "We were all on the bridge, gathering together before we caught the Military bus for City Hall, when Eve noticed that Lilly was missing. So, I called for her on the rig's broadcast system, but she was already on her way to the bridge. We all watched a little amazed as she sat down at the Communications desk and placed Dallas on it. "I'm going to smarten him up for the wedding." She said simply, pulling the Galley's small vacuum from the box she was carrying and started to vacuum Dallas very carefully. It started with a few chuckles and then it turned into laughter as she brushed and vacuumed the clearly appreciative cat.

Finally, I managed to say; "Lilly, you're vacuuming the cat!" The Chief clasped a hand over his face and muttered; "Lake Placid here we come!" But Eve thought it was great and especially laughed when Lilly fitted Dallas with a big silver lead; like dogs would wear. "We don't need to put him in that terrible cage thing [his cat box; which he disliked]; he'll happily walk on a lead." And he did.

It drew some strange looks when the crew appeared in the marriage chamber with a large cat on a lead. If anyone asked, we all replied with the same expression: we're from a Weather Service rig; they don't let us out much!"

Being a rig man himself, Gustov chuckled at that revelation, repeating the story to his wife Grace and anyone else who asked about the funny large cat and its friends. Jones and Eve danced together several times – which didn't go unnoticed by the crew - or the fact that Lilly and Peter also danced together though Lilly also danced with Dallas and most of the crew.

Kazza was explaining to the captain, the generous offer from his father-in-law about a position in his rig company, the new apartment and trips up to Taylor. Kazza was in heaven but admitted he would desperately miss the crew and the rig. Jones just smiled and was explaining about that strange little thing called 'responsibility' when his PA buzzed; he glanced down and saw the caller ID: Professor Jack Dawes. He walked over to Eve and Tom and whispered to both; "That's it, he's waiting for us."

Tom and Eve glanced at each other and rose from the table; this was the mystery man that Professor Jacobson had quietly recommended to Jones when he and the Chief had visited the old General Westmoreland. The three slipped away from the party and made their way to the old '8Gerald Webster' quarter of the city and a quiet alley where they found the little shop; "Jackdaw's." A bell tinkled as they squeezed into the badly lit room which was crammed from floor to ceiling with curiosities and antiques. Tom lifted a mask from a nearby shelf and closely studied it; "I think it's from Africa, back on earth, it's wonderfully primitive; superb."

"You know your masks; Mister Eddington?" From a dark curtain emerged Professor Dawes, he was quite a young man still with thick dark hair and cold green eyes; "It is African in origin and quite rare, a tribal death mask worn by the natives when they went on a killing raid. It's representing the spirit of death." He motioned for the threesome to enter through the curtain, and they followed him into a small office which was stacked with books and manuscripts. The professor squeezed behind his desk and held out his hand; "The old name tag please." He motioned them to sit, and Tom handed it over. In the still quiet of that musty office, Professor Dawes examined the old crew badge, at one point pulling a large magnifying glass from his coat. After nearly a minute he placed the badge down on the desk and sat back with a small smile upon his face; "Firstly, the aura I can detect from this artifact is not malevolent, quite the opposite in fact. I believe the entity connected with this was or is, somehow trying to help – how is anyone's guess - maybe trying to warn? Trying to protect? Trying to make contact perhaps?" The professor pulled a bunch of old-fashioned keys from his pocket and unlocked a drawer on the desk and placed a brown folder before them. "Secondly, the scene of those murders can tell more than one truth."

"Can there be more than one truth, is that possible?" Tom asked a little puzzled; "The truth is always the truth, isn't it?" Eve slowly nodded her agreement; "Facts and the truth must be the same, like evidence it has to be factual and true; doesn't it?"

The professor noticed that Jones said nothing but sat with his arms folded and grim faced. He had quickly realised what the professor was about to say, and the professor knew it. Quite an intelligent soul and quick thinking too, he could easily be a candidate the professor mused to himself. He then flicked open the folder and passed the photographs around; they were not pleasant.

"Actual photographs of the scene from forty years ago and what they can tell is another version of the facts or the truth if you prefer. When the original investigators made their report, they had only half the facts and the result is obvious: they got it wrong of course." He smiled and picked up two photographs that showed the dreadful scene in the Galley and kitchen area.

"Notice how, two of the bodies are sitting at the table; one at the top and another three chairs down. Then two more on the floor and another in the doorway. In the other picture, there are two more on the floor of the small kitchen area which is immediately adjacent to the galley. Seven in total."

Eve had a hand over her mouth and took a couple of deep breaths; "How did he manage to kill all seven without them resisting in some way or running away?"

"Good question Lieutenant and remember; no bloodstained clothing was found other than that worn by the dead. They had no body of Rollo Thames – he would have been soaked with blood splatters from all those bodies - so he must have been the killer that disappeared into the night. That was their truth. Which we now know is false." The professor tapped the photographs; "To answer your first question Lieutenant; the truth is the truth until new facts alter it. To answer your second question the original investigators concluded they were killed in a 'frenzied attack', almost if a Berserker had magically appeared and struck them down." He placed the photographs face down on the desk and lifted up two more; "The key is in these two."

That's the battery room." Tom muttered with some certainty and Eve agreed. Jones asked; "The battery room contained the answer which the original investigators missed because they weren't looking for it at the time, is that right professor?"

The professor smiled broadly: his hunch about the captain was right; definitely a possible candidate.

Eve and Tom studied the coloured photographs closely for some minutes and sat back shaking their heads; "I don't see anything unusual, there are the buckets Conway said he used as a toilet and the battery covers, he wrapped himself in...."

Eve stopped in midsentence and tapped the second picture gently; "On the wall, six marks indicating the days he was trapped; written in red crayon I think."

"Well done Eve, that is some coincidence that Conway also possessed a red crayon, the same as Rollo Thames. In fact, the little notebook's final words have never been confirmed as written by Thames, has it?" The professor asked Tom who agreed; "The red crayon found with Rollo was only half a stick, Conway must have kept the other half."

"Conway dropped it by the body when he scribbled in those final words, probably the next day after realising the full extent of the horror that had taken place and his part in it. Like his uncle, Conway practiced 'Black magic' and would have definitely been present at any séance; except they were not planning a séance at all." The professor sat back and added quietly; "Conway was Shriver's nephew, Shriver pulled strings to have his young nephew posted to the station."

"What were they really doing professor?" Eve asked lifting the second photograph up and studied it closely. That's when they noticed the change in Professor Dawes demeanor; he sighed loudly and after some moments, clasped his hands together tightly and lent across the desk, he spoke very quietly; "They were trying to summon the Devil; the ultimate aim of anyone who practices the black art."

There was silence in the small office. Eve placed the photograph face up on the table and tapped it gently; "The battery room floor has a distinct pattern on it, what is that shape professor?"

Professor Dawes was now impressed with both the Captain and this young woman, he coughed and outlined the shape with his finger; "A pentagram Eve, used as protection against evil; again the original investigators paid no attention to it because they simply weren't looking for signs of Devil worship! The battery room was the 'back-up plan' for the group; but what they conjured up that day overcame them far too quickly and only Rollo and Conway made it out the Galley alive and I suppose they headed for the battery room for protection, except only Conway survived." The professor sat back and ran his fingers through his dark hair. "Rollo states in his notebook that he wanted nothing to do with the supposed séance and I would speculate that Rollo realised that Conway had not returned to the battery room and went to fetch him, coming upon the horror that was taking place in the Galley; maybe he dragged Conway away and together they tried to escape."

"Except whatever had appeared caught Rollo and killed him as he tried to hide in the old store cupboard, probably after Conway had sealed the battery room before he could reach it; in panic and fear maybe?" The professor tapped the first photograph; "Conway survived because he reached the sanctuary of the pentagram, and he also possessed another potent weapon against evil incarnate."

"What weapon?" Asked Tom, peering closely at the picture, but the professor laughed and waved his hand; "I'm afraid it's not in the photo Tom – it was the station cat - 'Snuggles'."

"The cat!" Tom exclaimed with some surprise and laughed, shaking his head. It was the captain that answered Tom's unspoken question; "Cats have been protecting humans and their homes for nearly six thousand Earth years, why do you think so many families have them? Why so many rigs carry them? The Ancient Egyptians knew their worth, both in the world of living humans and the supernatural world."

The professor had a very broad smile, his initial feeling about the captain and the girl had been correct; they were both potential candidates. "Conway only survived because the entity that slaughtered those idiots could not breach the pentagram or pass by the protection offered by the cat. But the following day, the realization that he would be placed in the frame for the murders as the sole survivor, must have become apparent and he needed a plan. No investigation team would believe murder by demonic entity; so, Rollo Thames must become the killer and thus a simple, but clever plan emerged."

"That's how he managed never to slip up about his story; for the most part it was true." Eve spoke with a little amazement in her voice; both men were innocent! She now understood what 'the truth' actually means: whatever people perceive it to be!

The little shop bell tinkled, and Professor Dawes consulted his PA; "I've run over time my friends and the next visitor's really guard their privacy in all matters. Would you please exit through the rear?" Tom and Eve looked about; there was only one door!

But the professor stepped back and squeezed the desk leg nearest to him and the rear bookcase slid quietly back, revealing a small passage; "Follow it and you will appear at the rear of alley; goodnight my friends and I'll try and see you tomorrow." He shook their hands in turn as Jones led them into the tunnel, as they passed through the small passage Jones pushed the crew badge back into his pocket. The professor had passed it back to him when he shook his hand with the words;" Keep it. The entity that favours it may be of help."

They stepped into the dark and silent alley, then watched as the brick wall sealed up behind them so completely that none of them could even see a small crack. "Who the fuck is he skipper?" Tom muttered, and they quickly returned to the wedding party in silence.

23. THE PRESENTATION.

Jones held a hand over his face as he reviewed the crew assembled before him; "What a bunch of misfits! You look like you've bloody slept in those uniforms." The expression: 'collective hangover' came to mind and Jones sighed loudly. He glanced at the rig's clock and nodded; "Right, we have two hours before the show opens, I want those uniforms cleaned and pressed, food and coffee tipped down necks and aspirin for those that need it and back here in an hour for a final inspection; so get a grip and smarten up."

As the ragged group started to disperse, Peter held his brow and confided to Leon; "What lunatic arranges a Military parade and presentation the day after a wedding piss-up!" Leon simply groaned; "I don't know but the bastard needs shooting." Holding onto each other, they made their way to the galley where Frankie had put together a substantial breakfast and his dress uniform was immaculate under his apron.

The Chief was standing next to Jones, chuckling to himself and sipping coffee; his number one uniform was also immaculate [as was Jones's and Eve's] "I've seen Deep Vein Miners look better after a shift in the pits." He spoke quietly and smiled at Jones and the Doc.

"I'll get Lilly up to scratch, she needs help. I don't think she's use to strong alcohol." Smiling, Eve headed for the Ensigns cabin, stopping off to collect some painkillers and fruit juice.

AUTHOR NOTE:

"Make sure you get some food down her." Jones called after the Doc and sat back in his chair, sipped some coffee and started to eat his fried egg sandwich. The Chief lowered himself into the primary pilot seat and rolled his cup about in his hands; "Lilly will be fine, Eve will get her up to speed."

Jones sat quietly for a few seconds, deep in thought. Then he turned to the Chief and said softly; "They won't come, I called them twice, even told them that their accommodation and travel will be paid for. They refused. I will never tell Lilly what her father said, though I expect she knows well enough."

Jones pulled from his chair and stood staring at the dockside through the bridge windscreen; "When I said how proud we are of Lilly and that she would love to see them at the presentation, her father stopped me in mid-sentence and said; 'We don't have a daughter, we did have a son once but he is dead.' He hung up on me." the utter sadness in Jones was voice apparent.

"Bastards." The Chief grunted and added; "Yeah, but her new family will be there and proud as a dog with two dicks." Jones slapped Marcus on the back and smiled; "That's not quite the expression I would employ, but I know what you mean." Frankie appeared from the shadows; "You sent for me skipper?"

Jones noticed that the Chef was smartly turned out, even his regulation boots gleamed and his long hair was neatly hidden beneath his Military cap. Jones nodded, and with a smile to the Chief saic; "Yes I did Frank, I want you to carry the rig's Commissioning Pennant at the ceremony, is that ok?"

Frankie looked shocked by that statement and he said nothing for a few seconds, the rig's commissioning Pennant was normally carried by the 'leading' crew member – it was considered a great honour by all crews - to carry their rig's Pennant. "If you want me to Captain, it would be a real privilege to carry it for Miss Lilly's presentation." Jones nodded his thanks, and then Frankie stopped by the bridge ladder and added; "Best I run an iron over the fucker then."

The Captain and Chief burst out laughing and slumped back in their chairs. "What the hell were you and Gustov drinking last night? I could see it was quite a fancy bottle?" Jones finished his coffee and prodded Marcus; "Well, what was it?" He slowly repeated. Marcus smiled and held up both hands; "Just fancy old whisky liquor, that's all."

"Which fancy old whisky liquor are we talking about?" Jones asked and saw the sheepish look on Marcus's face, so he repeated the question. Marcus gave a big grin; "It would have been rude to say no, Gustov is a lovely man and generous too, so I joined him in a few drops of the stuff."

"What stuff?" Jones asked and Marcus sighed, he knew the truth would come out anyway, "Old Ma Crawford's Sipping Whisky." Jones placed both hands over his face and breathed deeply; "How many bottles did you talk him out of?"

"Only two." The Chief tapped Jones on the shoulder and smiled; "It's difficult to obtain these days you know, with all the Peace Guard raids, the health and safety people smashing bottles on TV and various fuckers claiming it sent them a little insane. It's hard to get hold of."

The Chief wasn't happy that the captain ordered him to keep the bottles in the 'Hazardous Chemical Store'. But at least he could keep them. 'Old Ma Crawford's Sipping Whisky' was legendary, especially amongst the rig crews who considered it 'their' drink. In mining and township bars, drinkers had bestowed upon the whisky almost mythical powers and despite various Government crack downs on the stuff, it had survived.

First distilled some two centuries ago, on a remote family farm near the North/South boarder, by 'Granny Crawford' who claimed the secret recipe came to her in a dream, the whisky was considered the State drink of the South; mostly by those who didn't think much of sobriety. It's famous 'tag-line' was a legend too; "Well its better than no Whisky'. Jones laughed to himself when he remembered the simple advice his beloved grandfather gave him, if offered a drop of the stuff: "Run."

The Grand reception area of the Southern Governors Palace was packed with dignitaries, invited guests, military personnel, media reporters and several groups of local school children and their teachers. The raised stage had several dozen chairs for the dignities and all the seven state flags of the Mars Federal Government hung from the walls: the Martian Flag hung from the ceiling.

A dozen Mars Marines formed a guard of honour for the Vice-president, who had arrived at the palace some twenty minutes behind schedule due to the railway station opening. He had received a rapturous reception from the crowds. Gaylord Prentiss was a very popular VP despite being an inveterate womanizer, gambler and drunk. He was originally from the South himself and he played up to his Southern roots and the crowds loved it. He always wore a white suit and shook hands gripping with both of his. The VP's catchphrase was: "Bless you, Mars and our mothers!" He had survived more 'scandals' than a box of cats had lives between them. Jones believed that back on 'old mother' he would easily be referred to as a 'snake-oil salesman'. But he was popular, both North and South which continually amazed Jones.

Jones led the crew of 'The Thor' into the hall, with Frankie beside him carrying the rig's commissioning Pennant. They marched to the front and lined up before the small podium which held the VP and Admiral Oscar Norrington [Commander of all Mars Southern Forces] and his flag officer, who carried the Silver Star in its presentation box.

"Thor will come to attention!" Jones barked the order, clear and precise: the crew snapped to attention. Jones stood before the podium and saluted; "Sir, the Thor is at attention." Admiral Norrington smiled and returned the salute; "Thank you Captain, stand them at ease please."

Jones ordered the crew 'at ease'. The Admiral made a short speech and called for Ensign Blissford to step forward. Lilly did the crew proud, despite her nerves, and marched up to the podium and saluted.

The VP then gave a speech and hung the Silver Star around the young Ensigns neck and the large audience exploded into clapping and cheering, Lilly gave a nervous little speech and looked quite relieved when Jones called the crew to attention as the VIP's filed from the stage.

"Now the good part." The Chief whispered to Eve as the crew was stood down for the after-presentation drinks and food; "Part two of the piss-up." He added with a big grin, full of happy anticipation. Lilly was happy to see that Bella and Kazza had delayed their honeymoon to attend but remained silent when asked about her parents. But the two empty chairs on the VIP stage didn't go unnoticed by the crew. The general consensus of opinion from them was the same as the Chief: "Bastards."

The after-presentation party was a hit; there were only a couple of fights and Eve, with Lilly's help, averted a major punch up between the Marines and the crew over Dallas. Apparently, the Marines had decided that Dallas should be a Marine Corp mascot and plied him with beer and dressed him in an eye-patch and 'skull & Cross-Bones' kerchief. But the girls had rescued him without a real fight starting.

"Our ladies are fucking fearless!" The chief was wiping tears of mirth away and between bouts of laughter explained to Jones how Dallas was almost press-ganged into the Marine Corp, but Lilly and Eve had marched over to the Marine's table and with lots of smiles and laughing [with some violence thrown in] dragged the cat back. But one big Marine had drunkenly protested, trying to grab Dallas from Eve and Lilly floored him with a single punch!

Strangely enough, not one of the remaining Marines objected to the girls walking away with the cat!

As a reward, the Chief gave young Lilly a couple of sips from his hipflask and 'Old Ma Crawford's sipping whisky' worked its magic; Lilly shouted a toast to the crew of the Thor and slid under the table, still clutching the happy cat, with the crew chanting; "Captain Dallas! Captain Dallas!"

VP Gaylord Prentiss had stayed for drinks, despite the attempts of Vice-Admiral Kellamann to escort him from the party – the VP had taken quite a shine to the young Ensign – that he had just decorated and watched the standoff between the rig's girls and the Marines with great interest.

"I see the Weather Service is upholding its reputation for

having some of the toughest sons-of-bitches that ever stepped onto the surface. You must be proud of them Everest." He was watching Lilly dancing with the cat and added; "Where do you recruit your ladies from? Deep Vein Mines by any chance?"

The Vice-admiral managed to smile and swallowed his drink down; "Our boys and girls do work and play hard Sir." He muttered watching the crew of the Thor leading the party in community singing of a very traditional rig song with some colourful lyrics. Even the Marines joined in, linking arms with the crew and dancing. The big Maine sergeant had recovered and grabbed Lilly, planting a steamer of a kiss upon her lips; Eve swore blind she could see sparks!

He confided to his Lieutenant; "I think I've just found my wife; what a fucking woman, it was worth a black-eye just to meet her!" He threw a couple of surprised waiters over some tables in celebration of his new love.

Jones led the toasts to the Marine Corp and their happy young officer reciprocated with several more toasts to the Weather Service Corp. Then two ladies from the Marines and the rig's girls danced on the table: the general opinion was that the dance appeared to be a Martian version of the 'Can-Can'. It received great applause and several shouts of 'ENCORE!' Including some from the VP himself, who was quickly taken away by his bodyguards before any scandal ensued; after he climbed upon the table and danced with Lilly. The big marine had taken exception to this and armed with a chair, also climbed on the table. To be dragged away by his colleagues; before any damage was done to the VP and the Marine Corp's hard earned reputation.

But a large party of MPG's [Military Peace Guard] had arrived and broke the party up after a few scuffles. Jones quickly took command of his crew and managed to get them onto their Military bus and ignored the bottles and glasses that appeared on the way back to the docks. The driver joined in the singing and was fascinated by 'Sunny' who insisted he admire her special 'presentation' silk stockings and suspender belt that she was wearing for the occasion. The grinning driver almost side swiped a passing tram and let Sunny drive the bus, sitting on his lap. That was until the Chief threatened to push his head through the steering wheel, if he touched her. Jones and Eve sat on the overprotective Marcus; they really didn't relish walking back to the docks in the middle of the night. Apart from that and Troy stripping down to his boots and hat, waving his testicles through the rear window at passers-by, the ride back to the Thor went without further incident. Well apart from Leon driving the bus using his feet and Sunny and the driver dancing slowly in the aisle. They were cheered and clapped by the crew until the big marine appeared from under a seat, trying to stuff Dallas into his kitbag: he was quickly and unceremoniously thrown from the bus, which didn't actually stop to let him off.

It's rumoured that Dallas – sitting on the now sleeping Leon's lap – drove the bloody bus back to the docks! But it's just a rumour apparently.....

24. M A KHAN.

Jones was sipping coffee and reading the National news on his PA, the bridge was quiet, and the Thor had a feeling of serenity about it or everyone was suffering their hangovers with great dignity. Leon was half asleep in the Primary Pilots seat; he had been the only choice to stand watch on the bridge, with the captain, because he was the only one of the crew who managed to get out of bed without falling over. He lay across the rig's dashboard in just his underpants and one sock, clutching a female Peace Guards hat. That was strange because there had been no female Peace Guards attending the celebration! Still, ask anyone and they will tell you that Mars is a strange place.

Jones patted his shoulder with pride; "Well done Leon, you're a good man to have in a tight spot." Leon raised his head slightly and muttered;" I'll get a proper job tomorrow mum." and drifted back to sleep. Jones sighed but smiled, he sniffed loudly: flowers! He could smell flowers! He sat bolt upright in his seat. Then relaxed back in his chair; Eve was placing a large basket of fresh flowers on the communications desk; "For Lilly." She said with a big smile on her face, adding; "From the VP." Jones now groaned quietly and ran his hands through his hair, that's all the rig needed, a horny Martian Vice President chasing Lilly about. He sipped his coffee and switched his PA to local news; he wished he had not bothered. A strange disturbing murder was headlines, with the terrible decomposed corpse found strangled sitting on his toilet wearing an E f's costume. The other headlines consisted of the visit by the VP to open the new rail station and a local Baker who makes bagels in the shape of people's feet. There was only a small paragraph about the presentation of a Silver Star to an Ensign for bravery, no names, no real story. No one was really interested in the antics of lowly weather service people; even the brave ones.

The last story was about the number of complaints received by Rossington Peace Guard, of a young man exposing himself from the back of an unidentified bus, late last night. Jones buried his head in his hands and simply muttered; "Shit!"

"Morning skipper, it's nice and quiet around here." The Chief dropped onto the spare Pilots seat and prodded Leon; "Is he dead?" Marcus sipped his coffee and looked like he never touched alcohol in his life, Jones shook his head in utter amazement, he could never work out how the Chief could be pissed out of his head at night and apparently stone cold sober the next morning?

"I don't think he's dead, he's still snoring." Eve tapped Leon on the head and smiled. Leon looked up and grinned broadly; "No thanks, I couldn't manage a whole plateful." And went back to sleep.

Lilly quietly sat down at the communications desk and admired her basket of flowers. 'Captain Dallas' leapt upon the table and started to nibble them, pulling petals off which floated about the bridge. Lilly stroked him and placing her head upon the desk went to sleep. Marcus sighed; "Is she dead?" Eve whispered; "No, but I think she wishes she was." The in-coming call buzzer sounded, and Lilly raised her head; "Good morning, this is the Thor, how can I help you?" Eve chuckled and lifted the receiver; "It helps Lilly if you're actually talking into the phone!"

It was Professor Jack Dawes for the Captain; Eve transferred the call across to Jones's desk and they spoke for some minutes before he slowly replaced the receiver and said to Eve; "Get your coat we need to visit an old friend." The Chief nodded; "You carry on skipper; I'll hold the fort here with great pleasure my friend."

As Jones and Eve departed the Thor, the Chief's shaking hand hovered above the 'Emergency Fire Siren' and with a huge smile on his face; activated it shouting; "Wakey! Wakey! You fuckers! Time to return to the land of the living!" He was laughing loudly; like a drunk who discovered he could fart the National Anthem without any 'follow-thru'.

Tom staggered onto the bridge clutching a fire extinguisher, dressed in just his shorts, and found the bridge crew all sound asleep, he slapped off the siren and dumped the extinguisher in the Chief's lap. "Thank you, Auntie Rose, I'll wear if for Founder's Day." Marcus muttered, salvia dribbling down his chin.

Tom noticed that Captain Dallas was still wearing his eye-patch and pirate kerchief and was asleep on Leon's head. "Fucking nutters." He whispered and holding onto the walls, made his way back to bed – past Troy stark naked on the floor of the crew corridor - clutching a traffic cone and still asleep despite the siren's best efforts. That's when Tom noticed the Traffic Cone was marked 'NYPD', he rubbed his chin with some amazement; there hadn't been a New York Police Department for over three hundred Earth Years! So, shrugging his shoulders, he quickly headed back to his cabin, thinking: see they are right about Mars being a strange bloody place…..

Eve and the Captain returned to the old 'Gerald Webster' quarter of the city and the quiet alley where they had found the little shop; "Jackdaw's." The bell tinkled as they squeezed into the room where Professor Dawes was waiting for them with another visitor; "I think you will know this gentleman." He introduced the young man to the pair.

Eve and Jones stood in total shock and silence; it was the previously deceased M A Khan, looking very much alive. "I think Research Station Thirteen just made séances obsolete." Jones whispered to Eve." Muhammad had the good sense to seek me out; he still has many questions about the real world of the supernatural. But just listen to his short story about what he uncovered whilst a guest at Research Station 13." The professor added: unsmiling.

Muhammad Ali Khan outlined his sudden death on the Space Passenger ship "Westworld" just before touching down on Mars, nearly a century ago. The description of his passing sent a shudder up Jones spine, but he and Eve listened with great interest as he spoke about what happened next. Muhammad had been revived at 'RS13'. One of just four successful Resurrections they had managed so far and after a period of rehabilitation was given a new identity and quietly moved to Rossington to work in a government office.

Muhammad had calculated that he was about 125 years old! But he wasn't the oldest person alive, that dubious honour fell to a young woman who could claim to be 154 years old now but was only 17 [Mars years]. Her body had been found by some archaeologists, in a small family graveyard of an abandoned farmstead. The farm had failed many years after her death and no descendants had survived, so she was a perfect candidate for 'Operation Cenotaph'. She also now worked for the Government: in Shackleton Tax office. But their stories of what happened after death were all similar; four dead people, basically describing the same collective experience of the afterlife, the professor quietly explained to Jones and Eve. "That can't be co-incidence. Four people who died at different times and didn't even know each other when alive, yet they still recounted – basically – the same story. Similar to those in the archive records of such experiences we still have from earth."

Professor Dawes tapped his desk; "This is the real interesting part; Muhammad, tell them what you overheard whilst still recovering." The young man nodded; "As I was coming round - I don't think the two in my room thought I was conscious, they were talking freely about a body found at a weather station and that the blame, luckily enough, [their words] could be attributed to the young Ensign and that it would not be exposed. What 'IT' was, they never said because they realised, I was waking up. Sorry."

Jack Dawes held up both hands and did not smile;

"Muhammad was already dead before the weather station killings took place, so his story can be believed." He rubbed his chin, thinking hard; "I think all this can be connected with the legend of the ruined city." That caught Jones and Eve's attention; what ruined city? They both asked with real interest. The professor explained about the stories that were whispered, after famous Bellman Easter's expedition returned from the Mountains and caves. Some members of his party mysteriously died in odd circumstances within months of their return. But not before they told stories about finding the very ancient ruins of a city buried deep in the mountain cave systems. The Government denied such a find and Easter himself called it 'total bloody nonsense'.

But the rumours persist to this day.

Jack leaned back in his chair and lowered his voice; "The stories stated the city contained something ancient and evil. That the city had been built solely to contain that evil, many millennia ago by the original inhabitants of Mars - who it is said were aliens to the planet themselves; Colonists like us - but not from Earth; not humans?" Jones and Eve didn't leave the curious little shop and its strange proprietor for a couple of hours. But they caught the tram for the Docks at about three o'clock and were surprised by the numbers riding the carriages, until they remembered that the rail station was now open. They sat in silence for the ride back to the Thor; the meeting with M A Khan, after his restoration to life under 'Project Cenotaph' had given both troubled thoughts.

Particularly what he said about being dead; "Death is nothing like a human could imagine." He had explained carefully and clearly, about his time dead and it had shocked the pair deep inside. They had no reason to disbelieve anything M A Khan said, he seemed a straightforward and honest man who had found himself a stranger in a strange new world.

The story about the weather station killings was grim enough; but a lost city built by aliens, who were trying to colonize an ancient Mars was food for thought indeed!

Eve broke the silence as the tram approached the South Dock Terminal; "I think I won't sleep too well tonight after that little discussion." She gripped Jones by the arm, and he agreed, but his attention was soon drawn to the dockside. There were a couple of Peace Guard Vans and two other vehicles parked by the Thor's dock, Eve pointed out a MPG van to one side and the entrance to Dock No.3 was closed off – there was a large group of people gathered outside the gateway - including reporters.

"What the fuck is going on!" exclaimed Jones as he and Eve jumped from the tram and headed for the Dock gateway, where "What the fuck is going on!" exclaimed Jones as he and Eve jumped from the tram and headed for the Dock gateway, where they were stopped by both the MPG and the civilian Peace Guard. The young sergeant asked for their identity cards and checked them through his PA, he then called up on his radio; "Inspector Random, we've got the missing pair here at Gate No.3, do you want them arrested?"

Jones and Eve exchanged looks of amazement, but before either could comment, the Inspector called back, saying that the Captain and his MO could come aboard their rig and escort them directly to the bridge; arrest wasn't necessary.

Eve and Jones were taken aboard the Thor under escort from two MPG's, on the upper deck they came across Leon, manning the Bridge External Pressure Door with yet another MPG. He looked tired and quite disheveled, but he saluted, and Jones spoke quietly to him for a few seconds. Eve stopped in the service corridor and whispered; "What did Leon say? What's going on?"

Jones gripped her hand and said quietly; "The civilian Peace Guard have arrested Peter and taken him away, they're now searching the Thor for evidence and taking statements from the crew." Eve looked stunned, and she exclaimed; "What the hell have they arrested him for?"

Jones opened the bridge door and ushered Eve in, stopping to whisper in her ear; "Murder."

ADVERTISEMENT BY THE AUTHOR.

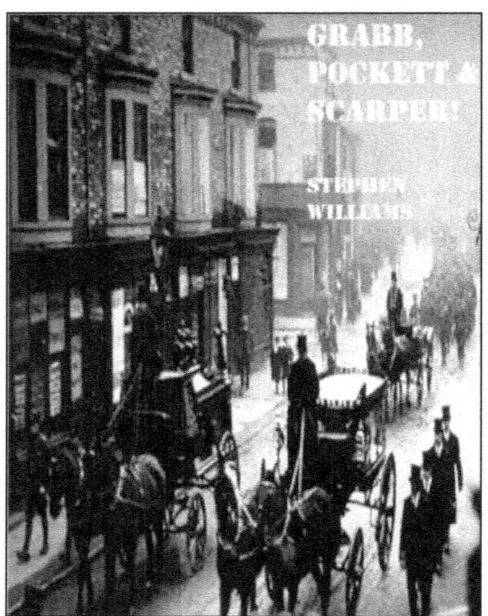

Will be available on 'AMAZON.COM' and all good bookshops! Historical comedy, fiction series set from 1900 to 1999 focusing on the Edinburgh Funeral Directors "Grabb, Pockett & Scarper" as they struggle with life in the midst of death!

Visit the author's website using this QR code:

EPISODE 9: "THE TRIAL OF Lt. COMMANDER PETER GRAVESTONE."

25. THE INVESTIGATION.

The Guard closed the door behind Captain Jones with a bang and the door locks clicked loudly. Through the small door's glass panel, Jones saw Peter wave and he held up his hand and nodded. Captain Jones couldn't put the past fifteen minutes visit in any order. Peter was coherent, then suddenly rambling, then he became sad and finally, smiling.

Jones walked quietly back to Inspector Random's office and found the Inspector standing in the doorway, arms folded with a half smile upon his face. "That man has no fucking idea what is going to happen to him." The Inspector laughed with real contempt in his voice; "He's looking at life, a minimum of 25 years in the Salt Flats prison and he can't even tell us, what he was doing on the day his ex-lover was strangled on the toilet wearing an Elf's suit!" He actually chuckled and headed for his desk and chair; still smiling.

Inspector Random slumped in his seat and shrugged his big shoulders, then tapped a brown folder on his desk; "From your rig's log, on the day the victim died, we have young Mr. Peter Gravestone arriving back on the Thor in a right state. From your very log Captain, I quote: Disheveled, distraught and in a total mess." The Inspector motioned Jones to take a seat next to Eve, who sat quietly with a hand upon her chin, she dabbed her eyes a little and placed the hankie back in her bag; "He had just broken up with the man who he loved dearly, of course he would be in a state."

The Inspector grunted and tapped the file again; "We have

the neighbour – who knew both men well – since she lived opposite the pair for a couple of years, placing young Mr. Gravestone at the scene that morning. She never saw him leave, but she saw him enter the apartment at about ten-thirty, that's just an hour or so before the victim died. That's going to be really hard to explain."

"If that's not damning enough, his DNA has been found on the body – case closed." The Inspector held up his hands and smiled, repeating; "Case closed."

Jones asked why the body wasn't discovered earlier and the Inspector shrugged his shoulders; "The victim had no real family: none that cared that much. He was a hotel Inspector and travelled all across Mars. It was the Travel office he worked for that finally reported him missing, but the address he had given was an old one; it belonged to yet another ex boyfriend who apparently didn't know anything about his current whereabouts. Adult missing persons are not a high priority for the Peace Guard; unless they're listed or reported as 'vulnerable' and he wasn't."

"How was he discovered?" Eve asked; she couldn't believe that a body could lie for weeks, undiscovered, in these modern times. The Inspector smiled and sipped a glass of water;" A bloody parcel delivery driver!" He chuckled to himself and added; "Apparently the same driver did the same route and had attempted to deliver on several occasions' finally speaking to neighbours who alerted us."

"What was in the parcel; if I may ask?" Jones spoke quietly; he was still devastated by the state Peter was in and wanted to know all the details of the dreadful story.

"It was a mask, a strange dark mask with horns. Maybe it was for a fancy-dress party, he liked those kinds of parties; so, neighbours have told us." The Inspector closed the file and sat back. It was a signal that the visit was over. The Captain and Eve were escorted from the Peace Guard Station and waited for Lilly to return with Dallas from the Vets [it was his thirty-week check-up]. They sat in 'Blind Charlie's Dinner & Bar' ordering a couple of coffee's and sitting in silence – the morning had cast a huge black shadow over Peter's case – the evidence against him was so strong, it would be hard to argue a suitable defense.

Charlie leaned across his counter and laughed; "Pic, I think your young lady is back with Dallas." Jones and Eve peered through the window and could see a gaggle of delighted children having their photographs taken with Dallas – while a very patient Lilly - held his lead and showed the children how to get a 'high-five' from the big cat.

"He'll soon have his own bloody fan club." Charlie added, still chuckling to himself, as he topped the coffee cups up and laid a fresh one out for Lilly; for when she finally managed to escape and squeeze her and the cat through the throng of happy children who didn't want Dallas to go.

"Sweet Mars!" She exclaimed, sitting opposite the quiet pair; "A twenty-minute walk from the Vets has taken an hour and a half!" She gratefully sipped her coffee and relaxed back in the chair, while a grinning Charlie placed a large saucer on the floor, filled with cold weak coffee. Dallas appreciated this kindness and started to lap up his favourite beverage with loud purrs

"The vet says he's fine [Dallas] but he needs to cut down on his beer, curry and cat biscuits." Lilly added with a smile; that statement made Charlie laugh out loud and he returned to his counter with a big grin, muttering; "Bloody weather service rigs!"

"The vet doesn't know the type of domestic cat he is, but despite being so big, he's really healthy. So, the vet thinks it's in his genes, maybe his mum and dad were big cats." Lilly placed her cup on the table and sighed; "I take it the visit to see Peter didn't go well?"

Eve nodded; "All the evidence points to Peter and nowhere else, even the Captain and I can see that."

Jones sighed loudly and sipped his fresh coffee; "His ex-boyfriend was murdered on the morning of Sol 156, Week 15, the day Peter came aboard in a right state, he only just made it, if you remember." Eve stroked Dallas and added; "The Peace Guard know this exactly because Nikki [the deceased] had been to a fancy-dress party, dressed as an Elf the night before. Forensics apparently confirms the same day of death, despite the state the body was in and a neighbour saw Peter enter the apartment that very morning." She held up her hands in despair and sat back in the chair.

 Jones nodded, adding: "Finally, if that's not enough, Peters DNA was found on the body. The Inspector summed it up really well: case closed." Jones placed his cup back on the table and checked his PA.

Lilly bowed her head and said quietly; "So he did it then?" The quiet pair opposite said nothing. "I'm going to see Professor Dawes and I'll meet you back at the Thor, Major D'Abaan that Military legal eagle, is stopping by to speak to those crew-members summoned to court." Jones left the table and thanked Charlie, paying the bill, while Eve and Lilly made for the docks; pursued by a gaggle of children wanting to play with Dallas. Jones sat on the tram deep in thought; the situation with Peter looked black as night and the weather service were considering manning weather Station Seven again. That thought sent a shudder through Jones; all those possible new victims for the evil entity summoned by the long dead crew. Then there was the Thor: there would be replacements for Bella and Kazza and quite possibly; Peter.

The tram came to a halt and several people moved to the doors, above which the sign read: "Gerald Webster quarter – Mayfield Square" and exited the tram. 'Next stop' thought Jones and re-read his PA: the message from Professor Dawes was quite intriguing: An offer for him and Eve to consider a little adventure outside the Weather Service. The professor was constructing a team for an expedition to the Easters, to locate the legendary lost city. He already had two crew members; his old friend Professor Solomon Jacobson, and Kech Tassi; a well-known conspiracy theorist and survival expert. What he really needed was a captain for the rig they had obtained and a medical officer; he hoped Jones and Eve would fill those positions. The remaining three members of the crew would need to be Rig Pilots and/or trained in military matters. He didn't specify exactly what kind of 'military matters' they needed to be trained in.

The expedition would consist of eight individuals and the rig was an old 'Mammoth' class; recently refurbished and bought up to match modern standards; she was called 'The New Argonaut'. He never stated where the money for all this had been acquired.

Jones had a pretty good idea that Eve would agree, and he had thoughts about the remaining three crew members that were required. He sat staring out the tram's window, deep in thought. Some minutes later, the tram came to a halt and Jones headed for the doors, above which the sign read: "Gerald Webster quarter – Downtown" he stepped off and made his way to Professor Dawes little shop, but not before he quickly glanced behind him and saw the two fellows on his tail. It took him a couple of minutes to leave them behind before heading for the Professors; whoever they were [Jones suspected they were Peace Guard officers] they were not very good at tailing someone in the busy 'Downtown' area. The Professor welcomed him with a smile; "There's someone here I think you should meet." Jones made his way to the little office and was re-introduced to Professor Solomon Jacobson, who shook his hand firmly;" Pic, I hope you have considered our offer to you and Eve very carefully."

26. THE TRIAL.

The Courtroom was packed with spectators and reporters: several members of the Thor's crew sat behind the defense council since they were not required to give evidence. Peter sat next to his two Lawyers with prison officers either side of him. He was wearing a nice grey suit and actually looked quite relaxed considering what was happening to him. He smiled at his colleagues and sat back and stared up at the ceiling.

Major D'Abaan shuffled papers about and spoke quietly with Mr. Harold Klien, who was presenting the case for the Defense; "The State has bought in Sarah Wells-Gordon, the proclaimed Queen bitch of the Prosecution, so we should expect a real dirty fight." Mr. Klien simply nodded and popped some peanuts into his mouth, pushing the packet back into his jacket pocket; "Me and her have crossed swords several times over the years." He picked up the water jug and poured himself a glass of water. "So you've beaten her before?" The Major nodded: smiling.

"No never." Mr. Klien sipped his water and waited for the Judge to appear. Major D'Abaan kept his thoughts about that revelation to himself and glanced across at Peter, who was talking with Lilly and Frankie; the case against the young man appeared water-tight and he had advocated that Peter pleads 'Guilty' and accepts the mercy of the court. But Peter had steadfastly refused, constantly saying he was innocent.

Through a side door, the Prosecution team entered the Court Room with Sarah Wells-Gordon at its head. She was tapping away at her PA and giving instructions to the clerk about booking lunch. She dropped into her seat at the Prosecution desk and looked directly at Mr. Klien; "Why is this not a damn guilty plea Harold?" Sarah held up her hands to signify some amazement, adding;" This is a two-day job, I have to be back in Taylor for the Drefyus killings; now that case has real potential for a good fight. This is over before we get in the ring." She chuckled, being handed several papers by her clerk.

"To answer your question, Sarah; the defendant claims he is innocent, so a not guilty plea was entered, sorry if that interferes with your plans for more publicity." Harold smiled and stood as the Court Bailiff announced the arrival of the Judge. Everyone stood and watched as Justice Wendell Jones made his way to his seat saying, "Bailiff, please bring in the Jury." The ten members of the jury [6 men and 4 women] filed into the Court Room and sat in the Jury Box without conversation.

Justice Jones called upon the Court Clerk to announce the case. The lady Clerk stood and read out the indictment: "Are you Peter Gravestone, born on Sol four hundred and eight in the forty-first week of year 309 after founding?" Peter said simply; "I am."

"How do you plead to the charge against you: that you did willfully murder a living human of full status: being Nicholas John Larrson; on Sol one hundred and fifty-six in the fifteenth week of the year 323 after founding? The clerk looked up from her papers and nodded.

"Not guilty." Peter replied and the Judge waved everyone to

sit; "Defense and Prosecution Councilors: are you both ready to proceed today without hindrance or procrastination?" Sarah and Harold stood and stated; "I am."

The Judge settled his bulk into the large chair and addressed Ms Sarah directly: "Madam Prosecution; you may begin." The Judge shuffled papers about and stared at the defendant and then his attention was drawn back to Sarah who had started to address the jury.

Outside in the waiting area, Captain Jones sat reading his PA whilst Eve was writing notes into a medical textbook. Leon was leaned back in his seat, eyes closed and his thoughts far from here. Troy sat head in hands and said nothing. The four were the only crew members called to give evidence and had been unusually instructed to appear in civilian dress.

Jones looked across to the three people who sat opposite: an elderly lady with bright peach coloured hair and Inspector Random with a young man who looked like he had been invited to his own funeral.

"That must be the woman neighbour, but who's that young man with the Inspector?" Eve asked quietly and Jones shrugged his shoulders and pointed to Troy, sitting the other side of her; "What's wrong with him: nerves, is it?"

Eve patted Troy on the shoulders and whispered; "You'll be fine Troy. All you have to do is tell the truth." Troy looked up with moist eyes and drew a deep breath, looking Eve directly in her eyes; "That's what I'm afraid of Doc; telling the truth." Troy returned his head to his hands and said nothing else.

Eve and Jones exchanged glances, then Leon gripped the captain's arm and whispered closely; "I recognise that young man from a picture Peter had in his cabin: that was Peter's boyfriend before Nikki came on the scene. To quote the Chief; the shit has really hit the fan."

Eve leaned across the Captain and whispered;"Why do you think they've called him Leon?"

Leon motioned for the three to have a little walk round the room; "Just stretching the legs." He commented to Inspector Random, who just nodded and continued chatting to the old lady about her pet cat. The young man stared at the three but said nothing. Behind a convenient pillar, Leon told the utter shocking truth to his colleagues; "That was Peter's boyfriend before Nikki; they split up over what happened after a party one night. Peter became angry because he thought Sean [the young man with Inspector Random] was flirting with another man and when they returned home, there was a fight."

Leon glanced about and with a grim look on his face said; "Sean alleged that Peter tried to strangle him in the bathroom but nothing came of it because Sean wouldn't charge Peter, but the incident must have remained in Peace Guard records."

Jones groaned out loud and ran both hands over his head; "For fuck's sake, that's what the prosecution says; that Peter strangled his ex in the bathroom because he was angry over being dumped!" Eve covered her face with a hand and whispered; "If that young man gives evidence like that, Peter is dead." She looked back at Troy and added; "What does Troy know that he really doesn't want to say?"

"I know." Leon wiped sweat from his face and spoke quietly, glancing about; "Troy was drinking with Peter at 'Sailor Mikes' one night, when we were docked in Dayburgh last year. He told me that Peter chatted up another man, despite still being with Nikki and the pair disappeared outside to an alley. After a few minutes Troy said that Peter came rushing through the club and Troy followed him out. On the tram, he said that Peter was laughing about the man he had picked up, that they had an argument about a condom and when he [the other man] tried to walk away, Peter grabbed him by the throat and tried to strangle him; but he was too strong and pulled away."

With that little revelation: they stood in silence for a moment, deep in their own thoughts.

They headed back to their seats and found that the old lady had been called to give evidence; they sat in silence, keeping their thoughts to themselves until Eve turned to Troy and said simply; "Troy, you have to tell the truth, even if it hurts a friend of yours. The truth is the truth, and a lie is unforgivable in a court of law."

Troy nodded and said quietly; "I know, but it still tears my guts up. Mr. Gravestone is good to me and many in my life are not, including my damn parents." He sat up straight and bushed down his jacket and trousers; "I'll do what I have too." He smiled sadly at Eve as the court usher appeared and said; "Mr. Sean Winstarr please!" They watched as the young man walked nervously into court. Inspector Random smiled at them sitting opposite, he raised his arms, then lowered them slowly; "Case closed." He said with a grin.

Eve and Leon went to the court restaurant and collected coffee and small sandwich packs. They returned in time to see the Inspector called into court. Jones took his coffee and nodded to the large doors of Court No.3; "The good Inspector thinks they'll have a verdict by tomorrow and it won't be the one Peter needs." He sipped his coffee and sat back in the seat; "This is going so badly; I don't think it can get worse."

"I think you spoke too soon skipper." Leon placed his coffee down and stood up to greet the couple who had just come through the Court's main doors. It was Peter's parents, who had made the long journey from Shenzhen [a Northern city] to attend the r son's trial. But before they could speak, the Court Usher re-appeared; "Mr. Leon Kamski please!"

Jones grasped Leon's arm and said; "Do your best Leon and keep on the straight and narrow. The truth will get out regardless." Leon nodded and waved to the couple before going into court. Troy shook Paul and Elle's [Peter's mum and dad] hands, introducing Eve to them; "This is Eve, the rig's new medical Officer. She took over after old Doc Greenspace retired."

Eve hugged Elle and gripped Paul's hand; "I'm so sorry about this mess, but he does have a good defense team."SheHe said nothing about the famous Prosecution lawyer. They sat talking until the dour Court Usher appeared and told them the case was adjured until tomorrow. From Court No.3, a stream of people passed them by until Eve saw Lilly and Sunny; "How's it going Lilly?" She asked quietly.

Lilly wiped a couple of tears from her face and whispered; "I think he's finished." Eve and Jones exchanged a sad glance: Lilly's news was not unexpected. The crew walked in silence to the tram stop and waited for tram No.13 that ran directly into the docks, no-one felt like talking except Frankie, who reminded everyone that he was visiting his sister, so they had to fend for themselves tonight, food wise.

"Mass fucking takeaways all round." muttered Leon with a sad smile. Jones stood and watched the tram slowly approach: he and Eve exchanged a glance again, but nothing was said.

27. THE VERDICT.

After a restless night the crew assembled to return to court;

except the Chief [who was required to stand watch on the bridge] and his apprentice 'Sunny' who really couldn't face another day in court watching Peter being broken down into little pieces. Jones understood her feelings and agreed to her heartfelt request. Jones and the crew had arranged a Rig rendezvous in 'Blind Charlie's Dinner and bar' for that night if the verdict comes in; either to celebrate Peter's freedom or hold a wake for a fallen comrade.

Vice-Admiral Kellamann had arranged a relief crew to cover for the night, from the old Battle rig: MSV The General Westmoreland, which had returned from patrol and was birthed in the Northern docks of the city. Jones understood that the Admiral would be in court to hear the verdict for himself and give support to the crew; whether he would attend the 'party' afterwards was another matter. He did have words with Jones over the Presentation party for Ensign Lilly and admitted he would have taken some discipline action over some of the incidents [especially Troy!] but for the VP, who thought it was: 'all good clean fun' - to quote the man.

Jones, Eve and Troy found themselves sitting in the waiting area for a second day as the trial reopened; the only person with them was Inspector Random who sat opposite them with a smile on his face, eating a large red apple very carefully and slowly. Troy was the first called into court and as he passed through the doors with the Court usher, the Inspector walked over and sat next to Jones. "It should be wrapped up by early afternoon, the Jury won't hang about on this one; it's not complicated. Clear case of he did it or didn't." The Inspector picked little pieces of apple from his teeth and placed the core in a nearby litter bin and wiped his mouth with a paper hankie. "You're a strange pair of birds to be hanging around with those mad Professors, especially Jack Dawes: the king of the supernatural and all things that are bloody crazy." The Inspector chuckled when he saw the look upon their faces.

"Be careful with Dawes, be very careful with that one. Gossip and rumour whisper that he's not all what he seems: has far too many connections with the Government up in Taylor and far too much money washing about his bank accounts; considering he has no real paid employment: it's odd that the stock of his little shop never seems to change." The Inspector stood up and walked towards the court, passing the Usher asking for Eve.

He looked back and said, "Your friend Jackie boy is involved with project Cenotaph, and I don't think his friend Jacobson is far behind him; don't look too shocked children; it's amazing what a dumb old Peace Guard Inspector knows, isn't it?"

He disappeared into court followed by Eve and the Court Usher, leaving Jones to consider the amazing disclosure from the Inspector, but it did answer one question; how Jacobson knew Dawes. If the Inspector is right in his suspicions. Jones was deep in thought and the Court Usher had to call his name twice before he realised it was his turn for the witness chair. With a heavy heart he walked into court and found it difficult to face Peter, knowing the stories told by Leon and Troy.

By lunch time, the Jury had retired to consider their verdict as directed by Justice Jones, who made a point of informing everyone that he and the captain were not related! A little ripple of laughter swept the court, more to relieve tension than appreciation of the Judge's attempt at humour.

The crew sat in the court restaurant having quiet little conversations amongst themselves. Their table was littered with coffee cups, soft drink cartons and several half eaten sandwiches. Peter's parents sat on a separate table in silence, the evidence given by Leon and Troy had shocked them: they had expected Sean [Peter's previous ex-boyfriend] to tell such a tale, but not people who Peter called 'friends'.

Eve had gone over to their table to see if they needed anything; but they waved her away without saying a word. Jones sipped yet another cup of coffee and noticed the time was 3.15pm; the Jury had been out for nearly two hours. "It's an amazing thought that ten complete strangers, people Peter has never met before has the power to save his life or basically end it." Tom said to no-one in particular and continued to eat his egg sandwich without really enjoying it.

Jones's mind was going over the evidence Peter had given in his defense; Peter claimed that he went to the apartment that morning to collect the last of his belongings and found Nikki was still dressed in a stupid Elf costume and still a little drunk from the party. Nikki had tried to stop him going into the bedroom to collect some clothes and he had pushed him aside. He found another man sitting up in bed, drinking coffee, a discarded 'Superman' costume thrown on the floor.

Nikki said he was called 'Solo' and they had met at the party. Peter repeated that he had left at that point to return to the Thor but found himself in a bar on the east side. He couldn't remember its name, but whilst sitting there had realised the departure time of the rig was quickly approaching and rushed to get back. He stated three or four times that Nikki was still alive when he left.

The Prosecution recalled Inspector Random to the Witness Chair who stated that his team had questioned most of the party guests and some could remember a man dressed as 'Superman'. But no-one knew his name. Most recalled the drunken Elf staggering about the place, being obnoxious to various guests and being told to leave at one point by the hosts. No one questioned could remember if 'Superman' left at the same time or just afterwards.

The Inspector also stated that his team could not find anyone with the name or nickname of 'Solo' in the city at the time. He did admit however, when pressed by Harold Klien, that this mysterious person could have left the city weeks ago and his whereabouts would be unknown, and many people have short memories. But the 'clincher' as the Inspector called it was only Peter's and Nikki's DNA was found around the flat; there were no traces of 'Superman'.

The Prosecutor: Sarah Wells-Gordon had mocked Peter's claim of a third person being present, telling the Jury: 'A fictional character inserted into a fictional story.' Even Jones winced at that cracking one-liner and Peter looked a doomed man rambling in the Witness box, at one point the flustered Court Stenographer had to ask the Judge to tell the defendant to slow down, she couldn't follow what he was saying, never mind write it down.

But it was her [Sarah Wells-Gordon] summing up speech that made Jones groan with the sense of hopelessness, she addressed the Jury directly; "Your decision is simple; either you believe the story of the 'Superman' or you believe the enormous amount of hard evidence presented by the State Prosecution Service and the Peace Guard?" She dramatically lifted her arms up and added; "Superman belongs in films and comics, not in a court case seeking justice for a brutally murdered young man."

She thanked the Jury for their attention and told the Judge that the Prosecution rests. Poor Harold Klien could only repeat his client's statement that he did not kill Larrson and there was a third man present at the time of the murder.

The Jury then retired to consider their verdict.

Jones had his thinking interrupted by Vice-Admiral Kellamann who strode over to the crew table, everyone stood; the dour

Admiral pulled Jones to one side; "Pic, my decision is made; if the verdict goes against Peter, then obviously I'll have to appoint a new XO, I have already sent for her. Now if Peter is fortunate, then I still must transfer him to another rig; you do understand that?"

Jones nodded but said nothing; he knew how the Military High Command functioned. The Vice-Admiral continued; "So either way, you have a new XO; Lt. Commander Margret Simms-Holder will join the crew tomorrow night from the Battle rig 'The Erwin Rommel'. I believe you and her have served together before?"

Jones nodded again; "I did time with her on the MSV: General George Washington; we were Ensigns together. She's a good officer and deserves the promotion I expect."

The Admiral smiled; "Not quite a promotion, she was XO on the 'Erwin Rommel', so this move is sideward's, I'm afraid. Now, I have your other two replacements assigned and they will report tomorrow evening as well. The following day, you ship out on 'Routine Duties' for at least three weeks. That'll give time for the air around the Thor and her crew to sweeten. That is all quite clear Pic?"

Jones nodded yet again; "Thank you Sir, but....." He never finished the sentence as Harold Klien appeared in the small restaurant doorway and said simply; "The Jury has returned. The verdict is in." he wiped his brow and didn't smile.

Everyone filed quietly back into Court No.3 and when all were seated, the Jury returned, and the Judge asked the Jury foreman to stand and give the verdict they have reached. Peter also stood and faced the Jury box. The Court Clerk asked the Foreman: "Have you reached a verdict in the case of Peter Gravestone verses the People and State of Mars

Federation?" The Foreman nodded and said, "Yes we have."

The Court Clerk asked; "Do you find the defendant guilty or not guilty?"

The Foreman glanced across at Peter and coughed, pushing back his long hair; "Not guilty."

The courtroom exploded into cheering and hugs as the crew heard the news, which frankly seemed impossible just minutes ago. Eve hugged Jones tightly; "How did they come up with that result in face of all the evidence? I'm so pleased, but that that's some bloody crazy decision I think!" she exclaimed, wiping away a tear.

Jones hugged her back and said it was wonderful news, but dark thoughts about young Peter Gravestone lingered in his mind and he suspected that Eve was having the same. But he shook them from his mind and hugged Peter who had tears running down his face, he gripped the captains' hands and whispered; "I thought I was dead and buried. It's a miracle. I'll never do anything bad ever again." Then he wiped his tears and broke into a huge grin shouting; "It's party time people! Blind Charlie here we come!" Peter hugged his weeping parents and turned back to Jones and smiled in a way that sent a shudder up the captain's spine. In that one look Jones knew the truth.

The Judge restored order to his courtroom and officially released Peter from State custody; Peter shook the hands of every Jury member and kissed the women with thanks. But Sarah Wells-Gordon asked the Judge for leave to appeal the acquittal; he turned that down. The look of disappointment was all across her face, especially when she had to say; 'well done' to Harold Klien, who appeared in a state of shock at his stunning victory. He sat with both hands on the desk with an incredulous smile on his face. If he lived to be ninety; he wouldn't not have heard a more lunatic verdict; considering the evidence presented against his client!

Eve and Jones trailed behind the rest of the crew as they poured out of the courthouse heading for 'Blind Charlie's to start celebrating Peter's great escape. Inspector Random walked up to Jones and Eve with a slight smile; he was eating yet another apple; "Have a good piss-up people, you may have won round one, but I don't give in easily. We [The Peace Guard] have been instructed to investigate further since the murder remains unsolved. You never know what we'll dig up now." He grinned and walked away to speak to the reporters that were following the group down the street.

As the raucous crowd tumbled into the small dinner and bar, Jones and Eve were stopped outside by a strange looking young man. But they both noticed his stunning blue eyes and powerful frame despite the shabby old-fashioned clothes he wore. He looked totally out of place and continually glanced about himself; then smiled at Jones and Eve.

Jones stared at the young man; there was something not quite right about him. Eve noticed it too. They both realised that the young man was a powerfully generated hologram of superb detail and quality; they were shocked to hear it speak directly to them. "Hello Sir, it is an honour to finally meet you in person." The stranger thrust both hands into the pockets of the shabby dark coat and with a big grin said; "I've waited a lifetime to meet my ancestor who started it all!"

Jones stepped back and stared at the smiling stranger; then realised how much he resembled his grandfather from the pictures when he was a young man; "Who are you?" Jones whispered. The stranger nodded his head and with a big smile quietly said; "I'm Temptation Jones - your great, great, great,

great, great, great - grandson." He counted the generations off using his fingers to make sure he had it correct. Then he added quietly; "I'm here to make sure that you live through the next four weeks!"

25. NEW CREW II.

Jones sipped his morning coffee and stretched his legs beneath the mess table; "Is the Doc about?" he asked Frankie who was refilling the coffee machine. "I've not seen her yet skipper, she usually has breakfast early when we're on the sand." Frankie wiped his hands with a paper towel and headed back to the kitchen; he needed to get her scrambled eggs on toast with fresh tomato and mushrooms prepared.

"I'll bring your breakfast skipper; it's the usual." Frankie called over his shoulder, disappearing into the small kitchen area, but Jones had not heard; his mind was kilometers away with Professor Dawes and Professor Jacobson and their offer to have Eve & Jones join their expedition to the fabled hidden city in the Easter Mountains. That would have to wait until some extended leave could be arranged for both. Then, the arrival of Temptation Jones had stood everything on its head; he claimed he had travelled from the Mars Year 604 to ensure that his ancestor [Picasso Jones] survived the next forty days and married Eve!

Now that revelation caused some amazement, especially to Jones and Eve; who laughed and joked about how preposterous that idea was; until they saw that Temptation Jones was standing with a look of utter horror on his face. "Come on you two!" He exclaimed with real concern in his voice; "If you two don't get it together I won't be born!" He then explained why his hologram image had jumped back in time; the future of life on Mars depended on a descendant of Picasso Jones who discovered the secret of rebuilding the planet's atmosphere; rapidly. Apparently, a descendant of

Picasso Jones who discovered the secret of rebuilding the planet's atmosphere; rapidly. Apparently, a descendant of Jones and Eve with the exotic name: 'Pharaoh Steadfast Jones' had discovered a chemical formula which allowed the atmosphere of Mars to be rebuilt in just two hundred years! But yet another discovery in the year 567 also changed everything; a machine that could display images from the past and future which contained alternative versions of both.

They also found that a hologram image of someone could be projected back or forward within the machine, and which would interact in real time with humans; they had discovered 'Time Travel'. But only for holograms because they were made of light and could travel at light speed. The machine could generate the image fully for about thirty minutes and then it would require recharging that could take up to a week. The hologram therefore spoke quickly; "You must not [speaking to Jones] take any risks during the next patrol on the sand. We have two versions of the past; in one you are killed in an eruption and so 'Pharaoh Jones' doesn't exist, and Mars has no new atmosphere. In the other, you survive and have children: with 'Pharaoh Jones' a descendant of your youngest son."

"You must avoid travelling or taking part in Professor Dawes expedition: it fails and the whole team and their rig vanish. But a few centuries after their disappearance another team under a self-proclaimed explorer and adventurer, Paris Smith, discover the ruins of an ancient city and the remains of two aliens in a state of hibernation. Your government knows already about the lost city and the aliens, that's why they commissioned 'Operation Cenotaph' in an effort to revive the aliens and learn from them. So heed my warnings Picasso Jones and take precautions." Promising to return when the projection machine has recharged, 'Temptation Jones' faded away. They made their way immediately to Professors Dawes shop; they needed answers and they sat in silence until Professor Jack Dawes muttered; "Well Pic, keep your bloody head down on the next patrol. I would like my great, great grandchildren to breathe and play outside!"

Both Jones and Eve omitted to tell Dawes about the fate of his expedition [according to the hologram] knowing full well he would go ahead with it regardless!

But it was the revelation about them that made awkward silences between Jones and Eve, as they walked back to the Tram station. Finally, Eve spoke up; "We best get to the party or Peter will be very upset." They exchanged glances and started to laugh together and sat talking on the tram, so totally engrossed they almost missed the station they needed.

Jones looked up from his daydream and was joined by his new XO; Maggie Simms-Holder. She was just a few weeks younger than Jones and very tall and slender. Maggie had dark black hair and brown eyes; apparently her ancestors had originated from a South American country back on Earth. She understood from family history it may have been Mexico. But she was puzzled about the Family legend; her name was old European and could be traced right back to Earth and a small island called 'England'. "Bit of a mystery; like my sideward's shift to this rig." She explained to Jones when they first met.

Clearly Maggie was not impressed with her move to the Thor after being XO on a big Battle rig. Jones had just smiled and said nothing; with 25% of his crew new, he would study and observe the newcomer's performance before commenting.

Harry Gelderfield, the new Meteorologist [Bella's replacement] appeared a solid recruit to the Thor, joining the Weather Service from University, working the rigs for some three years before taking a post at Weather Central [South]. He certainly knew his way around a weather chart! He also possessed the vital ingredient every rigger indeed for long patrols on the sand, a sense of humour. When asked by Jones why he had returned to the rigs, he said; "The wife. She's divorcing me and when she and her fecking blood sucking lawyer finished, I would have been sleeping in the tram yard; in my fecking underwear." Then he sat thinking for a few seconds and grinned; "Come to think of it – not in my fecking underwear – the bitch would have them too!"

Harry was quite a big man, easily matching Jones or the Chief for size. With a shaved head and strong green eyes, he had a strange habit of blowing his nose at least twenty times a day and his favourite expression was "Feckers!" Every sentence he spoke had the magic word; it was fecking clouds, fecking dust storms, fecking highs and lows and even the deadly Category one and two storms didn't escape: they were called 'Big Feckers!'

AUTHOR NOTE:
"Feck or Feckers was the soft version of 'Fuck' - should you wonder."

Jones believed that Harry and the Chief would become 'soul-mates'; they both professed a love of 'Old Ma Crawford's Sipping Whisky' and did not suffer fools easily. As Leon dourly commented, on seeing the pair drinking and laughing at 'Blind Charlie's Bar and Dinner'; "What bleeding nutter cloned the Chief?"

Harry quickly gained a crew nickname [always a good sign]: 'FeckCaster.'

Then there was the new Systems Specialist: Maxwell Tapp [Kazza's replacement] who became the Thor's second oldest crewmember [after the Chief] who was 23 years old; skinny and lacking in humour. He appeared to live in fear of 'ingrown toenails' – he had already seen the Thor's MO twice about them - he had been on board just one day!

"There's nothing wrong with them Max." Eve reassured him; yet again. Max left the Medical Bay, stopping to ask Lilly; "Miss Lilly, is our MO qualified to treat bad feet?" He asked anxiously and showed some anguish when Lilly replied in the affirmative. "Oh, I miss Gavin and Lynda; my Chiropodist and Podiatrist." He wandered off in his bare feet, shaking his head in apparent disappointment and was later found soaking them in the Engineering Office toilet.

Then: the 'Dallas' incident.

"Max was dozing in his office chair, barefoot as usual and must have been wriggling his toes whilst dreaming." Troy had to take deep breaths several times whilst recounting the story to his Crewmates in the Galley. "The doors open, and I can see old Max, slumped in his chair and sleeping. Then I see he's wriggling his toes on the carpet. Up the corridor comes Dallas and I give him a stroke and walk on; seconds later there is a blood curdling scream and Max rushes past me shouting; "That Fucking stupid big cat has savaged my poor fucking feet!" He disappears to find the Doc and I see Dallas saunter from the office and here is the real funny bit; if he wasn't a cat, I would have sworn he was smiling!" The captain exonerated the cat completely, telling an angry and distraught Max; "Dallas was doing his job. He clearly thought your toes were a mutant pack of rabid mice!" The entire crew voiced their agreement with that - the fact that many were laughing - didn't placate Max and he sulked for a week. He didn't appreciate his crew nickname either; 'tap toes.' Max sulked for another week over that cracker and finally Lilly asked him why he had returned to a life on the rigs, when he clearly didn't like it. His answer became a catch phrase on the Thor.

Max grunted and looking Lilly direct in the eyes and with great honesty said simply; "I can't stand being happy." But Max had one saving grace that all acknowledged; he was actually a very good systems engineer.

Miserable Max and his sickly toes quickly became a legend amongst the rig crews; once when the Thor docked in Dayburgh, a dock-hand asked Leon if this was the rig with the "big magical cat" and the miserable bastard with bad feet?"

26. AN OFFICER'S DUTY.

Even Jones raised an eyebrow when he heard the latest story about Dallas; apparently Lilly had taught the cat to play cards! 'High and low' to be precise and the captain watched in utter amazement as Dallas won three dollars from Troy over several games in the packed Galley; the cat being cheered on by the incredulous crew. Dallas took another two dollars from a grinning Harry, who insisted on checking the cat's paws for hidden cards which caused raucous laughter for some time.

"Best fecking two dollars I ever spent on entertainment." Harry chuckled, pushing the money to Dallas with a big smile, adding; "And that's two dollars the bitch won't get her fecking claws on."

Jones also stood smiling; Dallas was very good at his primary role; no mice or other vermin had ever been seen on the Thor and he was even better at his secondary duty; keeping up crew morale!

Jokingly, he asked Lilly what Dallas was going to do with his winnings; "Eve and I are keeping them in a specimen jar in the Medical Bay, I think he [Dallas] wants to save for his retirement." Lilly smiled broadly and wandered off with the big cat following. Jones and the Chief exchanged glances, and both shrugged their shoulders, the chief commenting; "At least he's thinking about his future, not like those dimwits Troy and Sunny!"

The captain had to agree with that, then stopped halfway down the service corridor and muttered to himself: "The cat is saving for his retirement!" He shook his head in disbelief and then reasoned: if time travelling Holograms from the future could drop in, then Dallas could save for his retirement. With that thought Jones headed for the bridge – grinning.

The Captain was sprawled in his bridge chair staring through the windscreen; it was a beautiful day [for Southern Mars] and he sipped his coffee and relaxed a little. The Thor was making good time towards Weather Station Six and they would soon leave the Prospect Plains behind, heading into the High Easter Mountains to complete the inspections on Stations six and nine. 'Working the line' was the expression for this particular service mission.

Jones always assumed it was some kind of rhyme created by the early weather service riggers: 'working the line/three, six & nine.' listening intently to radio traffic and he smiled with satisfaction: Sunny could have been a major problem. When at the Officer's meeting, the entire Chief's doubts about his young Engineering Apprentice surfaced and the painful truth about Sunny's lack of ability and failure of the Engineering exam was the only talking point.

The Chief came to the point; bluntly and honestly, he informed Jones that Sunny would never pass with sufficient marks to gain a Scholarship to Engineering University and the Training Officer will end her apprenticeship upon the Thor's return to Rossington. Jones read the Training Officer's report and assessment with some sadness, but he really couldn't disagree with the findings that were clear and concise; Sunny didn't have the ability or technical knowledge to be an future Engineering Officer and the Training Department's Head's recommendation was termination of her Apprenticeship and departure from the service and the Thor.

They sat in silence for a few seconds, and then Eve spoke up; "Couldn't she move apprenticeships? I mean, she is still young enough to qualify for another chance surely?" Lilly agreed with some enthusiasm, adding; "All we need to find is what exactly Sunny is good at?"

"Now there's a real challenge." Grunted the Chief, but with a smile. Sunny may never wear the little silver spanner on her Rank Patch – but she could always wear another badge - he mused to himself and looked across at the captain. The Rank Patch Jones wore caught his eye; three silver Bars indicating a Captain, a silver spanner for his Engineering Degree, a Silver Star [Lilly and the Chief also possessed that decoration] and a bright blue pyramid – a very rare award: The Presidential Medal of Honour for bravery.

The Chief knew that only three other persons, currently serving in the Mars Military, who carried that award. The captain was in elite company there: two were Admirals and the other was Marshal Edward Kinghorn; head of all Mars Military forces.

Whilst Jones rarely spoke about the award, the Chief and the crew knew how their Captain won such a Medal; by sheer courage and dedication to duty when he was a young Ensign on the old battle rig: MSV 'The General Conway'. There had been an explosion in the forward turret corridor and a fierce fire raged towards the pulse shells stored there; had the fire reached the turret, the rig would have been ripped apart in seconds with mass casualties. The Fire Suppressant system spluttered and worked in spurts; it was clearly faulty.

But Jones had kept his head and with calm courage pulled the two injured gunners from the turret to safety. Then with absolute guts and determination, Jones went back in and fought the fire, managing to keep it in check and away from the shells, until the fire party arrived and extinguished the blaze. But Jones didn't escape without pain; he still carries the burn scars upon his back, right shoulder and left leg.

Within a few weeks of leaving hospital, Jones received his promotion to Lieutenant and then stood nervously in front of the Martian President as he hung the Presidential Medal of Honour about Jones's neck; watched by his very proud Grandfather. Neither his mother or father bothered to attend and Jones never forgot that either.

At the Presentation party afterwards, the First Lady asked Jones why he took such a risk to himself; Jones said simply: "It's an Officer's duty to protect his crew and his rig Ma'am." Everyone present knew that Jones was already earmarked for high position within the Military, especially his old Rig Captain La Strade, who commented; "If that's not a future Marshal, I'll eat my boots." Few disagreed with his assessment of the young Lieutenant Jones.

Now Jones was looking at a very different assessment and the quiet conversation turned again to Sunny's abilities and skills; or rather lack of them. But it was Eve that pulled the Genie from the bottle, she had been sitting deep in thought when she suddenly clicked her fingers and grinned; "Sunny is a very good cook!" The Chief nodded vigorously; "Bloody hell Eve, she actually is. Her cakes are excellent!"

Lilly clapped her hands together and shouted; "She made that vegetable curry you loved so much skipper!" Jones watched the three officers' breaking into smiles and nodding their agreement to each other.

"A really good idea, but for Sunny to transfer to another apprenticeship would need an Admirals signature on the form." Jones rubbed his chin and was already considering the possibly of Sunny being placed on a Chef's Course. "Maybe a little chat with Admiral Kellamann would produce a solution." He re-read her Training Assessment and tapped the desk with his fingers. "Frankie is the key to this." The Chief said, leaning back in his chair and smiling; "Just above the little silver brassier on his Rank Patch [indicating a trained chef] are three silver stripes and they are the real key to this plan." Lilly looked puzzled and asked the Chief to explain. "Those little stripes mean our Frankie is a Class 1 Chef; rare to find one of them serving on a rig, but it also means that Frankie is fully qualified to teach and examine students. All Sunny would have to achieve is passing the four-week Chef Preparation Course at the Military Catering College. Then she can easily complete her course right here on the Thor under Frankie's guidance. Finally, another four weeks at college and she passes her final exam and gets posted as a Chef!"

"That is simply brilliant Chief." Eve patted his shoulder and Lilly nodded her total agreement. Jones looked up from the form he was reading and sighed; "Frankie would have to agree to teach her and that is an awful lot of extra work to take on for no real reward; well, not in the monetary sense anyway."

"He'll agree." Both Eve and Lilly said as one: then laughed together. The Chief leaned forward, clasping his big hands together and said quietly; "Oh Frankie will agree if Lilly asks him." Everyone looked at Lilly who blushed a little and spluttered out; "Why on Mars would he agree just because I asked him?"

"Because he thinks the sun shines out your bum; that's why!" Eve slapped her on the back and laughed again. Lilly was about to protest when the captain held up his hands and spoke softly; "Right it's agreed: we'll point young Sunny towards a career in catering. Lilly, your job is persuading Frankie to teach her, Eve and Marcus: you work on our young lady to agree to all this and finally; I'll work on Admiral Kellamann for a little signature. That's it folks, back to our duties as Officers."

The Officer's meeting broke up with everyone relieved and happy with the decisions made. Now Jones would have to bring Margret into the loop; with some diplomacy and tact, otherwise she would feel slighted that such a major personnel decision was taken in her absence.

AUTHOR NOTE:
"Margret would have been manning the bridge as directed by Military Regulations: there must be always a qualified officer on the bridge - the three qualified on the Thor were her, the Captain and the Chief."

But the plan had worked better than Jones and the other conspirators could have dreamt of, firstly; Frankie had agreed without hesitation to help young Sunny when asked by Lilly; that caused a few rumours and smiles among the crew.

Secondly, Sunny had seen merit in the scheme and she really didn't want to leave the Thor just yet and finally; Admiral kellamann had only thought for a few seconds about the Captains request before he agreed it; "If she's recommended by you Pic, then that's good enough for me." Now that did raise a few eyebrows about the rig; gaining a second apprenticeship was rare, almost unheard of and Jones had managed it for his young crew member and the decision was welcomed by the entire crew including 'Tap-Toes' who grunted; "I don't agree with happiness, but others seem to enjoy it."

Yes, miserable Max was definitely a legend amongst the rig crews!

Jones was disturbed from his happy recollections by Sunny's nervous sounding voice; "Captain, Weather Central South has just issued a 'CODE RED ONE' for the South Cydonia and deep South regions. The Volcano 'Beano Houseman' has erupted in South Cydonia and its bad."

30. ERUPTION.

The bridge was packed for the captain's briefing on the situation, but t was Harry who was talking about the eruption of the volcano 'Beano Houseman' on the Southern desert of Cydonia and its far-flung effects.

Harry pointed to the pictures and graphs being projected on the bridge windscreen and outlined the extent of the huge explosions and ash clouds. An area of some four hundred square kilometers had been completely obliterated with fire and lava – luckily - this part of southern Mars was not really inhabited and so far, no casualties had been reported. But drifting down South was an enormous cloud of ash and with terrible coincidence; a Category 2 High storm was pushing north from the Ice Shelf. The pair of monsters collided over the Deep South with terrible effect over townships and rigs north of the Easter Mountains. The Emergency Control Centre in Rossington had announced several fatalities and many people injured; thus all military resources had been called to the area to assist in rescue operations. The Thor had been dispatched, now travelling at speed, heading north towards the Easter Mountains, one of only two military rigs in the location which could render assistance to anyone in need - the other being MSV: 'The Jennifer O'Donnell - the supply rig which was to due to rendezvous with the Thor.

The Captain now took over the briefing and outlined the

Thor's new mission; the rescue of surviving crew members from a large cargo rig; CV: 'the Moon Queen' which had been hit by debris from the marriage of the eruption and the storm. She lay crippled at the Northern tip of the Easter's, with the two survivors managing to send an SOS before barricading themselves in Cargo Bay 3 and now awaited rescue. But as Jones pointed out; the life clock was ticking, the pair had only a few days of oxygen left and little or no food. With no Environmental conditioning they suffered the heat of the Martian day and the cold of the Martian night; they needed immediate rescue.

"We have about 24 hours left to affect a rescue, otherwise it's a corpse collection job and we've already done our share of those." A grim-faced Jones addressed his silent crew and then sipping some lukewarm coffee, continued; "Their only chance is if we get there quickly and currently with all the debris and poor visibility around, we are simply not going to make it with Thor. She's too big and too slow for the conditions we're facing, so the Chief and I have come up with quite a radical plan; it just might work!" Jones managed a smile and really breathed deep, then announced the simple plan of rescue to a stunned crew.

The plan was simple and dangerous; 'Little Thor' would be equipped with rescue equipment including a pressurized survival tent and cutting gear. Then she would dash across the surface, achieving speeds that the Thor could never manage and arrive at the crash site with just two hours to affect the rescue. The Thor would follow at safe speed, and they would rendezvous at Valley La Mort, when the oxygen supply of the 'Sand-Cat' would almost be exhausted. "It's all about time." Muttered the Chief as he loaded the flatbed trailer with Troy and Leon's assistance, whilst Eve put together a medical supply kit and Frankie filled flasks with hot water and coffee – Sunny made up ration packs, putting packets of sweets in each from her personal stash of goodies.

Harry worked on new weather charts and the best route available with lots of 'fecks' thrown in. Max calibrated the 'Edison', a device which allowed conversations to take place through solid steel walls and bulkheads. Tom and Margret remained on the bridge with Lilly, who monitored the radio and video traffic streaming between the Emergency Centre and various townships and rigs asking for assistance.

When asked by Tom what was happening, she said simply; "There are a lot of desperate people who need real help." He nodded his agreement and didn't ask again, checking the 'scope' and Seismic gauges repeatedly as the Thor progressed towards the disaster zone. Just before darkness fell, all the preparations were completed; 'Little Thor' was ready for her dangerous dash across the sand; all she needed now was a crew.

"It has to be volunteers." Jones announced to the crew, quietly assembled on the bridge for the second time that day. "I'll lead the mission, that's not up for discussion Chief." He smiled at the disappointed old man who said nothing but nodded his sad agreement. Jones looked about the faces. He sighed and added; "Firstly, we need a medic because there may be injuries, but not the Doc. I think any qualified medical personnel will be like gold dust in the days to come. So you're staying here." He pointed to a very disappointed Eve who stared at the floor and like the Chief; said nothing.

"I understand that we have a Battle Trained First Aider on board and I'm hoping they'll volunteer." Jones looked straight at Lilly and smiled. Lilly glanced about the bridge and raised her hand; "That's me skipper, I'll get the medical kit." Everyone chuckled with Leon saying, "The captain has quite a way when picking volunteers!"

Jones smiled broadly at Leon; "Apart from me, the Chief and Harry, you're the only crew member who's done the training course for a pressurized rescue and those two are just too old and ugly to go."

The crew laughed, shouting their agreement with Jones. Leon shrugged his shoulders and muttered; "Yep, the Captain has a real skill for picking bloody volunteers!"

"Finally, we need someone young and fit to help with the rescue and someone who can drive the 'sand-cat'. One of you fits both job descriptions and since there's only one seat left, I'm hoping you'll volunteer Troy. You're about the best 'Sand-Cat' driver I've seen in some years, are you with us?" Jones slapped Troy on the shoulder and nodded his head, waiting for Troy's agreement. Troy looked about at his crew mates and grinned; "I do know how to handle that baby and she loves it."

Everyone chuckled and started to disperse, saying their goodbyes to the rescue crew who made their way to the suit room and prepared to quickly descend onto the surface and walk to the waiting 'Little Thor'. They suited up in silence.

When fully suited apart from helmets, the four stood quietly in the Surface Suit room and Jones held out his hand and said; "That's it friends, we go to save life. It's a dangerous gig and I couldn't ask for three better friends to jump into hell with." Troy, Leon and Lilly nodded their agreement and each placed their hand upon the captain's and the foursome shouted; "The Thor!"

They fixed helmets and Jones gave the thumbs up to the camera. On the bridge, the remaining crew all watched the suit room monitor in silence until the Chief said quietly; "They'll be alright. Pic knows what his doing." Jones was last into the elevator and turned back to the camera and slowly mouthed some words; as if they were spoken directly to the watching Eve, who caught the gesture and sat back, hand over mouth. She looked about the bridge and noted that everyone else was already watching the external cameras; to see the crew board the 'Sand-Cat'.

Eve brushed a little tear from her face and breathed deeply, then with cold shock, she remembered what 'Temptation Jones' had said: "You must not [speaking to Jones] take any risks during the next patrol on the sand. We have two versions of the past; in one you are killed in an eruption and so 'Pharaoh Jones' doesn't exist have children: with 'Pharaoh Jones' a direct descendant of your youngest son."

Eve watched the rescue crew enter the 'Little Thor' and a deep foreboding fear gripped her, but she said nothing to anyone else. They had descended to the surface and made their way to the 'Sand-Cat' – the storm was now kicking up dust and debris - and they gratefully clambered into the relative shelter of 'Little Thor'. Troy eased into the pilot's seat and started to check his instruments, the captain sat next to him and punched the crash site co-ordinates into the on-board 'Navicom' and pressurized the 'Sand-Cat' for her perilous journey north.

Lilly checked the medical supplies and rations, finding the sweets from Sunny and a little note; she read it quietly and folded it carefully, placing it in her suit pocket. Leon had eased back in his chair and waited for the captain to confirm it was safe to remove helmets. The internal lights dimmed to night vision and the external lights bathed the surface in a yellowish glow.

"We're ready captain." Troy said simply and Jones gave the thumbs up. Troy fired the engine and the 'Little Thor' pulled away, accelerating into the darkness. The silent Bridge crew watched her departure with some emotion: especially Eve. The Chief sat next to her and gripped Eve's hand; "When he gets back, I think you two should have a nice long chat about life and stuff like that." The Chief smiled and released her hand, heading for the Engine room.

Eve looked down at the floor and found Dallas sitting there; she leaned down and stroked the big cat, feeding him a couple of cat biscuits from the bag Lilly always kept on the Communications desk.

Tom called across the bridge to no-one in particular; "I've got them on the scope!" He could see the little green dot moving north, accelerating away from the relatively slow-moving Thor's position. "They are making good time, but they won't hit the Disaster Zone for at least three hours." He added, accepting a fresh coffee from Sunny, who tapped the little green dot gently with her finger. "Good luck, my dear friends." She whispered and returned to the Galley for more fresh coffee and to help Frankie with the evening meal; not that many would have an appetite.

Margret sat in the captain's chair watching the gathering gloom through the windscreen; the fate of the Thor and its crew now rested on her shoulders and she felt the heavy responsibility weighing her down already. She sipped her coffee and stared out at the darkness and thought about the 'Little Thor' struggling through debris and storm. She thought about its very brave crew, Lilly, Troy, Leon and the Captain.

The captains whispered final words came back to her; "The Thor's in your hands now Maggie, just get the boys and girls home safe." She glanced down at the little green dot moving into danger and swallowed hard, she couldn't let the crew see her shed a tear; not yet. Sitting up with a jerk, she wondered why that thought had appeared: 'Not yet.' Maggie looked across at Eve, sitting in silence on the Communications desk, listening to the radio and video traffic about the disaster that had unfolded. She wished they had known each other longer, just so they could sit and chat, so that she could unburden herself about certain matters. But she pushed the thoughts from her mind and asked Tom for a status update: 'Little Thor' would be rolling into the Disaster Zone any time now.

Harry stood behind her and spoke softly; "Ma'am, an update has just been flashed to all weather offices, it will appear over the air soon." Maggie spun round in her chair and accepted the paper from Harry, for a moment she thought his hands were trembling; she read the paper and lowered her head in despair.

Before she could comment; Eve called out from the busy Communications desk, her voice breaking with real emotion. "Weather Central South has just issued another 'CODE RED ONE'. The volcano has erupted again, and ALL personnel must clear the Disaster Zone immediately!"

Everyone stared at the 'scope' and the little green dot passing rapidly into the Disaster Zone.

EPISODE 11: "AFTERMATH."

31. THE DISASTER ZONE.

The 'Little Thor' was dipping and rolling as she sped across the sand, the nights darkness was illuminated by bright flashes of lightening and no stars were visible because of the ash cloud that hung above – visibility was limited - but she didn't slow.

 "Nothing but bloody static on the radio and no signal on the MSN; both Military and civilian sites are offline." Leon shouted and attempted to sip his coffee whilst it was still hot. Troy nodded and peered through the windscreen; "The sand is really starting to fly captain!" He smiled at Jones, adding; "This baby loves a challenge." Jones checked his PA and found that the 'No Signal' sign was still up. They had another three hours of this before they reached the wreck site. Lilly passed Jones a cup of coffee and he sipped it through the lids hole, the 'Little Thor' was rolling like a ship at sea. "I've checked the equipment again: it's strapped down tight." Lilly had staggered back from the rear observation window after checking the flatbed trailer. "We can't afford to lose any of that kit." She added and dropped into her seat behind Jones and popped a mint into her mouth. Sunny had placed a packet of her favourite sweets in the medical kit and Lilly really did appreciate that gesture.

Jones checked the Navicom again and tapped Troy on the shoulder; "Correct your course 2 degrees North-East, the winds are making her drift a little!" Troy nodded and adjusted his route, keeping a careful eye on the Compass as Leon tried to make contact with the Thor over the radio.

"Still fuck all Skipper." Leon sighed and sipped his coffee
which sloshec about in his cup; "This storm looks like it's just
kicked off; you don't think the fucker has erupted again?"
Leon was peering through the windscreen, watching the
lightning flashes exploding in vivid colours against the black,
ash filled sky.

Jones looked over his shoulder and nodded his agreement
with Leon's reasoning; "I think your right Leon. This is worse
than when we left the Thor!" The crew lapsed into silence and
the sand being driven against the 'Little Thor's' hull, sounded
like a giant drumming his fingers. Lilly broke the silence by
dishing out the sandwiches that Frankie had packed, and the
conversations started up again; particularly when they
discovered Frankie had made the captain Curry sandwiches!

Just half hour from the wreck site, the 'Little Thor's' radio
came back online, and Eve's voice could just be heard above
the static. They listened without comment to the dire news of
the second eruption and finally Lilly grabbed the microphone
and responded; "Eve, we just minutes away from the wreck
and we're continuing on; the skipper says we've come too far
to turn back now!"

The decision made by the crew of the 'Little Thor' was
accepted with few comments on the bridge of the Thor; the
Chief just shook his head and said quietly; "The skipper knows
what he's doing, they'll be alright." But Eve sat in silence,
arms folded, watching the Communications monitor which had
the details of the eruptions and their aftermath playing; there
were 164 confirmed fatalities and over three hundred injured.
This was followed by the story of the attempted rescue by a
weather Service rig: The Thor, which made everyone gather
around the little screen and watch the news bulletin.

Everyone cheered as the names of the Rescue crew were

broadcast and the Chief squeezed Eve's shoulder and smiled; "They'll be fine, they have a couple of hours to get those two poor bastards out of the wreckage and head for home." Eve nodded and patted the Chief's hand and they both watched the story unfolding on the late News.

Jones and Leon climbed carefully from the hatch of the 'Little Thor' and struggled to reach the flatbed trailer against the driving wind which kicked up dirt and black ash. Visibility was still fair and the pair could see the wreckage of the cargo rig some meters from their position. "Troy's done a great job getting us this close!" Leon shouted into his helmet's small microphone as he operated the crane which lowered the Rescue Tent onto the swirling dirt. Jones and Lilly manhandled the bulky piece of kit and lowered its wheels.

"Let's go!" Jones signaled the rescue attempt was on and with Lilly's assistance began the short, but dangerous journey to the wreck; followed by Troy and Leon hauling the additional rescue gear.

"Cargo hold number three is located just behind the second tyre on the starboard side." Jones panted, pulling the Rescue Tent with Lilly, the damn thing seemed to get heavier by the minute and he glanced across at Lilly who was also panting loudly; but they were now approaching the dark and shattered rig. The CV: 'The Moon Queen' lay broken into three pieces with the bridge smashed open and the Port side ripped apart; the rear was simply torn into little pieces, scattered about the swirling dust and ash. "What the fuck did that?" Leon shouted as they slowly approached the walls of steel; broken and blackened.

"Projectiles thrown out of the volcano, they travel a lot further than on Earth because of the thin atmosphere and they are far bigger and a lot more bloody dangerous!" Lilly answered between pants and waved her free arm about, adding; "This place is littered with them." Leon looked about and could see several large dark rocks embedded in the dirt: still smoking from their deadly flight. "Oh shit!" He said quietly and very nervously searched the skyline, but only saw the approaching darkness in the ash filled air.

"Leon and I will get the tent ready, whilst Lilly and Troy check the bridge for any other survivors." Jones commanded and the team stopped next to Tyre No.5, which was just blackened steel strands hanging around the wheel's hub. Lilly and Troy made for the bridge, their powerful torches lighting up the dark wreckage.

Jones plugged the 'Edison' into his helmet socket and placed it against the wall; "Got 'em!" he exclaimed as quiet voices filled his helmet. The captain then shouted the Rescue crew's arrival to the trapped survivors.

Jones gave the survivors clear instructions on how the rescue would unfold; firstly, they would secure the Rescue tent against the hull and pressurize it. Then they would use cutting gear to open a small hole through which the trapped crew could crawl to safety in the tent. Finally, after any injuries had been treated, they would don emergency pressure suits and then everyone would make it back to 'Little Thor'. If they succeeded in all that, it would be a cramped and difficult return to The Thor.

Lilly and Troy had returned with a grim report; the other three members of the crew lay dead amongst the wreckage of the bridge; apparently in two or three pieces each, such had been the force that struck them. Jones nodded and they worked to get the Tent strapped against the hull, whilst Leon prepared the cutting gear. That's when the two trapped inside the hull informed Jones through the 'Edison' that there was a third crew member that required rescue!

"Shit! We only have two fucking suits!" Troy exclaimed and the rescue crew stood in silence; they could only save two people. Then one of the trapped managed a strained laugh – the rig's mascot was the 'third crew member' - a cat called 'Lucy'. "We'll have to leave her; we can't transport her to the 'Little Thor', as we have nothing to put her in." Jones spoke quietly, clearly not happy about leaving the poor creature to her fate, but what choice did he have? He sighed deeply and leaned against the steel wall. Lilly tapped the captain on the shoulder and smiled; "Dallas's old pressure box is in the storage drawer of the 'Little Thor', he's too big for it, so the Chief and Tom made him a new one; now that's what I call luck, she'll be alright if she behaves herself!"

One of the survivors shouted that Lucy was a big cat and very intelligent, just tell her what's happening, and she'll be fine and they didn't mind waiting; while someone fetched the damn box. Lilly set off immediately and returned with the pressure tube which was bright red and had 'DALLAS' painted on the top side and 'HANDLE WITH CARE – CONTAINS A CAT!' printed on the lower side.

The rescue could now go ahead, and Leon cut a not so neat hole in the hull and Lucy was first through; the surviving crew had not exaggerated about her size; she could be Dallas's sister, except she was a patchwork of vibrant colours with a smoky grey tail and face.

"She's absolutely gorgeous!" Exclaimed Lilly and stroked her, giving Lucy some water in a coffee cup lid and produced cat biscuits from inside her suit; much to Leon's amazement; "Do you always carry cat biscuits inside your survival suit?" He asked incredulously. But Troy simply laughed and stated that the Thor's Ensign was quite nuts; so, she fitted in with the rest of the crew; quite nicely. Even Jones had to chuckle at that, especially when Lilly didn't deny the 'allegation'. The two survivors were pulled through the hole and Lilly treated their cuts and bruises, one had a broken arm which required stabilizing and the other a broken ankle. They both gulped down cold water and thanked everyone. Cole Janiski and Tabs Wong had been deckhands on the cargo rig and had their lives saved, simply because they were in the cargo hold when the rig was struck. Tabs stroked Lucy and told Lilly that quite unusually, she had followed the pair; normally she was laid about the bridge. Tabitha Wong wiped tears from her face and smiled; "Eight to go old girl!"

But Jones knew they were on a very short timeline and ordered everyone to suit up. Leon sealed Lucy in the box, she just squeezed in and he checked the pressure and air twice before giving the thumbs up. The relieved and tired group left the tent and headed back to 'Little Thor' across the swirling sand and dark sky, which was punctuated with vivid flashes of red, orange and white. The storms crashing together were very dangerous, but spectacular and colourful.

32. THE LONG VOYAGE HOME.

It was quite a squeeze, six people and a cat, in a 'Sand-cat' designed to carry four persons. But no-one actually grumbled about the situation; especially the rescued pair who were accommodated on an air mattress at the rear of 'Little Thor's' crew cabin. Lilly had given them some pain control and they were both sleeping for the first time, after almost two days and nights in the hold of their dead rig.

Lilly had Lucy sprawled across her lap; the big cat was also sleeping. Lilly ran her hand down her neck and back and received a spluttering purr in thanks. Troy was sipping coffee and leaned across to give the cat a stroke; "I really do think that Dallas and our furry friend here will hit it off." He grinned and Lilly nodded her agreement; "They should be the best of friends." Leon glanced towards the pair and laughed, then adjusted the drift of the 'Little Thor' as the winds grew and fell in strength.

"I estimate at least six hours before we reach the rendezvous point with the Thor, if she doesn't show up within four hours of our arrival, we're in the shit!" Jones shouted and tried the radio again; nothing. The storm had renewed its strength and all communications were down again. The visibility was poor, and Leon had to slow the 'sand-cat' on numerous occasions as great gusts of sand and ash flew against the windscreen.

"It's like trying to drive with your head in a bag!" He called to Jones who smiled and checked the Navicom yet again. "We'll change over in another half hour, and you can get some rest. I'll take it for a spell." Jones tapped Leon on the shoulder and sipped his coffee, and then scoffed down the sandwich which Frankie had made chicken curry and fries.

The big cat stirred and sat up on Lilly's lap; she dropped her paws upon Jones's shoulders and sniffed at his sandwich. Jones pulled a little chicken from it and fed Lucy; she ate it with some gusto. "Oh, fuck another Dallas! She eats curry!" Troy exclaimed as everyone started to laugh, Lucy also ate from Lilly's cheese and tomato sandwich and then lapped, just like Dallas, plenty of weak cold coffee from Lilly's mug lid.

"They have to be related, through Lucy is a lot prettier than our mangy old bugger." Troy muttered, pulling the cheese from his sandwich for the cat who now sprawled across both he's and Lilly's lap, purring with happiness. "With those two in hospital who will look after her?" Troy asked.

Lilly tapped Jones on the shoulder and spoke quietly; "I'm

going to tell our guests that whilst in hospital and then convalescing, we'll look after Lucy; so they don't have to worry about how she is being cared for. Is that O.K. Captain?"

Jones grinned and nodded his agreement; Dallas will love that sort of company!

The radio came back to life, but only for a few moments at a time, but it was enough for the crew to appreciate the extent of the disaster and now Jones prayed hard that the Thor can make the rendezvous on time; if they missed it, then the rescue crew and survivors wouldn't last more than a couple of hours. The weather conditions had added more time to their mission and time was not on their side.

Oxygen was the deciding factor; the extra time that the weather conditions placed upon the mission sucked up the precious reserves and whilst they can recharge the batteries through the roof solar panels, they couldn't manufacture oxygen.

If they used their suit oxygen as a last resort, they could add a couple of hours to their survival time; but the figures were grim. Originally, they had worked on having at least eight hours of oxygen after arriving at the rendezvous point; a very good safety gap.

But the renewed strength of the eruption had stolen three or four hours from that and now the travelling conditions were becoming so bad, they may have to stop because visibility was nearing zero. But any delay waiting on the sand simply meant death. But if they can't see – they can't drive - and Jones groaned as the sand and ash slapped against the windscreen and the wipers struggled to cope. "We can't keep going much longer." He muttered.

I'm sorry skipper." Leon whispered as he peered out at the

swirling storm "What's that little dot on the' Mini scope', about thirty Kilometers South-East of us?" Troy tapped Leon on the shoulder and pointed towards the 'Mini-scope'. There was a small dot blinking, stationary and some thirty kilometers from the approaching 'Little Thor'. It displayed no digital identifying signature and Jones reckoned it was about the same size as the Thor; without her trailers. "Head for it." Jones said simply and the 'Little Thor' trundled over the violently moving sand, rolling and pitching like a cork in a filling bath. It took about an hour to reach the mysterious dot and what they found surprised and stunned the crew.

They parked up some forty meters from the derelict hulk; a wall of steel plates loomed through the flying sand and ash; the strange contraption had the old fashioned 'caterpillar' track system and was indeed about the size of the Thor without the trailers. The odd-looking tubes and pipes running down the roof and sides betrayed its identity.

"Sweet Mars! It's a bloody old Geo-Harvester!" Exclaimed Jones with real amazement in his voice; "It has to be nearly a hundred years old. They stopped using these babies almost a century ago." He couldn't make out the faded name, but the logo appeared to be some kind of bird in flight. Troy was already tapping in the details and sat back; "It's a Class 3 'Geo-Harvester', the last one finished operation and headed for the scrap yard on Week 41: Day 402: Year: 234 and it states that over the years worked, they lost at least two dozen of these machines to storms and catastrophic mechanical failures - whatever that means – and finally the decision was made to pull them. It states that over fourteen of these machines simply disappeared - with their crews – on Southern Mars alone."

"Well, we've found one." Jones muttered, rubbing his chin and then he turned to Troy and smiled; "What did these big old beasties use for oxygen?" But Leon had already checked the Engineering archives on his PA and nodded; "Its bottled oxygen; lots of bottled oxygen!" and jerked his thumb up.

"I'll get my helmet and Troy can drop the 'little Beaver'." Jones said quietly and Troy grinned broadly.

Jones and Leon crouched low behind the 'Little Beaver', both machine and men struggled against the wind driven sand. "From what I remember at Engineering College, the external pressure door is on the roof. So, get ready to climb!" Jones shouted through his headset and Leon gripped the rail of the 'Little Beaver'; "I'll climb bloody Olympus Mons for fresh oxygen cylinders!" He laughed between pants; this was hard going.

They climbed the starboard ladder, buffeted by flying sand and ash, to the roof deck and crawled on their hands and knees to the pressure door, which had both a manual and digital opening operation. Jones ran his glove over the access panel; it was, as expected; dead. He gripped the star shaped, manual opening lever and began to turn – like the short walk from the 'Little Thor' – it was hard work. They dropped down the inside ladder and stood on the bridge; "Sweet fucking Mars!" Leon whispered looking at the Geo - Harvester's young Captain, sprawled back in her chair, the face quite calm with a hand gripping her throat, whilst the other lay at her side.

He glanced to the floor, where a young man, no more than mid-twenties, lay face up with both hands clutching his throat, a piece of paper lay next to the body. Jones scooped it up and read it with interest. "It's directions to a cave system in the Easters." He nodded at the bodies; "Batteries were notorious for failing and if the crew didn't react really fast......." He waved his hand at the corpses; "This happened and that's why this whole class of Geo – Harvesters was scrapped."

"Not quick enough for these poor bastards." Leon muttered and thought the long dead Captain was very pretty and he glanced down at her name tag and was quite puzzled; "Skipper, where the fuck have I heard the name 'Caroline Palmer' before?"

The walk back to 'Little Thor' was silent; the little Beaver was weighted down with several oxygen cylinders and both Jones and Leon clung onto it, as the winds tried to push them back. "Skipper, we've identified the Geo-harvester; she's ''Sullivan's Stork' and was reported missing in a really bad storm back in 231, but the really amazing thing is her skipper was called..." Jones interrupted Troy's transmission; "We know; Caroline Palmer. We've just seen her dead body."

They had found five dead bodies in the derelict Harvester, not including the rig's mascot; a large exotic parrot whose name was; "Arnold'. They had all died apparently of asphyxia, caused by the leaking batteries. When Jones tested the rig's foul atmosphere it was still lethal after all those years. They had left the bodies as found; an Investigation Team would be dispatched after the latest disaster calmed down and Jones didn't want to disturb any evidence too much. He sat in the cab of the 'Little Thor' and watched the storm; occasionally she would roll and shift with the wind. But they could now afford to wait for better visibility. Leon sat eating a packet of fruit balls – a little gift from Sunny – and offered them to Jones, who picked an apple flavoured ball.

"Now that is some co-incidence; Caroline Palmer is the Medical Officer at Weather Station Seven in 233 and just bloody well disappears, no trace found. Then we find a Caroline Palmer, who's a Geo-harvester skipper, stone dead; apparently bumped off by toxic gas in 231. They even had the same name and same age." Leon grinned and dropped another fruit ball in his mouth.

"This one had a map of some caves in the Easter Mountains, who are located on the edge of the Iceshelf and Weather Station Seven, where the other one was to disappear?" Jones said quietly and rolled the fruit ball around his mouth; "Is that another co-incidence?" He studied the Map again; Valley La Mort and the Prospect Plains, then Weather Station No.7 clearly marked.

"Do you know what else is really odd about our derelict harvester?" Jones smiled at Leon and pushed the map back into his suit pocket. Leon shook his head; he didn't know.

"They had apparently worked that area for three weeks, from the rig's log that I downloaded, and the hold was empty; totally fucking empty. So, what the hell, were they really doing, out there on the sand?" As Leon realised what the captain was saying that they should have had a full hold, he simply muttered; "Fuck!"

The wind had dropped, and the 'Little Thor' set off for the rendezvous point at some speed with Jones driving. They listened to the scale of the disaster on their radio in almost silence.

33. THE SERVICE OF REMEMBERANCE.

The President of Mars had declared a 'Day of Remembrance' for the victims of the eruption, which numbered 404 dead and 2,361 injured. There were plans put in process to have a 'Memorial Wall' built in the Southern Mars Capitol which listed the dead by name. The location would be the entrance of the new railway station at Rossington.

The crew of the Thor had been given Liberty to visit family and friends; so, the only crew remaining aboard her was Jones, Lilly and Troy. The captain had no real close family and other members of the 'crew' who stayed were Dallas and Lucy. The two big cats were quite inseparable and were always found together somewhere around the rig. Their antics delighted the crew – even old 'Tap-Toes,' - who apparently had forgiven Dallas for the 'Toes' incident.

Frankie had taken to Lucy [as had the entire crew] and she was fed and watered from Dallas's rations; topped up after a very generous collection was taken from the crew!

Like Dallas, she was groomed and checked by Lilly and Eve. To everyone's amazement and amusement, she even allowed Lilly to vacuum her fluffy big coat, just like Dallas. The big cat had been easily accepted by the crew and now was loved as much as Dallas always had been.

Jones had brought Tom, Eve and the Chief up to date with the saga of 'Caroline Palmer' or rather the 'Caroline Palmer's'. Leon was now interested in the story and sat in on the meeting. The other visitor was Professor Jack Dawes, who visited the Thor whilst she was docked at Rossington.

The professor had done some homework on the two Caroline's, but admitted that the Military had informed him, that both files were still 'classified' and would remain so until further notice. "I actually believe there is only one Caroline Palmer and she died on the Geo-Harvester in 231, but why a military crew was working a harvester is a whole different question." The Professor had discovered that the entire crew of the 'Sullivan's Stork' rig had been current serving military personnel. No mention of this had been made at the Inquiry into the loss of the Geo-Harvester. No one at the company who owned the rig [at the time] knew that the rig was off course by nearly five hundred kilometers. They had searched the area she was supposing to be working and found nothing at the time.

"Little bleeding wonder that they found sod all [at the time]
she was five hundred Kilometers from her last reported
position!" The Chief grunted; in all his years of service, he had
never heard of a commercial rig operated by the military.

"They must have been doing something during their three
weeks stay on the sand. It certainly wasn't harvesting sand
and minerals; the bloody hold was empty." Jones informed
the group and Tom asked the Professor why he believed there
was only one Caroline Palmer, as there are two years between
the death on the harvester and the disappearance at the
Weather Station.

"Simple my friend, if Caroline Palmer and her crew – all
military - but working a commercial rig, were on some
classified mission, then her death on the rig was never
reported The crew was never identified by name at the only
inquest held about the loss of 'Sullivan's Stork'. I would further
believe that someone was posted to Weather Station Seven
under her name some two years later but was involved in
some unexpected incident and vanished; probably killed by
person or persons unknown."

"So, the missing Medical Officer was never Caroline Palmer
because we now know she died on some secret mission,
running a Geo-Harvester near the Easter Mountains." Eve
muttered and added; "So who the hell is missing?"

On that note, the meeting broke up and Jones reminded
everyone about the remembrance ceremony at the Governor's
palace in the morning – best dress and sobriety was the order
for the day. Following the ceremony, the Thor's crew would
depart on leave for an entire week.

Professor Dawes was concerned by the no-action of Jones and
Eve regarding the revelations made by the apparent time-

travelling hologram, 'Temptation Jones'. He quite liked the idea that his great, great, great grandchildren will be able to live outside in Mar's brand-new atmosphere, thanks to a descendant of Jones and Eve.

"He got the eruption spot on Jonesy; how the hell did he know about that before it happened?" Professor Dawes held up his hands and grinned broadly, adding; "So stop bloody procrastinating and marry the damn woman so we can all breath easily in the future!"

 Jones had to smile at that and shrugged his shoulders with a sheepish grin; "I'm working on it."

The professor nodded and returned to his small shop to study the case of 'Caroline Palmer' further. The crew of the Thor was all present at the ceremony of remembrance held in the Grand reception area of the Southern Mars Governors Palace. The service was simple and dignified; the names of each person who had died in the disaster were read out by a family member and a candle lit in their memory.

Jones met Eve and her mum; Maggie, in 'Blind Charlie's Bar and Diner' where the crew had arranged a 'quiet' drink to celebrate surviving the disaster; even Margaret, the Thor's new XO turned up and even more amazement was expressed when Max Tapp arrived and joined the party. The guest most welcome at the little party was the newest member of the crew: Lucy. Lilly had bought both cats to the party, it appears Lucy also walked on a lead and enjoyed a small beer, just like Dallas! The crew welcomed the pair with cheers and bottles raised and old Charlie just had to smile.

"It must be the breed. They are all similar, I expect." Charlie muttered, as he poured the cat's beer with a huge grin on his face and his wife; Joy fed the pair with chicken pieces and cat biscuits, fussing over the pair like a mother hen.

The crew had a really good party and then dispersed for their leave – Jones and Eve had quite a long goodbye – it should be noted and that Maggie [Eve's mum] actually invited Jones home for the week.

But one qualified Officer must remain with the rig; even when docked. That responsibility fell to Jones and Eve knew it. The following morning Lilly was up early and Jones found her in the galley cooking breakfast for him, Troy and herself; she had already fed the two big cats, who chased each other about the rig for the remainder of the morning.

"I took a call for you this morning Skipper, it was from that Professor Dawes; he said he would drop in at lunch time with some information for you. I thought we could get pizza take-away for lunch?" Lilly slapped some more scrambled egg upon Jones's plate and smiled. Jones slowly nodded his agreement about the pizza's; as long as they came from 'Monkee's', the little pizza and burger shop near the Dockyard's Peace Guard Station. He really liked their vegetable and egg pizza with plenty of chili's. Lilly wrote up his and Troy's order, pinning it next to the Communications desk, before setting off to meet Eve and Sunny for shopping.

The Professor turned up early and joined Jones on the bridge; they drank coffee and discussed what the Professor had now discovered about the mysterious 'Caroline Palmer': The 28-year-old had been in the military for five years before her death in 231 and her entire file was still 'Classified'.

"We know she had trained as a Medical Officer but took up 'other duties' [not specified] during the Invasion war and apparently did not return to her studies. It appears she has no living relatives and so her body will be passed onto the team of 'Operation Cenotaph." The professor stated. That made Jones shudder - he really disagreed with the purpose of that project and could see no merit in the scheme.

The Professor was really interested in the map Jones had found by the body of the young man, on the bridge floor of 'Sullivan's Stork'. "It appears to be an entrance to the caves, from the Valley La Mort, that lay deep under the Easter Mountains. But what do this numbers and letters mean?" He stared at the paper and wondered if they were – maybe some sort – of reference points inside the cave system, but where did they lead too? Or perhaps, what did they lead too?

Jones had noticed the mix of letters and numbers every few centimeters on the flimsy drawing; 'AX34 - AY21 - CT84 etc.' Jones shook his head; he had no idea what they could mean. Both he and the Professor came up with various ideas, but none seemed to ring true and were very easily dismissed; they would have to remain a mystery for now.

Both men wondered if her death and that of her crew had any real connections with the legend of the ruined city, hidden deep in the Easter Mountains. But neither man could produce any reason or evidence there was indeed, a link. The only exception being the map with the code letters and numbers; but they remained unknown for the moment.

Professor Dawes left the biggest surprise to last; he pulled a photograph from his briefcase and slid it across to Jones and smiled. Jones looked hard and then realised who was in the Military Graduation photograph.

"Class 7 Alpha of Rochester Officer's Academy in the year 226, the nine officers' in the picture have just graduated. The other two are instructors, but do you see who number three and number eight are?" The professor tapped the photograph and said quietly; "Number eight is Lt. J.E. Stanner and number three is Lt. Caroline Palmer; they must have known each other."

Jones considered the Professors words for a few seconds and spoke softly; "Stanner's apparently committed suicide in 227, during the Invasion War and Palmer apparently died in 231 of gas poisoning: how can they be connected?"

The Professor placed both hands upon his head and leaned back in the chair; "Do you think that Palmer was leading some kind of secret mission to recover the weapon that Stanner hid in the cave system?"

Jones shook his head; "No one knew about the weapon until we viewed that old communications device and saw Stanner's video." He stood and paced the floor, then clicked his fingers with a broad smile; "Maybe our friend Stanner survived, made a little map and then somehow got it another officer he could trust: Palmer? Who he knew from his Military Academy days and maybe they kept in touch after graduation: that's entirely possible I believe."

The Professor had to smile at that reasoning; "That would explain why no-one knew about the Geo-harvester mission in Military Command [at the time] but someone high up in the Government certainly must have authorized such a mission?"

Jones nodded and wondered what the hell happened to bloody Stanner if he didn't die in the caves of the Easter Mountains?

EPISODE 12: "THE NEW ARGONAUTS."

34. THE TWO PROFESSORS.

Troy stared for some time at the plate of food placed before him, he rotated the dish on the table and looked closely at the meal and after a few seconds declared; "What the fuck is it?" He looked up in puzzlement at the young Chef, who folded her arms and rolled her eyes. "Cabbage and rice risotto with celery pieces." She said sighing and then walked back to the small kitchen. Leon started to laugh quietly and pushed his plate to one side; "They trained her for nearly a year to produce crap like this; it must be a joke." He muttered and then smiled broadly, as did Troy, when the Chief entered the galley, rubbing his hands in anticipation of lunch.

"Bloody Sunny could have knocked up better." Leon said and wondered how she was getting on, with her basic Chef's course at the Military catering School in Rossington.

Marcus dropped into the chair opposite them and stared at their plates; "What on the lunch menu today boys? – I skipped breakfast; it looked quite strange." Troy and Leon shrugged their shoulders and pushed the plates towards the Chief; "Total crap Chief; does the captain agree with this rubbish being dished up?" Leon asked and folded his arms. The chief poked the meal with a fork and sighed. "She's just out of Chef School and is following their recommendations for a healthy food regime; doesn't know any better I suspect. The captain is going to speak with her this afternoon, I know that."

The Chief chuckled and pushed the plate away and looked up

as Lilly stuck her head around the Galley door and smiled; "I don't know if anyone is interested, but Eve and I are knocking up fried egg sandwiches in the Medical Bay." She said simply and disappeared. Marcus, Leon and Troy exchanged glances and quickly followed Lilly towards the medical bay.

The young Chef appeared in the galley clutching the Chief's lunch and was a little surprised to find it empty; even the two big cats turned their noses up at the food on offer and headed for the Medical Bay, where they both knew Eve and Lilly kept a stack of cat biscuits and other treats.

The medical bay couldn't fit too many more of the crew inside and so Tom and Harry stood in the corridor outside, clutching their precious fried egg sandwich's and sipping Lilly's freshly brewed coffee. The small kitchen within the medical bay had never been so busy and the fry pan was turning out constant fried eggs; to everyone's delight.

Picasso had found the galley totally empty – apart from the bewildered Chef – which was unusual because it was lunch time! The noise from the service corridor caught his attention and he found most of his crew there and in the Medical Bay. The smell of fried eggs also caught his attention, and he joined the queue with a slight smile upon his face.

Everyone certainly missed Frankie on this trip; he had been granted two weeks compassionate leave to attend the funeral of his beloved sister Katherine, who had died suddenly at home. His replacement: Chef Louise Koch was straight from Training School and the Thor was her first posting – she followed Military nutritional guidelines like they were gospel – and the crew was not happy.

Thus, it was decided by Captain Jones that he would have 'quiet' words with the young Chef and get curries, chips and chili's back on the menu; before he had a full-blown mutiny on his hands! On a rig like the Thor – and most other rigs – food could make or break morale. All the crews looked forward to food time and it was one of the most important events of the day; whilst out on the sand. You couldn't send for a bleeding takeaway; so it had to be good!

Thankfully, the young Chef did understand just how important the meals were to the crew [particularly for morale], after a very careful and diplomatic discussion with Captain Jones. Louise shuffled through the recipes left by Frankie and set to work.

That evening, a very apprehensive crew started to assemble in the Galley, but the gorgeous smell of curry filled the air, and they began to relax and chatter amongst themselves. The curry was excellent and young Louise received a full round of applause for her efforts; even Jones had to admit that it wasn't too bad – as a substitute for Frankie's curries - which were almost worshiped by the crew. The Chef was a little surprised that Dallas and Lucy also tucked into the food; accompanied by a bowl of cold beer.

After dinner, she raised the matter with the Chief, who was sprawled across two chairs in the Dining room, sipping a little 'Old Ma Crawford's' from his hipflask. He smiled and said simply; "They're Rig cats – they'll eat anything." Then he thought for a moment; "Just don't let the buggers have beer with every meal; it makes them fart. Give them weak cold coffee and some water now and again." A very amused Chef returned to her little kitchen to plan tomorrow's meals, chuckling to herself and stepping over the two big cats asleep on the floor, curled up next to each other. She sighed; the Chief was right about the farting and switched the extraction fans back on.

Jones and Eve sat in the corner of the Galley, opposite each other and sipped their coffees quietly. They were both quite disappointed that their application for extended leave had been rejected; the two professor's expedition to the Easters would now go ahead without them.

Vice-Admiral Kellamann had been quite apologetic whilst refusing their applications – following the eruptions of the volcano – all military personnel had been placed upon 'High Alert' and the Thor had been dispatched to complete the serving of weather stations three, six and nine, there were no real replacements, readily available, for Jones and the Doc.

Thus Professor's Jacobson and Dawes expedition to locate the fabled ruined city of the Easter's had commenced without the pair. The two professors had leased an old 'Mammoth' class rig and put together a small team of eight – the expedition was already underway - when the Thor had left Rossington Docks to complete the interrupted service schedule.

Jones had kept a quiet eye on the 'scope' and watched the dot, which represented the old 'Mammoth' cargo now renamed 'The New Argonaut', as it progressed towards the Easter Mountains. He had calculated that the Thor and the New Argonaut will cross paths south of the Easters, upon Prospect Plains, just before they [The New Argonaut] entered the foothills of the mountain range. He would arrange a visit to the 'New Argonaut' when the two rigs meet up on Prospect Plain; probably in a couple of days. The Thor was on route to Weather Station numbers three to complete the service schedule colloquially known as 'working the line' [three, six & nine]. There had been no further information regarding Caroline Palmer, but Jones had given Professor Dawes a copy of the suspected map, that he had found near her body, in the old geo-harvester. The professor had promised to keep Jones, Eve and Tom in the loop. The two professors believed the entrance, of the cave system which held the fabled ruins, lay some nine kilometers west of Valley La Mort and that's where their expedition would commence the search. Dawes had confided to Jones that he had some serious unspoken reservations about a couple members of his team, particularly the Rig's captain: Norman Bannister. Jones believed he knew the name but could not recall why. Only later when he casually mentioned the name to the Chief did he realize that Captain Bannister had been involved in two nasty incidents with rigs he commanded: mostly for being drunk. He had his Rig Masters certificate [RMC] revoked on two occasions and was suspended for a year each time. A very close eye would have to be kept on him. The other crew member the professor had doubts about was a former Mars Marine, who admitted he had been dishonorably discharged from the Corps, after an incident in which a fellow Marine died. He was also suspected of being a little too much reliant on alcohol. The remaining crew members appeared quite solid; a student in their last year at medical college, a former XO [who still has his RMC] on a big cargo rig who had retired early, a survival expert and a Government Surveyor, taking extended leave. The planned expedition had left Rossington some days before the Thor departed for service duties.

35. JOURNEY INTO THE UNKNOWN.

The Thor had been parked for some hours outside weather station number three and the Chief, with Tom and Max were the service team working inside, completing routine service and maintenance.

Jones sat on the bridge with Leon, sipping coffee and chatting about the two mad professors and what they hoped to find in the caves. Eve was gossiping with Lilly on the communications desk, having set up the Surface Suit monitoring system, for when the service team cross the surface back to the Thor. Maggie was reading her PA in the Pilots seat and occasionally checking the odd instrument read out.

Lilly answered the internal phone and called over to Jones; "Skipper, Louise says that lunch will be ready at twelve. There's chili, chicken salad or Pizza on the menu today and there's ice-cream for dessert." She grinned broadly and Leon nodded his approval; "That must have been some little chat skipper!" Everyone chuckled and Jones just smiled.

Harry appeared and bent down to Jones with a concerned look on his face, he spoke quietly, and Jones immediately turned to Lilly; "Can you get onto weather central and get an update for the weather at the Easters and the Ice-Shelf please."

Harry folded his arms and stood quietly next to the busy communications desk, while Lilly called up weather control. "I can't understand why they are not flashing a warning for us, if a dumb feck like me can work it out, surely they can." Harry spoke directly to Jones who could only nod his agreement. A possible Category 2 (Low) storm was no laughing matter, especially near the volatile Iceshelf.

It took several minutes before Lilly received a reply; a serious storm warning for their region was indeed underway; Harry had simply worked it out a lot faster than they did. Jones patted Harry on the shoulder; "Good work Harry, I'm glad that someone knows what they're doing!" The bridge crew unanimously voiced their agreement with that.

It was clear that a category 2 (Low) storm was just a few hours away and it was carrying electronics. The lunch would have to wait, and the service crew needed to be recalled.

Jones was already working out a placement plan for the 'Lightning canisters and the best place to park up the Thor. A small valley some kilometers away, near the Easter foothills, offered the best cover. When the service crew was recovered successfully, the Thor was immediately diverted and made her way to 'Hudson Valley'.

Already the sky was darkening above the Easter Mountains and far in the distance could be seen small flashes of white and orange. The Chief swallowed down some cold water, followed by fresh coffee and watched through the windscreen, as the small valley entrance appeared. "I think we'll have just about an hour to place some canisters, with a reasonable safety margin for working on the surface." He spoke to Maggie who was now in command of the bridge. Jones, Leon, Troy and Lilly were already in the suit room, getting ready to deploy. Tom and Max remained in the corridor; they were still suited up, having returned from the weather station. Louise had arrived with coffee and water for them, which was gratefully received and said that hot food would be served, upon the captain's order, when they returned from the surface. Maggie parked the Thor up, just inside the valley and after Eve had checked the readouts of the surface suit monitors; gave the go ahead for canister placement.

The team hit the sand some minutes later and Leon rolled the canisters from the cargo bay external door to their waiting grasp. It took thirty minutes to place the lightning canisters and all the surface crew returned safely to the Thor.

That's when Maggie drew Jones attention to the scope; the New Argonaut rig was still on the move inside the foothills of the Easter Mountains. "What the fuck!" Muttered the Chief adding; "The other three rigs on the scope are stationary, probably deploying canisters as I speak. What the fuck is this one up too?"

Jones rubbed his chin and nodded; "Maybe he's running for

cover, perhaps to one of the big cave entrances." Jones turned to Lilly adding; "Try and call them up Lilly; before we close down for the storm." Jones stared through the dirty windscreen at the quickly approaching darkness and lightning flashes. Once Lilly had made contact with the New Argonaut, he would order the close down of the rig, with deck furniture [aerials and satellite dishes] folded away and shields dropped.

"Can't raise them captain, sorry." Lilly looked quite concerned, adding; "There's nothing wrong with the signal or equipment and they are receiving our call; they're just not replying." Jones grunted and ordered the Thor's closedown for the duration of the storm. Tom asked for the order to fire the lightning canisters and Jones nodded: affirmative.

Everyone could hear the muffled explosions, each in in turn, as the canisters were activated by Tom. "All are up and running correctly skipper." Tom called out to Jones, who dropped into the captain's chair and watched as the shields came down slowly over the windscreen. He turned to Lilly and told her to announce that lunch could be taken; that would put smiles on grim faces.

The storm arrived some minutes later with hurricane strength winds and serious amounts of lightning; everyone could hear small rocks and stones slamming against the Thor's hull and running across the roof.

Jones ate his lunch sitting on the bridge with Leon [who also had his lunch bought to him by Louise] and chatted about the storm and the professor's expedition. Maggie rejoined them after dinner, praising the young chef's chicken salad dressing, which also received recommendation from both Lilly and Eve. Jones and the chief had chili; as did Leon, Harry and Troy.

There was lots of conversation and a little laughter on the

bridge as they sat out the storm. Jones was happy that morale was good, and he reached down and stroked Lucy, who sat at his feet, whilst Dallas was sprawled across the communications desk, being fussed over by Lilly and Eve.

Suddenly, there was a huge bang and the Thor rocked from side to side; one of the canisters had apparently been hit and was totally destroyed. Tom switched off the 'collision alarm' and checked his instruments. "The North canister has been obliterated. That must have been some lightning strike!"

Leon looked up from his panel and slightly smiled; "Hull integrity is 100% skipper. But should I prep the life-rafts?" Jones nodded. The Chief and Troy left to physically prepare the life-rafts by opening ingress hatches and switch on their internal systems. "Better safe than sorry." Jones muttered.

Leon activated both rafts from the Bridge and Jones punched in his security code, setting the rafts for automatic launch and Lilly sounded the 'Go to life-raft' stations alarm. The two rafts quickly filled with the non-essential and apprehensive crew; Raft 1 had the Chief in command with Lilly, Troy, Harry and Louise; the other place was for Maggie. Raft 2 would be commanded by the Captain with Max, Eve, and Leon on board. The two big cats were also placed inside, and Eve amused them with a couple of soft balls. The crew in her now waited for the captain and Tom. On the bridge, Maggie turned to Jones and tapped the scope; "That's really strange skipper, they have simply vanished off the scope; just gone."

Jones and Tom stared at the screen. She was right; the three other rigs, which were within the two-hundred-kilometer range of the scope, were clearly shown. The New Argonaut had disappeared from the screen. The captain ordered a recalibration of the scope which Tom completed in about ten minutes. The result was the same; the new Argonaut had simply vanished from the screen.

36. THE MISSING AND THE LOST.

"They could be hiding inside one of the really big caves that litter the foothills. That could easily close the signal off, especially with this bloody big storm knocking about." Tom eased back in the co- pilots seat and shook his head; "I think we don't have to worry until after the storm and if their signal doesn't return." Tom added and scrutinized the scope again, still no signal.

Jones knew that nothing could be done during this storm, and they must wait it out, hopefully the New Argonaut would come back on line when the storm has finished. He told Tom and Maggie to take their places in the life-rafts and he would join them soon. He set the Thor on automatic pilot and the rafts would be automatically sealed for launch; should the need arise!

Jones was now alone on the bridge, so he pulled a couple of sheets of paper from his shirt pocket and sat quietly reading in the captain's chair. They had been print-outs sent by Professor Dawes to Jones, the day the old rig had left for the Easter's. Jones sat and read about the Expedition Members.

The two Professors [Dawes and Jacobson] were both known to Jones, and he quickly moved on to the other six names upon the sheet: Ketchi Tassimi was a 16-year-old [29 on Earth] 'survival expert' who specialized in training commercial rig crews to survive on the sand, should the rig fail them. His nickname was 'Ketchup' and apparently had a good sense of humour – he wrote a 'conspiracy' column - that appeared on Mar's internet, called 'Strange Tales.'

Norman Bannister was 27 years old [48 on Earth] the Rig's

captain and was definitely a dubious character and that really did concern Jones, known for his drinking habits and double suspension for incidents on his previous rigs. Surprisingly enough, his RMC was still current. [Rig Master's Certificate.]

Ian Kennedy was 18 years old [32 on Earth] a former Mars Marine, who had admitted being dishonorably discharged from the Corps. He had been unable to hold down various jobs since leaving the Marine Corps and was expected to provide security and military experience to the group. Jones knew he liked a drink – whatever the circumstances - and that was definitely not a good sign.

Christine Fletcher was 14 years old [25 on Earth] and a qualified Surveyor, who normally worked for the Housing Directorate of the Federal Mars Government. Fletcher appeared quite solid, a student in their last year at expedition. Christine also wrote articles for a couple of 'Conspiracy' sites and was a self-declared 'fitness freak'.

William 'Billy' Doyle was 30 years old [55 on Earth] and had recently retired from working the rigs, where he had held XO [Executive Officer] positions on several big cargo rigs. His RMC was still valid, and he was a qualified engineer. Jones believed he was a solid recruit for the professor's team.

Finally, apparently on board for communications and medical needs, was Elizabeth 'Lizzie' Pushkin aged 15 years [27 on Earth] who was in her final year at Medical University and was taking a sabbatical to join the expedition. She professed an 'interest' in various conspiracy theories, particularly about the ruined city and Research Station 13. But her favourite was about a certain 'Project Cenotaph'.

Jones finished reading and pushed that sheet into his pocket, he read the next with real interest. Professor Jack Dawes had sent Jones the proposed schedule for the expedition and clearly marked the large cave entrance that interested him and Professor Jacobson. Jones sighed and was nearly thrown from his seat as another huge explosion was heard outside.

Another canister had been struck; they only had one left to protect the Thor from serious and probably fatal damage. That was not very good odds and Jones switched off the 'collision alarm' again, checked the Thor's hull integrity; it was good. Then he headed for raft number 2 ensuring all the pressure doors across the rig closed behind him; sealing off each compartment. Eve gave a big smile of relief as the captain climbed through the hatch of raft no.2 and sealed the heavy door behind him. He slumped into the seat next to Eve and smiled; "This could get very hairy; a second canister was hit." Tom swore loudly and pushed his fingers through his hair; "Another strike like them two and we would have to launch skipper; right?"

Grim faced Jones said "Yes." And turned to the small control panel by his seat and slid the protective covering down. He could see that the Chief had already sealed raft number 1 to go. He flicked down a couple of switches and sealed the raft. "Buckle up boys and girls." He said quietly and pushed back in his seat, watching Eve and Tom placing the cats into their specially constructed survival cases and strapping them down.

Everyone was now strapped in their seats and Max passed some water bottles around, which were gratefully received; there was no conversation.

The minutes seemed like hours and Jones could feel the sweat running down his face and back, his mouth was dry despite the water he sipped and reached across and gripped Eve's free hand. She managed a smile and raised the bottle in salute; "For once I could even go a drop of Old Ma Crawford.

Where's the Chief when you need him!" They all chuckled; even Max.

Another huge explosion rocked the Thor and the lights dimmed and failed; Jones heard Max swear loudly and he knew that the Thor had been struck.

Then darkness.

In the Control Centre at Rossington, the Duty Military Transit Controller; Major Maurice Applegate stared at his monitor and wiped his face slowly and deliberately. He turned to Lt. Caroline Huskman and said quietly; "Get me Vice-Admiral Kellermann urgently on the secure line."

After a few minutes Kellamann appeared on the video caller. The grim-faced Major clasped his hands together and said simply; "WSV the Thor is apparently lost with all hands and a commercial cargo rig called the New Argonaut is also missing; both in the Easter Mountains region during the current Category 1 storm. I'm very sorry sir."

Jones was falling through the darkness, arms and legs moving rapidly like he was swimming in the blackness. He was shouting but couldn't hear his own voice. Then it stopped suddenly and a confused Jones lay face down on something soft. Groaning, his fingers dug into the soft yielding soil and he eased himself up onto his knees.

He stared about in utter disbelieve and closed his eyes for a few seconds, then opened them again. He slowly stood with his legs trembling – no, they were shaking – and fell back onto his knees. He could feel the strange warmth of the bright sun through his suit and now was sweating badly. He lifted his right arm and stared at the readout and shook his head again. He managed to whisper – despite his dry mouth – "That's bloody impossible!" His survival suit was telling him about the surrounding environment he was standing in and to quote Jones: 'it was bloody impossible!'

He slowly stood and took in the scene before him: The mountain range was enormous, covered with grass and huge trees. Its peaks disappearing into white-grayish clouds that hung like curtains in the light blue sky. That's when he saw the mighty river, flowing about a kilometer from him, being fed by an incredible waterfall and he could imagine the noise of all that falling water. But for now, he stood in a strange, but beautiful, silent world. That's when he saw movement between the thick forests of trees that spread down from the mountains. He stared hard as the beast darted between the trees with some grace. Then he realized it had two legs and two arms: it was a human wearing some kind of animal skin, complete with the strange creatures head still attached. He also immediately noticed the long spear gripped in one hand. The figure crouched down and was lost in the tall grass.

Jones hadn't realized that he had taken several steps backwards and almost fell over the figure laying in the grass and dirt. He knelt and turned the body over: it was Max and his helmet visor was cracked and broken. Jones shook him and Max's eyes fell opened and rolled closed again. Was he dead? Jones couldn't tell and Max's instrument panel was certainly dead, showing nothing. That's when a hand touched his shoulder and Jones jumped up: it was Eve, helmet off and speaking, gesturing for him to remove his bloody helmet!

She knelt by Max, pulling off his helmet and unzipping the top of his survival suit. Jones slowly removed his helmet and the heat, wind and noise hit him. "He's still breathing skipper!" Jones could hear Eve's sweet voice and he breathed deep. "What the fuck happened?" was all he could reply and turned to see the Thor standing between several huge trees with the starboard side [facing him] broken open, blackened and burnt. Leon was sitting with his back to the wreck, with no helmet and raised a hand.

Eve shouted for Leon to help with Max: get him back to the Thor. Jones asked her if she knew what happened and Eve didn't smile; "It appears that some of the crew were somehow thrown from the rig: you, Max, me, Tom and Leon. There's no trace of anyone else apparently." Between Leon and Jones they managed to carry the unconscious Max back the relative shade of the Thor and get him into the medical-bay. Eve went to work as Leon handed Jones a very welcome bottle of water, saying grimly: "She's dead: totally. No bloody power whatsoever. Then....then everyone but us five is.... well, missing, and gone. No trace of them. Raft No.1 is missing but our one is still attached. The Chief's must have fired off before...." He shrugged his shoulders and drained his water bottle. He had no idea what had really happened, how he was 'thrown' from the Thor, finding himself a stranger in a very strange world.

Jones watched Eve rummaging through her medical kit and asked where Tom was. Leon managed a smile; "He's around the stern, he's going to try and winch 'Little Thor' down by bloody hand but the mechanism appears stuck. But the 'sand-cat' appears bloody undamaged!" Jones nodded at that and sipped his water, asking Eve if Max was alright. She looked up and shrugged her slim shoulders, "He doesn't appear injured – on the outside – but appears to be in some kind of deep coma. There's no apparent cranial damage, so it could be shock."

"We are not alone, I saw something...well, I think it was human dressed in some kind of animal skin...." Leon quietly interrupted Jones, "Yeah, me and Tom saw that. I think it is human. It has bloody arms and legs after all." Tom appeared in the doorway, dirty and sweating, but smiling broadly. "Thanks for the sodding help mates! I managed to manually winch the bloody 'sand-cat' down and she's undamaged and the fucking engine started!" Jones gave the thumbs up and asked again about Max. Eve shook her head, "Nothing is apparent that I can treat. It must be some kind of deep coma, probably caused by shock."

Jones stared about the room and sighed, "If the Thor is dead then we'll have to abandon her and use the 'sand-cat'. If we can get the flat bed out...we can load it with supplies and head...." He stopped talking: where the hell do we go! They all looked at each other thinking the same thing: what the hell happened and where the fuck do they go? Finally Leon voiced what they were all thinking. "Have we been thrown back in time? Is this Mars of old?" No-one answered him because they simply couldn't believe it.

Jones drained his water bottle and stared at Max. "I don't know Leon but I think we're still in the same place – at the foothills of the Easter Mountains – except maybe in a different dimension ....or time. Somehow we have been transported through....space and time maybe. The Chief must have activated his life raft before the Thor was hit and they are probably laying on the sand waiting rescue." He took a deep breath, adding, "I bloody hope so."

That's when they all stood stock still as the loud ferocious roar drifted over them. Jones rubbed his chin and gestured to the bridge; "I think we'll be a bit safer in here for now." No-one disagreed with him and Jones made his way to the silent bridge. Jones stared through the dust covered windscreen and gripped tightly the back of his seat as the beast wandered slowly into view and he knew what it was almost immediately: It was some kind of dinosaur! The slow moving beast was huge, easily the size of the Thor and covered with reddish brown scales. Had Jones known anything about the dinosaurs that once populated 'old mother earth' he would have quickly identified the beast as a cross between a Tyrannosaurus Rex and some kind of primeval crocodile.

It seemed to stare at the Thor, and then simply wandered off as if quickly realizing it couldn't eat the damn thing! Jones eased into his seat: his legs were shaking a little. "What the hell has happened?" he said and ran a hand over his face.

"THE ADVENTURES OF CAPTAIN JONES AND THE CREW OF THE THOR CONTINUE IN 'RED PLANET TRUCKERS!' SERIES 2."
Stephen Williams.

SOME INFORMATION ABOUT COLONISED MARS.

1. Introduction to "THE RED PLANET TRUCKERS!"

"It might be helpful to realise, that very probably the [Grand*] parents of the first native born Martians are alive today."
— Harrison 'Jack' Schmitt, Apollo 17

When Commander Margret Taylor first stepped onto the surface of Mars on 3rd May 2032 [Earth Time] she, and the other six personnel of the 'Mars Colonisation Team' knew they had come on a 'one-way' mission. There was no going back, they were here to stay.

* My little addition!

On Mars that historic date is recorded as Week: 33 Sol: 337 Year: 1. [This week and day was the actual date using Mars's position in its long orbit of the Sun.]

Over the next fifty years [Just under 90 Earth Years] many immigrants arrived yearly, bringing construction crews and supplies, and the first families.

Michael Foster-Roberts; Born: Colonisation Unit 1 (Northern Mars) W: 7 S: 68 Y: 2. Died: aged 43 in the year 45 {Earth age:77], was the first real Martian, born in the medical unit of the main habitation some 72 weeks after colonisation began.

The adventures of the mighty THOR and her crew begin in the Martian Year 323, that's some three hundred and twenty three Martian years after Commander Taylor placed her foot on the

Mars surface, which means approximately 581 Earth years have lapsed since that historic date.

Mars now has vast cities, mines, farms, townships and even holiday resorts.

But there's always the Martian weather, on Mars you always wanted to know about the weather and the reports had to be accurate, up to date and continuous, otherwise someone could get killed. The weather on Mars has become increasing unpredictable since early attempts at 'terraforming' failed at the turn of the first Martian Century.

WSV: "THOR" is a weather station maintenance vehicle; she travels Southern Mars on service and repair missions with her crew of twelve, sometimes spending weeks away from her home port of Rossington [The Southern Mars Capitol City]. The "THOR" is one of three such rigs employed by the Martian Weather Service to service the 26 weather stations scattered across the Southern hemisphere.

In the heavily populated North, the Weather Service employs another three such rigs, with an additional 'flyer' workshop for real emergency work, to service the 33 weather stations located there of which five are manned stations. Whilst three of the Southern weather stations are manned, the remainder are automated.

"The Thor" was a 'Titan' Class Rig, weighing some 200 tone, equipped with two huge Dyson rig engines and with a full specification that made your mouth water. Standing nearly 6 meters high with full external armour and a double hull; The Thor was designed to withstand whatever weather Mars threw at her. The Thor could haul two, 70 tone trailers with ease over the harsh and unforgiving Martian surface. But the two trailers she normally hauled were specially built for her and the weather service. One contained a fully operational weather station and fitted workshop for the twelve crew members who serviced the vital weather stations scattered around Southern Mars – a task that was so necessary for the survival of humanity on the planet, that the military controlled the weather service. All the weather service personnel were, in-fact, in military service.

The second trailer contained a full medical suite, high quality living modules, a ship's mess and galley with a small cargo storage area. It also carried a couple of drones for observation and exploration. The Thor boasted two fully equipped survival rafts that could carry 16 persons between them and keep the crew safe and alive for up to 5 days. It also carried a small 'Sand-Cat' – a four-person tractor that could travel very quickly over the Martian dust, she was highly maneuverable and basically, a great deal of fun to drive! Her nickname was 'Little Thor' amongst the crew – there never was a shortage of Volunteers to take her out for a spin.

THE CURRENT CREW OF "THE THOR":

Officer Commanding:
Captain Picasso R. Jones - Age: 16 years [29] Born: Kiev (Southern Mars) W: 33 S: 322 Y: 307

Executive Officer: (XO)
Lt. Commander Margret Simms-Holder - Age 16 years [29] Born: New London (Northern Mars) W:61 S: 614 Y: 307

Chief Engineer:
Lt. Marcus J. Enders - Age: 28 years [50] Born: Taylor (Northern Mars) W: 11 S: 106 Y: 295

Medical Officer:
Lt. Eve M. Votech - Age: 14 years [25] Born: Rossington (Southern Mars) W: 51 S: 504 Y: 309

Ensign:
Lilly Blissford - Age 10 years [19] Born: Taylor (Northern Mars) W: 3 S: 28 Y: 313

Specialist (Engineering):
Thomas R.E. Eddington - Age: 18 years [32] Born: Normandy (Northern Mars) W: 25 S: 247 Y: 305

Specialist (Meteorologist):
Harry Gelderfield - Age: 17 years [31] Born: Taylor (Northern Mars) W: 47 S: 473 Y: 306

Specialist (Systems):
Maxwell Tapp - Age 23 years [41] Born: Rossington (Southern Mars) W: 33 S: 334 Y: 300

Deck Hand:
Troy T. Humbleson - Age: 11 years [20] Born: Shackleton (Southern Mars) W: 31 S: 305 Y: 312

Deck Hand:
Leon A. Kamiski - Age: 12 years [22] Born: Taylor (Northern Mars) W:51 S: 509 Y: 311

Chef:
Franklyn F. Fingermann - Age: 21 years [38] Born: South Paris (Southern Mars) W:35 S: 347 Y: 302

Rig Apprentice:
Summer 'Sunny' Yelsin - Age: 9 years [17] Born: New London (Northern Mars) W: 22 S: 219 Y: 314

Rig's Mascot:
"Dallas" - Age 1 & 1/2 years [3] Born: Unknown. Y: 321 [?]

FORMER CREW MEMBERS:

Executive Officer: (XO)
Lt. Commander Peter Gravestone - Age 14 years [25] Transferred to MSV: "The John Garfield."

Medical Officer:
Captain [Dr.] Patrick Greenspace - Age: 30 years [55] - retired on grounds of ill-health.

Ensign:
Yoki Hali-Hussain - Age: 12 years [22] - promoted to Lt. and transferred to MSV: "The Neil Armstrong."

Specialist (Meteorologist):
Richard Halstrome - Age: 17 years [31] - left service to run family farm.

Bella C. Limbstronn - Age: 15 years [27] - Left service due to family matters.

Specialist (Systems):
Kazzamondo Yassimini - Age 13 years [23] - Left service and joined a private Rig Company.

Deck Hands:
Lora Kapasiki - Age: 12 years [22] - left service, whereabouts unknown.

Jean-Paul Bamphine - Age: 10 years [19] - left service, returned to college.

Rig Apprentice:
Tony Barr - Age: 11 years [20] - Completed apprenticeship and received paid Military Scholarship to Fort Benjamin Engineering University.

*[00] This gives the equivalent age in Earth Years.

A Brief Summary of Mars Dates & Times.

For the sake of clarity, differences between Martian Dates and Times, as against Earth equivalents, will need some extra explanation:

"Time on Mars is easily divided into days based on its rotation rate and years based on its orbit. Sols, or Martian solar days, are only 39 minutes and 35 seconds longer than Earth days, and there are 668 sols (684 Earth days) in a Martian year. For convenience, sols are divided into a 24-hour clock.

Unlike on Earth, there is no leisurely-orbiting moon to give Mars "months," and while there have been many imaginative calendars suggested for Mars, none is in common use. The way that scientists mark the time of Mars year is to use solar longitude, abbreviated Ls (read "ell sub ess"). Ls is 0° at the vernal equinox (beginning of northern spring), 90° at summer solstice, 180° at autumnal equinox, and 270° at winter solstice.

On Earth, spring, summer, autumn, and winter are all similar in length, because Earth's orbit is nearly circular, so it moves at nearly constant speed around the Sun. By contrast, Mars' elliptical orbit makes its distance from the Sun change with time, and also makes it speed up and slow down in its orbit. Mars is at aphelion (its greatest distance from the Sun, 249 million kilometers, where it moves most slowly) at Ls = 70°, near the northern summer solstice, and at perihelion (least distance from the Sun, 207 million kilometers, where it moves fastest) at Ls = 250°, near the southern summer solstice. The Mars dust storm season begins just after perihelion at around Ls = 260°.

The coincidence of aphelion with northern summer solstice means that the climate in the northern hemisphere is more temperate than in the southern hemisphere. In the south, summers are hot and quick, winters long and cold."

Therefore, no months exist on Mars. They have weeks consisting of 10 Sol's (Martian Days) and Years that average 66/67 weeks. The Martian year consists of 668 Sol's, and that is equivalent to 684 Earth Days - Therefore a single Martian year is worth nearly two Earth Years - 1.8 to be precise. Which means giving Martian ages could raise a smile to Earth People [if any still existed]. For example, Captain Picasso Jones was born some 16 Martian years ago, which means he's approximately 29 years old - if Jones was on Earth. But, of course, Martians see nothing funny or odd about a Rig Captain aged 16 years - No living Martian has experienced Earth dates or times - so they mean nothing to them.

Thus, Martian ages and birth dates appear quite normal to the average Martian!

Important Birth dates that Martians celebrate:

3 years [5] - The age children start formal schooling.
5 years [9] - The age children attend senior school.
8 years [14] - The age a juvenile can attend college.
9 years [16] - Considered an 'Adult' in Martian Law.
33 years [60] - Allowed retiring on basic pension.
45 years [81] - Big birthday celebration by families and friends, 45 years is considered a real achievement, also means an increase in Pension and other State Benefits.
50+ years [90+] - Recognised by the State as a real achievement, includes Medal presentation by President.

Martian days of the week are named thus:

Newday [the first day of a Martian week]
Monday
Tuesday
Wednesday
Thursday
Friday
Saturday
Sunday
Tayday [named after Commander Taylor]
Enday [the last day of a Martian week]

3. About the "THOR."

The "THOR" was powered by two large 'Dyson Liquid Solar' Engines, affectionately called 'Sun Cups' by the crew's engineering staff, these engines were the heart of the rig and capable of delivering the enormous amounts of power required by such huge rigs.

Basically, some seventy Martian years before, a brilliant young engineer [Lawrence Comfort Dyson - Born: Taylor (Northern Mars) W: 34 S: 337 Y: 231 Died: Europa (Northern Mars) W: 56 S: 558 Y: 270 aged 39 years] invented a process to 'liquefy' sunlight that was captured through solar panels [the main form of power for everything on Mars] and store it safely.

This simple process revolutionised travel on Mars, simply because it increased the power ratio up to 10 times that was previously available, and that made it possible to built such rigs as 'Mammoths, Titans and Goliaths'. These engines could handle enormous weight and provided the metal giants with the power to achieve good speeds on the Martian surface and they were incredibly reliable.

Previously, a trip from Taylor [The Capital city of Mars] to the

Military base Fort Benjamin, some 7000k from the capital, would have taken 8 days and nights of constant driving - it now took just 4 days to complete. The new engines also allowed more armour and bigger crews, with far better living and working conditions that the 'old riggers' could ever imagine. The giant engineering works and township of Dyson - on the North/South boarder is named after this young genius with great pride.

The "THOR" is a rig with 12 'tyres' and each of her trailers boast a further eight tyres. These tyres are quite unique to Mars, designed specifically for the Martian surface, at first appearance they look like normal heavy load carriers. But they were actually made from millions of strands of steel wire, which allowed dust to pass through them, reducing drag and increasing the speeds achievable. If a rig had been sitting some time on the surface, a good Captain would 'blow' his tyres before setting off. This was achieved by blowing a pressurised gas mixture through them - with the legendary sense of humour that rig crews were famous for - it was called 'the captain's blow job'.

All Military rigs carry a chef because there is very little processed food available on Mars, that type of food was usually available only in 'Emergency Ration Packs'. Nearly everyone ate fresh meals, prepared with organic produce supplied from the numerous enclosed farms scattered about the planet. Food was expensive, and obviously, vital to life on Mars. So on a rig like "The THOR", you needed a Chef, otherwise each crew member would have to prepare their meals from scratch, two or three times a day, and with twelve people on board, that's a serious waste of man-hours.

Fresh water had to be conserved and thus, the "THOR" contained a small recycling plant to ensure that very little of this precious commodity was wasted. All the showers aboard her were referred to as 'Misty's' since they worked by spraying water droplets, which covered the body like a hazy mist and apparently they are quite effective in getting you clean.

The toilets stored waste in the rear of the vehicle, and the septic tanks were emptied with regularity since this waste constituted the main source of organic fertiliser available on the planet and could achieve good returns for the service. A little saying amongst the truckers was "We shit and they get rich!" The Martian toilet paper is worthy of note; it's edible. As part of the organic recycling process, all toilet paper has to be produced to a certain standard, which bizarrely, makes the paper edible; though all Martians will tell you to try it before you actually use it!

The air re-circulation system present on the "THOR" is a little masterpiece of engineering, providing a breathable atmosphere for the crew at all times. Based on liquid oxygen, the system functions at such a level of efficiency, that even working at 20% capacity, the crew will survive.

Every Military rig that did 'sand-time' was required to carry a 'Medical Officer' to cover emergencies and maintain the crew's health and fitness during the long journeys over the Martian surface. Whilst many were not fully qualified Doctor's, their training was such that they could even perform minor surgery if required. Most MO's were part qualified Doctors and would normally only complete their mandatory one year of 'sand service' before moving on. But some do return to service and continue their Military career as MO's, aboard the many military rigs that traverse Mars, because they enjoy the life aboard the rigs. The rigs 'Doctor' had their own private cabin, contained within the medical suite which also included a small morgue and laboratory.

The three senior staff on the rigs are usually well respected by the crews, The Captain's; because everything was in their hands; including your life! Next, the Chief Engineer's; because if the engines failed [and without immediate rescue] you were very likely to die on Mar's hostile surface, and finally, the rigs 'Doctor's'; because they could save your life when you were ill or injured - simple as that!

Sometimes, the "THOR" would carry the maximum crew allowed by Military Regulations for her class [which is 16 persons] this was normal if she was carrying a relief crew to one of the manned weather stations and returning with the relieved crew.

4. Martian Names and places.

After Martian Independence in the year 60 [Martian Years] there was a great clamour to change the old Earth given names to more concurrent and appropriate titles. Thus, nearly all the old 'Latin' inspired names disappeared; replaced with more Martian titles. In the years following Independence, the process accelerated and in Year 63 a new Martian Globe was issued, and all maps had to carry the new names.

For example, 'Valles Marineris', the grand valley of Mars which extends over 3,000 kilometres long, spans as much as 600 kilometres across, and delves as much as 8 kilometres deep is now known as 'Cutters trench' after Professor Wilson Cutter, who was the first human to actually enter the Valley, when his expedition spend two years surveying the place in Years 59 and 63. Few old Earth inspired names exist today. There are some exceptions; 'Cydonia' retains its old name, as does 'Olympus Mons' Mountain, which still holds the honour of being the largest Volcano in the Solar System.

5. Independence Day.

Mars became a independent sovereign state on Week: 25 Sol: 255 Year: 60 and the day is celebrated all across Mars to this day. It is a National Holiday in all seven states of the Mars Federation.

6. Currency.

The Currency Unit of Mars is the Martian Dollar [$MD] which consists of 100 Cents and the notes are issued in straight denominations of 1$MD, 5$MD, 10$MD, 20$MD, 50$MD, 100$MD, 500$MD and on rare occasions; a 1,000$MD bill [normally used by the State Governments to pay Government Contractors and other States].

The coins consist of a 1, 2, 5, 10, 25, & 50 cent pieces. Each coin has the head and shoulders image of one of the first 'founding' crew that landed on Mars: Commander Taylor is on the reverse of the 50 cent coin.

To get some idea of the notes value; Captain Picasso Jones earns roughly 2700$MD a year as a rig captain, whilst Deck-hand Leon Kamski would collect about 1600$MD. A cup of coffee in 'Blind Charlie's Dinner & Grill' would cost about 15 Cents. A three-course meal in the same establishment would cost about 1$MD and 70 Cents; Written simply as $1.70.

The WSV: 'The Thor' cost around 250,000$MD's to build - the big battle rigs cost a lot more!

Government Income Tax is currently 7% per employed person. Everyone who works pays 2% of their total income into the Mars State Government National Pension Scheme and 33 [60 Earth years] is the normal age for retirement, though many do choose to work on a little longer. Company Tax is about 11% of total Profits.

7. State Property.

90% of Martians rent from the state, which means serious money is returned to the State Treasuries and does not go to private companies and Landlords. Some 'Super Rich' people have constructed their own 'small 'villages' to reside in. They are called 'Castles' in Martian slang. Some big corporations and Mining Companies have also built townships; normally attached to a mine or farming community and charge subsidised rents to their workforce.

8. Religion.

There is very little 'organised' religion on Mars. Most people keep their religious beliefs to themselves and have services in their own homes with just friends and family. There are Federal Laws preventing the 'preaching' of any religious beliefs and upon conviction the offenders spend time at the asylums in Lake Placid. The Government and people of Mars secular position was one of the major causes of the 'Invasion War' of 227 with Earth and that position remains to this day.

Contains a listing of some of the major works by the author that are or have appeared in a book format: please scan the QR code below to visit his blog.

AGE RECOMMENDATION.

THE TEMPORAL DETECTIVES.

"THE TEMPORAL DETECTIVES. – SERIES 1."

"THE TEMPORAL DETECTIVES. – SERIES 2."

"THE TEMPORAL DETECTIVES. – SERIES 3."

"THE TEMPORAL DETECTIVES. – SERIES 4."

"THE TEMPORAL DETECTIVES. – SERIES 5."

"THE TEMPORAL DETECTIVES. – SERIES 6."

"A GUIDE TO THE SERIES: 2024."

 **AGE RECOMMENDATION.**

THE RED PLANET TRUCKERS!

"THE RED PLANET TRUCKERS! "

 **AGE RECOMMENDATION.**

THE GRAVEYARD CHRONICLES.

"THE GRAVEYARD CHRONICLES."

 **ADULT CONTENT SERIES.**

MISS DOROTHY HADDEN.

"MISS DOROTHY HADDEN – SERIES 1: The Early Edwardian adventures – Part 1."

"MISS DOROTHY HADDEN – SERIES 2: The Early Edwardian adventures – Part 2."

"MISS DOROTHY HADDEN – SERIES 3: The Late Edwardian adventures – Part 1."

"MISS DOROTHY HADDEN – SERIES 4: The Late Edwardian adventures – Part 2."

"MISS DOROTHY HADDEN – SERIES 5: The Great War years."

"MISS DOROTHY HADDEN – SERIES 6: The London adventures."

**AGE RECOMMENDATION.**

CRABB, POCKETT AND SCARPER!

"GRABB, POCKETT AND SCARPER: THE UNDERTAKERS STORY!"

**AGE RECOMMENDATION.**

HARRY BARFIELD.

"HARRY BARFIELD."

**ADULT CONTENT SERIES.**

SAM DANTE.

"SAM DANTE."

 ADULT CONTENT SERIES.

THE ADVENTURES OF ALEXANDRA.

"THE ADVENTURES OF ALEXANDRA: SERIES 1."

"THE ADVENTURES OF ALEXANDRA: SERIES 2."

"THE ADVENTURES OF ALEXANDRA: SERIES 3."

"THE ADVENTURES OF ALEXANDRA: SERIES 4."

"THE ADVENTURES OF ALEXANDRA: SERIES 5."

"A GUIDE TO THE SERIES: 2024."

 ADULT CONTENT SERIES.

FATHER PARADISE ADAMS.

"FATHER PARADISE ADAMS."

IMPORTANT NOTE:
"**NOT** ALL BOOKS ARE CURRENTLY AVAILABLE OR STILL IN PRINT – SORRY ABOUT THAT!"
Please enquire about availability at your local bookshop or contact the author at:
stephen.williams24@btinternet.com.

——— ⋆★⋆ ———

www.ingramcontent.com/pod-product-compliance
Lightning Source LLC
Chambersburg PA
CBHW071436200726
48294CB00002B/670